Libel the Dead

Also by John Fink

The Leaf Boats

John Fink

Libel the Dead

A Thomas Dunne Book

St. Martin's Press New York

 For information, address St. Martin's Press, 175 Fifth Avenue, New York, N.Y. 10010.

Design by Judy Stagnitto

Library of Congress Cataloging-in-Publication Data

Fink, John.
Libel the dead / John Fink.
"A Thomas Dunne Book."
p. cm.
ISBN 0-312-07617-7
I. Title.
PS3556.I475L53 1992
813'.54—dc20 92-5065
CIP

First Edition: August 1992

10 9 8 7 6 5 4 3 2 1

To Marilla, and to Paul, and to Paul Bradley

Libel the Dead

One

Morton Brock didn't seem like the type to kill himself. At forty-eight, he'd made it big as a private detective. He had offices in New York and L.A., and a new book out about his adventures in Hollywood, protecting famous people from others and from themselves. He was a roaring, clawing success, a real down-to-earth guy who didn't mind getting his fingers in slime if that's what it took to accumulate a pile of money. And oddly enough, attractive to women—even to attractive women. Go figure.

On the other hand, it looked to me as if he'd been trying to do himself in, very slowly, for a long time. Picture this slouching form, with a round head growing out of sloping shoulders like a cabbage. Obese. No exercise, smoked too much, always complained he felt too punk to answer hard questions. Didn't like himself a lot. Hidden there in the sleepy, puffy eyes, in the thick, heavy body, in the dung-brown-green suit, all of him, the one time we met, grudgingly going along with gravity, disappearing behind his desk. Hiding from me because he'd blown his chance at some good publicity by bragging too much, then not being able to back it up, losing himself in a smoke screen of clouded fact, crouching someplace in there. Well, that was his chosen profession, working undercover: concealment.

Brock and I had our only meeting one sunny morning in March, one of those breezy Manhattan weekdays when you'd rather go for a stroll in the park, so I walked from my office on Lexington to Brock's on upper Broadway. Beside me was Noel Flynn, a big, noisy, hard-drinking thirty-year-old free-lance writer in a ratty sport coat whose byline had appeared in some of the best places and a few of the worst and whose series of four articles about Morton Brock was about to be cut in half. Naturally, Flynn was upset. This had never been done to him before. And since as his editor I was the guy who was doing it to him, he was being awkwardly deferential, letting me decide when to step off the curb against the light and when not to, things like that.

Usually I don't like being deferred to. It smacks of obsequiousness. But Flynn wasn't used to deferring, either, and he's such a big guy, it was like having an argument with a bear. Besides, I knew he was nervous. Hell, so was I. I was going to tell Morton Brock, private eye, that he was a liar, and we both knew that Brock sometimes packed a .45 and could be dangerous. Flynn was acutely conscious of this because he had followed the detective around for three or four months, researching the story. My nervousness was vaguer. I was only an editor and didn't get out much. Working in the offices of a sleek, well-financed magazine insulates you from the outside, keeps you from feeling threatened by what's tawdry and menacing on the street. No, I was mostly concerned about remembering what I was going to say. I had it memorized.

Maybe what was worrying Flynn most as we crossed Times Square and headed into the upper Fifties was that although he trusted me as his editor, he wasn't sure I could handle Brock. I'm younger than Flynn is, and although I'm nearly his size, he had never heard me raise my voice above a mild cry of reprimand. What he didn't know was that I had just taken a short course in intimidation from a master of the art. I'd spent the previous hour with Bob Struiker, the magazine's libel lawyer, and I'd learned my lines. Not only that, I'd gotten the voice down just right. I was primed. At that moment I *was* Bob Struiker. Or put it this way: I was all of him I was ever going to be.

Brock, of course, was brooding behind his desk, already sniveling a little, part of his act, being formidable and pitiable at the same time. I remember his door was open and we walked right in, sat down, and started to talk. Brock didn't have a secretary. He was a very private man. Flynn said he answered his own phone and did his own filing and brought in secretarial help from an agency when it was necessary, and he left his office door open because he didn't want anybody breaking it down. Besides, Flynn said, there was always that big .45 in the desk drawer.

I wasn't intimidated and I felt no pity, and this surprised me, because usually I'm looking around anxiously, wondering whose problems I can solve next. I wasn't me, though; I was Bob Struiker, and to Bob Struiker, Morton Brock was an asshole, pure and simple. So I sat down and started yelling. I let Brock have it, just the way Struiker had said.

"You lied to us," I shouted. "You lied!"

Brock flinched, no doubt wondering what was up.

It was working already. Good. I felt great.

But first let me tell you about Mr. Kim.

The only part of me that wasn't enjoying this whole thing was the vivid memory I had of this man. Mr. Kim was a young, enthusiastic Vietnamese who occasionally wrote for local Vietnamese newspapers and wanted to spread the good word about his people to the larger world. He had come to see me about a year before, shortly after I'd gone to work for the magazine, and proposed an article. He would take readers on walking tours of various cities across the United States, he said, explaining the Vietnamese cuisine and the Vietnamese work ethic and the Vietnamese point of view. He would make the Vietnamese so admirable that they would be welcomed wholeheartedly into the

American version of the brotherhood of man, even in New York City. That was a joke, the part about New York City. Mr. Kim was very proud of his sense of humor. He laughed recklessly and shouted in my face, and ordinarily I would have kicked him out of my office, but I rather liked him. Besides, he was thin as a reed and obviously starving from lack of work. He seemed so desperate, I couldn't imagine what would happen if he didn't leave with an assignment from me. Disintegrate? Would he just disintegrate? Grab his skinny throat and strangle himself?

The article, he went on between laughs and shouts, would be highly entertaining. Its centerpiece would be a leader of the Vietnamese community right here in Manhattan, a dentist who was not only a very funny fellow in his own right but a great mountain climber.

"You are a great mountain climber yourself!" he yelled at me.

I was somewhat puzzled. I had never climbed a mountain in my life. Then it came to me. "You're talking about my boss," I said, "the editor in chief." Mr. Kim's face fell. One hand reached for the knot in his tie. "But," I went on, "I have a great admiration for people who climb mountains." It occurred to me that he probably owed the dentist a lot of money.

Encouraged, he laughed his hilarious, half-strangled laugh, demonstrating to me that his teeth were in tip-top shape, gold crowns and all. "The article," he shouted, "it will be very funny. People will be highly amused!"

People were not amused. The dentist wrote us a letter in which he said that he had been publicly humiliated by tales about him that had no basis in fact. I sent the letter along to Bob Struiker because it looked litigious. Other letters flowed in from his outraged countrymen, most of them probably patients of his like Mr. Kim. Bob Struiker called up and said, "Get Mr. Kim or whoever it is over here." I showed Mr. Kim the letters and he laughed with joy, claiming to be greatly pleased. Yes, he explained, he had made up the stories about the dentist going climbing and falling off the mountain and generally making a fool of himself, but it was sometimes necessary to exaggerate in order to be read, and the dentist would come to see what a great favor had been done him. He insisted, all smiles, that his article was both entertaining and enlightening. It had made our readers feel good about themselves and the Vietnamese. He laughed and shouted, celebrating this crowning achievement of his life.

But by the time we sat down with Bob Struiker, he had stopped laughing and Struiker was doing all the shouting, if you could call it that. Struiker never shouted, not really. He didn't have to. Even in ordinary conversation, his voice had a certain weight and rasp, as if he was poking at you to keep you listening, prodding you off balance. As his voice grew louder, it became more penetrating, like a surgeon's knife, but it never lost its clear articulation and insistent reasonableness. It merely rose a notch, like a steady, irresistible wind of gale force, driving the argument before it. There might be anger in it, even outrage or contempt, but the anger was always harnessed, always controlled. Still, his voice could slice like a razor. It could make an incision the length of your arm before you knew it.

So as Struiker began, his voice low and rumbling, like a distant pounding surf, Mr. Kim grinned brightly, but in his eyes was a glassy, gaseous fear, and a quaking, as if he sensed something ominous in the air. I had more or less stopped breathing. Struiker always scared me half to death, especially when he was just warming up, because I knew what might lie ahead.

We didn't have to wait long before Struiker moved in on Mr. Kim like a tidal wave about to crumple a coastal village, his voice rising and his sallow face becoming dimly fuchsia. "Don't you see what you've done?" he said. "This is the press of the United States of America, not some dinky neighborhood rag. You told lies about a respected man in your community, held him up to ridicule. You lied to

Beyond magazine and Mr. Lindenthal here. You cheated us, and now you're going to get what you deserve."

Mr. Kim shuddered forward in his straight-back chair, almost stood up. "But it was funny stories!" he screamed, and then fell back. It was the only thing he said. Struiker may have viewed himself as a surgeon, cutting away corruption in the system, but to Mr. Kim, I have no doubt, it must have felt like being mortally stung, rendered helpless, and watching your life ebb away.

Because now Struiker was on him like a scorpion, relentlessly stinging and stinging. "It was lies, Mr. Kim, lies! And because you have lied and cheated in an attempt to ingratiate yourself, and because you have stolen our money, we can no longer protect you. I want you to go back to your community and beg forgiveness. Tell them you'll never do that again. Swear by your ancestors! And then put it in writing to that dentist and send a copy to me. That's all, Mr. Kim. Now get out of my office. And I hope to God your ancestors forgive you."

Mr. Kim sat with his chin on his heaving chest, crying silently. I glanced at Struiker. Behind his great desk, he showed no emotion, almost no life, as if it was he who'd been poisoned and immobilized. But in his neutral-gray face, his eyes flickered with what seemed like amusement. I was appalled by that, but I was wrong. I think it was just a moment of fulfillment, just a satisfying sense of winning.

Now I knew what that kind of satisfaction felt like, watching Morton Brock sag behind his desk, a great brutish toad sinking into a quagmire of his own making. That's how I saw him and that's what I felt. What more can I say?

"You lied to us," I said triumphantly, my voice ringing, "and that was wrong. That was stupid! You came to us begging us to tell your story, and then you didn't even have the decency to tell it straight. Just one example, Mr. Brock. You made certain claims about your recent confrontation with the district attorney and you said you had it all on tape. So far we've seen no tape, we've heard no tape; there isn't any tape! The district attorney's office says you're a liar. You leave us no alternative but to kill the rest of the series."

He jumped up, waving a couple of cassettes, his eyes wild. "I've got it all on the record," he cried, "anything you want!"

I stared back, obviously unconvinced. He blinked. I felt exultant. "But when we ask to hear the tape, you never play it. It's the wrong tape or you haven't got time or you left it at home. We've heard nothing, nothing at all to substantiate what you say."

He sat down heavily and mumbled, "The Feds. You talk to the Feds?"

So I gave him what little was his due. "The Feds say you're okay, you've helped them with a number of cases. But they have no information to back you up on this. Now I have to explain one thing to you. You don't lie to *Beyond* magazine and walk away from it. Fortunately, we've been able to kill the last two articles, but if we get sued for anything we've already printed, we're going to take every penny you've got, every stick of furniture, every suit and tie in your closet. Because we trusted you and you took advantage of us. And that means you've broken one of the golden rules of journalism, Mr. Brock, the promise implicit between a publisher and a source of information that they can trust each other, that they'll play fair. You lied to *Beyond* magazine, you lied to Mr. Flynn here, and we can have nothing further to do with you. Good-bye, Mr. Brock."

I felt good. I was thinking, It's about time. I had a strange feeling of gratitude to Bob Struiker, as if he were the guardian angel I'd always wanted to take me under his wing, make a man of me. I led Noel Flynn to the nearest bar and bought him a drink. I needed one. I needed to hear him say, a little awed, "God, Mike, I didn't know you had it in you."

I was so entranced by my performance, I almost didn't hear him add, "Mike? Mike, you don't think I had anything to do with this, do you? I mean you could think I tried to put one over on you, tried to slide one by. I wouldn't want you to think I'd do anything crooked."

What could I say? I was forgiving. "No," I said, "I don't think you're crooked, Noel." And then, because I held all the aces, had a lock on truth and principle and the golden rules of journalism, I added, "Just stupid." And I didn't look at him, tried not to hear the small sigh that escaped him. And then I went back to my office and removed his card from my Rolodex, as I had once removed Mr. Kim's.

Two days later, like I say, there was Brock's picture in the *New York Blade*, his lifeless body occupying most of the floor behind his desk, the .45 in his hand, dead, he would have put it, as nails. I don't know how the *Blade* got the picture, but I wasn't surprised. The *Blade* was the last living example of the old *Front Page* tradition in which practicing journalism was like leading the charge of the light brigade. And of course it seemed fitting that the *Blade*'s libel lawyer was the one who had coached me on how best to convince the late Morton Brock that he was just below the level of a louse.

"Brock may have made us liable to legal action," Bob Struiker had told me the morning I met with Brock, "and to make him see that, you have to forget you're this nice, literary editor who works with sensitive authors on their crappy stories. Brock has to believe he's dead in the water and it's his own fault, because it is. And if we get into court on any of this, he's got to be willing to say whatever we want him to say; otherwise I'm going to throw him to the wolves. All I care about is that he may have damaged us, and so should you. He doesn't deserve your sympathy, he deserves your contempt." I'm a quick study, and, as you see, I got my role down pat.

It was hard to feel contempt, though, once Brock was dead. Any more than I was able to feel contempt for Mr. Kim, who was still alive, I guessed, but mortally wounded. I admired Bob Struiker. Sometimes I wished I could be more like him. But now I had this thing gnawing at me. For a while, it was a real personal conflict down inside. Part of it was guilt. Not because Brock had killed himself. I didn't think he'd done that because I'd called him a liar. But I hadn't checked out Mr. Kim's funny stories, and I'd okayed the series on Morton Brock despite the fact that by all accounts, including Flynn's, he was a lowlife who occasionally made improbable statements he couldn't prove.

Sitting in my living room, looking at his picture in the *Blade*, I had another drink, and then I phoned an attractive former citizen of France I know named Panky Janvier and took her to the country for three days. But all that long weekend with Panky, I was clumsy and inarticulate. I could do nothing right. I kept seeing Morton Brock's dead, puffy eyes and Mr. Kim's scared ones, and way down in my stomach, I had this funny feeling I couldn't get rid of. It kept ticking in there like a battery-operated alarm clock that was about to go off.

Two

Bob Struiker wasn't a big man, but he was lean and hard and had the presence of a naked rapier. Let me clarify that. It's rapier, like a sword. Nothing to do with sexual intimidation, rape, raper, rapist, no, nothing like that. Except for Mr. Kim, of course. It seemed to me that Mr. Kim, being delicately, you might say vulnerably, wired, had experienced some kind of invasive violence, and that even now, six months afterward, he was somewhere suffering from postassault syndrome.

This morning, Struiker was sitting across the room in the offices of the magazine, with the staff gathered around, the tall and the short, the fat and the lean, the wary and the trusting, lounging on chairs and desktops listening to his assessment of a Manhattan private eye's unexpected suicide, and none of them was bored. Struiker had been speaking softly, in short sentences or in rambling, legal-sounding ones full of detachable phrases, and now he was winding up his summation.

"So remember this," he said, "Morton Brock shot himself with his own forty-five, which as you all now know can do a lot of permanent damage, because, for whatever reason, he could no longer live with himself. That's all there is to it. So my advice to you is to forget it and get on with your work. It's Brock's problem, or it was. It has nothing to do with you, now or in the foreseeable future." He glanced slowly around the room. Then, satisfied that he'd been heard, he leaned back and shut up.

Anton Black nodded several times, letting the message sink in, and then stood up. It was Monday, and as the magazine's publisher he had called this special meeting to minimize the emotional spillover from the Brock affair. He was a slight, wiry man, a smaller version of Struiker without either his muscular shoulders or his mesmerizing gaze. A dagger, not a sword. Anton Black could look hard at you. Struiker glared. Struiker worked out every day. He swam, he boxed. Black went for a tramp along the Hudson every spring. Struiker was a pet of Manhattan's moneyed class, lionized as the coldest, most arrogant and efficient libel lawyer in town, representing not only *Beyond* magazine and the *New York Blade* but one of the cable television networks and a slew of other magazines. Black had been trying to worm his way into New York society for years, but so far he'd made it only as far as opening night at the Met.

Neither of them attended the regular staff meetings, of course. These were run by the editor in chief when he was around. Nels Barbidoux was a tall, rangy type with fuzzy blond hair who'd been in and out of *Time*, *Esquire*, *New York*, and *Travel & Leisure*, and in and out of a couple of them again. After eighteen months at the magazine, I still didn't know Nels very well. He was away from the office much of the time. He really did climb mountains, and he sailed his ketch down the coast. He'd written two books about climbing and several articles, two of them for *National Geographic*. Nels had a friendly smile and a quick mind. We all liked him. We weren't so sure about Anton Black, the money man. But we did like the way he made the ads roll in.

As executive editor, I found myself doing whatever Nels didn't want to do, and more and more this seemed to include whatever got us in trouble with readers, especially legal problems. Although the Morton Brock series had been his idea, Nels had been out of town when it was sent to the printer's, so I got the responsibility and the follow-up. But apparently he still felt possessive about it, because now he was saying we ought to run the remaining two articles, taking out whatever might be litigious and pegging them on the end of Brock's controversial career. Anton Black wasn't so sure.

"Advertisers run like hell from the stench of death," he argued, shaking his head. "Anyway, by the time it gets into print, readers won't be interested."

"Wrong," Nels said simply. "Readers love the stench of death, no matter how old and fetid." He smiled cheerfully at me. "Mike, what do you think?"

I looked away. I didn't want to hear any more about Morton Brock. "Leave me out of it. I feel too close to the corpse, almost like I pushed him over the brink."

Struiker, whose demeanor up to that point had been low-key, even dour, grinned. His grin was always so unexpected, it won you over. "Come off it, Mike," he said. "You just got there a little early for the wake."

Everybody laughed. It was agreed to get the two remaining articles rewritten as a single piece, and Struiker had no objection. "Flynn will do it, won't he?" Nels asked me.

"Sure, as long as we pay him," I said. "And if he forgives me for calling him an idiot."

Struiker, still amused, said something to Anton Black I didn't catch. Black looked over at me.

"Speaking of idiots, Mike," he said, and winked at somebody in the crowd, I guess trying to keep it light, "I got a letter this morning objecting to something in that article on California you assigned."

The article had just appeared, along with the second piece in the Brock series. I was mystified. I couldn't imagine a more inoffensive, sanitized article. It seemed so harmless, I'd even toyed with the idea of not running it at all. But it was beautifully written, an old-fashioned essay in the spirit of the new journalism of the fifties and sixties, like Tom Wolfe's pieces for the old *Herald Tribune*. And because it was about the Southern California lifestyle, Anton Black had been interested in seeing it appear, not only for the advertising it promised to draw but because Southern Californians were a big chunk of our readership, they and people like them in other parts of the country who spent time and money savoring the outdoors and improving their health and looks. In fact, *Beyond* had been titled just for them, upscale readers whose interests and budgets went past the ordinary, the humdrum, people who couldn't stand to be bored. Anton liked to identify with these people. He sometimes wore bizarre blazers. He threw picnics in Central Park. He drove a Mercedes convertible, repainted red.

"This broadcaster in L.A. thinks you've maligned him," he said, holding up a copy of the latest issue. "He has a very high opinion of himself and thinks his reputation's been sullied. He can't figure out why we'd do a thing like that. Neither can I."

His tone was sharper now, and I know I blushed. It was the kind of thing that should have been said to me in private, not in front of the whole staff. Nels, interceding, said, "Be specific, Anton. What's he complaining about?"

"Well, it's just a little thing in here, but apparently we got it wrong. Wasn't this quote checked out, Mike?"

I didn't remember the quote at all. I vaguely recalled something about a TV talk-show host shooting off his mouth on the air, but what he'd said hadn't made much sense, a typically outlandish West Coast remark buried in high-flown verbiage. "Can you read it to me?" I asked. "Give me a clue?"

But Anton wasn't listening. "Apparently it wasn't checked. His name is Bangor Laudicek." He began spelling it out, *B-A-N-G-*, and then everybody was looking at Nels because Nels was spelling it out right along with him.

"I know him," Nels said, "a little bit. Nice man but pompous, and infatuated with himself. Has this talk show on public television, likes to make gratuitous, self-serving statements, little State of the Union messages summing up the current social crisis." He flashed me a grin. "I met him several years ago at a party out there. Nobody else could get a word in." He looked at Black. "I read the quote. What's wrong with it? It sounds exactly like him."

Anton thrust the magazine at him. "Maybe you should read it aloud. It's circled there, in red."

Nels leaned back against a desk and read the paragraph silently, smiling to himself. Then he read it to us. It said that "among the more articulate kooks in the land of sunshine and smog" was this "self-adulatory TV host" who was "in love with the sound of his own heartbeat" and was given to "blithely recommending to his viewers the advantages of drugs in achieving higher states of mind."

Nels looked up. "Wrong?"

Black nodded. He wasn't trying to lighten things up now. "Wouldn't you think a statement advocating the use of drugs in this day and age would be questioned? Just a little, teensy question?"

The staff was looking at me now, especially the three fact checkers, who were undoubtedly wondering whether they were going to be fired, or whether I was.

"Well, I assumed it had been checked, of course," Nels said. He stood up and handed the magazine to me. "I asked myself, Why would he be quoted at all as an example of the idiocy of L.A. if he hadn't said something idiotic? Anyway, it was said on the air. We can get a transcript and see. The writer's supposed to be good. Who was it, Mike? Trill something?"

"Trilla. Trilla McGuffy. She started out here, may even have done some pieces for *New York* when you were there." He shook his head. "Now she's in L.A. writing film scripts, but I think she mentioned having an assignment from *Es-*

quire. I'll get her on the phone and check it out." I looked at Anton Black. "Can I see the letter?"

He handed it to me without a word. It was on legal-looking letterhead and signed by a lawyer on Sunset Drive. It asked us to reconstitute the broadcaster's ruined reputation instantly or he'd sue the pants off us. It denied that he had ever recommended the use of drugs to anybody.

"He denies it," I said for the benefit of the staff, and handed the letter to Nels. Somebody laughed, as if I'd intended it as a joke. Maybe I had. I wanted to wipe that scared look off the fact checkers' faces.

"I just want to say—" It was Struiker. He was sitting back in his chair, with one hand against his cheek, his legs crossed, and he looked as if he'd just awakened from a nap. Though he spoke quietly, as usual he got everybody's immediate attention. "—that we have a serious problem here, and if you don't mind"—he glanced at Black—"I'd like to go about resolving it in a different setting. With all due respect to the staff, now that we've had this fascinating discussion I'd prefer to keep the matter between me and Nels, informing you as necessary, Anton. You can't have thirty people noodling on something like this. And of course nobody's to talk about it outside this room, not a word, please, until it's settled."

He swung his chair around, and his gaze flickered around the room. "I will repeat, just for emphasis, that this is a very serious matter. Even if the man said something that could be construed as recommending drugs, he apparently has a sterling reputation that could seem to have been besmirched in this chatty, lighthearted article, especially to a California jury. I want to say a word about California juries. Everybody hates the press, and California juries especially hate the New York press, which is always sitting in judgment on our California brethren. Now, this author's stuff may thrill readers of *New York* and *Esquire*, but her tone in this piece is not reassuring to me in terms of its effect on a jury. In fact, I have just read it and I think it's a frivolous piece of writing by a smartass author who ought to know better, and I think that's how a jury will regard it. Because this Bangor Laudicek, or whatever his name is, is highly regarded as a TV commentator out there, a fellow Californian who doesn't deserve this shit. Now, that's a preliminary reaction, but I just want to point out that when you're putting out a magazine for general consumption, you do have to think about more than just getting your jollies. That's all I think I should say to you all until this is over, but I would like a word with Nels and, uh"—suddenly he was having trouble remembering my name—"Mike here."

Anton Black dismissed the class and excused himself, pleading a business lunch. The three of us went into Nels's office and sat down.

"Two things first," Struiker said, leaning back with his hands behind his head. "Talk to this flaky author and find out what she knows. Then get a look at the TV transcript. Don't ask the station in L.A. for it, because I don't want anybody to get the idea we're worried. Isn't there a public-television station in this town? You must know somebody there, don't you, Nels, who can ask L.A. for it without mentioning us? And then we'd better think about asking Bangor Laudicek to come to New York as our guest and sit down with us like gentlemen, see if we can ease his mind. Him and his crappy lawyer. I want to make a grand gesture, maybe agree up front that he's been treated unfairly, that his remarks were wrenched out of context, if that turns out to be the case. You know, here's a man of wide renown whose rampant generosity toward those who seek release and enlightenment through harmful drugs has been misinterpreted, and so he deserves not only some form of recompense—not necessarily monetary—but also emotional reassurance. Because what he really wants, you understand, is to get this author out of his hair, make sure he never has to worry about her again. Okay?"

Nels sat and looked at him. Finally, he spoke. "You want to sit down with Bangor and put him at his ease?"

"Yes," Struiker said. "Do it quickly, before he gets testy."

Nels shook his head. "Then I'm out." He turned to me. "It's all yours, Mike."

Struiker said insistently, "I need you there, Nels. The distinguished editor, experienced, open-minded, and fair. Not some twenty-five-year-old punk who looks like a copy-boy." He grinned at me. It stung, but I grinned back. I couldn't help myself.

"Can't do it," Nels said. "I might as well tell you, although I don't imagine he'll bring it up. I knew his wife before they were married, and Bangor Laudicek's a very jealous man."

Struiker stared at him. "You know what a jury would do with that?"

"I know. I'm sorry. But it's not that way. We're just friends." Nels looked at me. "This writer, it's just possible that I may have met her. When you talk to her, ask her if she was ever in Nepal."

I nodded. I already knew the answer.

Struiker said, "Christ," and closed his eyes. He looked completely relaxed, but I felt a jolt of sympathy for Trilla McGuffy. I recalled how Struiker had gone after Mr. Kim, jaw clamped, eyes burning in the gray face, nose twitching in impatience above that grim slash of mouth, his brain spinning like a gyroscope and his voice slicing the air. Like he'd just been through hell at the head of Genghis Khan's army and had wasted the place. You know, a man who knew all the world's darkest secrets, things I could never guess, and that compelling air of rendering final judgment, no matter whom it hurt.

He said, "We'd better go to California instead of asking Bangor to come here. Mike, I'll have my secretary call you with the details, but start packing. Call McGuffy and tell her not to talk to anybody. Go and do that right now."

I looked at Nels and he nodded, so I left. I'd never seen him look so Nordic and blond, so kind of sad, so pale. Like a child who'd never been allowed to go out in the sun. He couldn't have been doing much mountain climbing lately, and if he was still seeing Mrs. Bangor Laudicek, it must be in New York, not sunny California. When? How often? Where? Was that where he went sometimes when he was out of the office? To be with her? And how well did he know Trilla McGuffy?

I got back to my desk feeling dirty and disgusted—not with him, with me. A week ago, I'd been telling a low-life private eye he was a liar. Then I'd been Bob Struiker's alter ego. Now I was beginning to think like the late Morton Brock.

Three

I couldn't imagine what Trilla McGuffy looked like. I'd never asked her. Somehow it seems unethical for an editor working with a writer of the opposite sex to get that personal. This has nothing to do with sexual harassment around the office; it just interferes with the working relationship. But I'd been curious about McGuffy from the start because on the phone she had the voice of an angel, as if she'd sung in heavenly choirs. But more than her looks, I'd been curious about her mind. She was obviously bright and perceptive, but she had a way of putting things that made me wonder whether she was quite earthbound. It was a fey quality that came out when you least expected it. If she were an angel, I'd said to myself, that could mean she'd been off the earth quite a while, long enough to forget what it was like here. It hadn't occurred to me then, though, to ask her how she felt about misquoting people in today's litigious society. I'd just wanted to find out whether any of the strings in her harp were missing.

"What did you do after that last piece for *Rolling Stone* in New York?" I'd asked her months before, while we were discussing her assignment. "You start doing movie scripts right away?"

"No, Mike," she'd said on the phone from L.A., "I blissed out in Nepal for a while."

Nepal? A long way from home, I thought. Originally, she'd come to Manhattan from an exurb of Chicago, by way of the University of Michigan. She'd made a quick reputation in *The Village Voice*, then written a whole lot of memorable articles in *New York* and *Rolling Stone*. After that, there were sporadic appearances in *Interview*, all of them, yes, datelined Nepal, curiously offbeat little pieces that sounded as if they came from the world's outer reaches, someplace in the neighborhood of Shangri-la. Altered mind states, psychedelic drugs, out-of-body stuff against a background of soft temple bells and cataclysmic mountain ranges. She must have been there for a year or more. Then, in California, only random magazine assignments to keep her name alive. And shared writing credits on three or four money-making films, which I might not have known about if it hadn't been for Harv Wallace, the Hollywood gossip columnist.

Wallace, a reporter for the *Los Angeles Inquirer*, had sold a book of his livelier reminiscences to the publishing house I worked for then. I became his editor. A year or so later, when I was hired on at *Beyond*, he told me he wanted to do a piece on L.A., but when it came time to assign it, he said he was too busy working on another book. He'd suggested McGuffy. Said he'd work with her on it. Said she was becoming a major screenwriter. Said she was a looker. Come to think of it, maybe that's where I got the idea she might be an angel. Harv Wallace liked his women young and swift-winged. His books touched on his sexual conquests among the stars, famous Hollywood names who'd been his for a night or a noon hour. The implication was that along the way lots of aspiring, star-struck young women had added themselves to his collection, in return for a column mention, of course. Harv Wallace was not a nice man. But he was intelligent and funny, not to mention pink-cheeked and portly, and I'd enjoyed working with him on the book. And he'd been right about McGuffy. Whatever the other qualifications that interested Wallace, to us she'd seemed absolutely right for the California piece, someone who could get beyond the shoddy faddism and eccentric flash of the place to its essence. Her drawly prose had bite and style, and she was young and adventurous, with a rare blend of Midland conscience, coastal sophistication, and Eastern mysticism. She was said to have been both a protégée of Norman Mailer, the curmudgeonly old drum major of the march on the Pentagon, and a disciple of the new Walt Disney—Steven Spielberg. I wondered what influential guru she'd attached herself to in the Far East.

"What were you doing in Nepal?" I'd asked her on the phone. "How was it?"

"Weird," she'd said, and then an explanation that explained nothing: "The scenery and the people were wonderful." And almost as an afterthought: "Tricked me right out of my skull." And she'd laughed, like bubbles sparkling in the sunlight, and mentioned manifestations of Buddha consciousness, purging the ego, and the radiance around us right now.

I had steered her back to the article, but she'd seemed uncertain about exactly what tone we wanted her to strike. "If you're trying to build circulation and advertising out here, I guess you have two ways to do it, by being nice and polite or by being totally opinionated. Either way, you'll get people's attention. I know you want to get beyond nice, but on the other hand I haven't seen too much in your magazine that was, you know, sophisticated and outspoken and clever. If you poke too much outrageous fun, you're going to make a whole lot of people out here really angry. You ready for that? Or you want to play it safe?"

"Both. Neither! Look, Trilla, you just play it straight and let us worry about the fallout."

"Huh! That's what they told the reporters on the press plane over Hiroshima. And call me Trill."

I'd done an audible double take. "There was no press plane over Hiroshima!"

"Just a joke," she'd said. "Literary license."

More shades of Mr. Kim. This unexpected debate had started to worry me a little. What was she after? Reassurance? I'd decided to give her some. "No, Trill, just do your usual workmanlike job and we'll be very happy. It's a great satisfaction to me to have your hardheaded reporting and exuberant style in the magazine. We don't always get both."

"Wow," she'd said, "thank you! An editor after my own heart."

Fine, Trill, I'd thought, now just go get the story.

But now, calling to ask her about Bangor Laudicek's views on using drugs, I was hoping the quote had not been another case of literary license.

Her voice was breathless, and a little edgy. She said she'd just gotten out of the shower, where she'd been trying to participate in the world with joy, not fear or desire, the way things had been for her back in Nepal, and then she said, "Oh, what the hell, you're calling about Bangor, aren't you? I was trying to pretend it was another assignment or a Pulitzer Prize or something."

"I don't think they give Pulitzers to magazine writers," I said.

"Then, okay, it's Bangor. Listen, it started ten days ago. Ten days of this shit!"

"What started?"

"These calls! My phone service couldn't figure it out. Some weird lady calling me every day, they said, leaving messages. They thought she was calling from the state of Maine, but she wasn't. She finally got me in the middle of the night, and it was Bangor's wife, and she said, 'What are you doing to Bangor?' I knew I was in for a dark night of the soul."

"Bangor? Oh, I see, Bangor, Maine." I didn't see at all.

But she said, "Exactly. The first place his parents saw

when they flew over to this country from Europe was the rocky coast of Maine. He was five years old. As a patriotic gesture, they changed his name from Frederick to Bangor. This was nothing to what they might have called him, maybe Buddha or Siddhartha or something, because his father was a noted scholar in world religions. Papa Laudicek wound up teaching at a small school near La Grange. That's in Illinois, outside Chicago. I grew up there."

"You knew him?"

"Not him, no, not then. I knew his parents because they lived down the street, but Bangor was older and already at the University of Michigan by the time I was born. His parents encouraged me to go there to school because I was interested in communications and Bangor was becoming a big wheel in the department. Radio-TV."

"You mean a professor?" The guy was accumulating more credentials all the time.

"Yes, almost unbearably distinguished and adored. Every December, he'd stand up in the auditorium and read *A Christmas Carol* to the student body. He also had a sideline, seminars on inner peace and the new transcendentalism. I knew he was a phony from the start, doing Scrooge in that big, sonorous voice, with his big head of gray-flecked hair and those glowing actor's eyes. A really marvelous head, but not as much in it as you'd think, looking at it. Anyway, he left a couple of years after I got there."

"And went to L.A."

"Into show business, yeah. Talk-show host, celebrated spokesman for social causes, great brain. Big bullshit artist."

"You don't like him."

"How could you tell? Listen, that quote in my story was right on the money, Mike. He's a jerk, a twirly son of a bitch. He said it publicly on his TV talk show, and I've got the quote and the date here someplace. It's written down on a cocktail napkin." I could hear what sounded like a file drawer opening. She seemed to be collapsing into bales of paper.

"Can you get a transcript of the broadcast?" I asked, and she said, "Sure, why not?"

But by that time, Bangor had sent us a detailed summary of his remarks, typed out from memory on his own typewriter, and while it didn't specifically recommend taking drugs, it did seem to play fast and loose with their possible effects, sliding over the worst of them, and if not condoning drug use, at least in awe of those who were using them, hell-bent on finding nirvana in an age that sorely tried the soul. I couldn't see that he had a case. What exactly did he want us to retract?

But of course Struiker cut through the mystery the next day, explaining again about California juries, slicing into my peace of mind. "Furthermore," he said, "it doesn't seem to me that he's recommending the use of drugs to anybody, and that's the crux of it." It looked as if I was going to drag myself out to California with my hat in my hand. I didn't look forward to that. I was born there, in L.A. My parents had only recently moved down the coast, to Laguna Beach. My sister still lived around there when she wasn't in college up in Oregon, and my brother was just up the road in San Francisco, in marketing. It was on a visit to my brother's that I'd met my girlfriend, Panky Janvier, who had jetted out for a weekend with an old college roommate. Panky isn't her real name. I call her that because she wants me to. Her real name is Gisele, but as a new American she believes that all really modish young women should have names that sound as if they came out of the eastern educational mill. She works for a fashion house on the Upper East Side and she's very beautiful. I call her whatever she wants but I always think Gisele.

"But," Struiker was saying, "there are other factors that may be just as damaging. Nels messing around with Bangor's woman, even if it was all in the past. And no wonder

Bangor wants to get McGuffy out of his hair. Are you aware that she's done this to him before?"

"No. When?"

"The first time at the University of Michigan, in the school paper. Unkind remarks about his annual reading of Dickens, a hallowed event she made light of, and some fairly scurrilous reviews of his discussion shows on the campus radio station. But she didn't stop there. Just last year out in California, in an alternative paper, more so-called levity at Bangor's expense. And now she's going around spreading the word that she's destroyed him in the national media."

"That doesn't sound like Trill. She's a professional."

"Well, I want you to tell her to keep quiet from now on and be prepared to meet with us out there next week. Tell her if she opens her mouth about this again, she'll see me in court and I won't be defending her."

"I'll tell her."

"Have you found the tape?"

"I'm working on it. The local station hasn't gotten back to me."

"All we need is a copy of the passage that so offended Miss McGuffy. And don't discuss the case with her. The less she knows, the better."

"All right."

I called PBS with a reminder and then Trill, and she said, "I had a meeting with Bangor."

Oh, shit, I almost said. "What about?"

"His lawyer called and set it up. Listen, what's going on? I don't know how much more of this I can stand—I mean it, Mike. In Nepal, I learned to sit for four hours without moving an eyelash and forget things like this happen, but in the last two weeks my nerves and my rapture have been shot to hell. I'm twitching all over."

"Yeah, that's terrible, Trill. But what happened? When was this?"

"Yesterday after you called, his lawyer called. We talked

over tea. The great man brought up something I'd forgotten about that you ought to know. A year or so ago, I helped write a piece for the *L.A. Primer*, the alternative newspaper, you know? They were putting out a gag issue, and we, a guy I know and his wife, concocted a review of a nonexistent CIA documentary film in which a talk-show host turns his viewers into mind slaves, kind of intellectual TV rape, and as a result they go out and rid the world of Lebanese cabdrivers and save the country from mass destruction. Silly, isn't it? Anyway, Bangor reminded me. What happened was, we were trying to think of what to call this talk-show host, and this guy, or maybe it was his wife, came up with the name Gangbanger Blankcheck. Bangor says, 'Why did you do that to me?' I said, 'Do what?' I'd forgotten about it completely! Obviously he thinks of me as his nemesis or something."

"Well, are you?" I said. "What about the University of Michigan?"

"Yeah, that's another thing! Hey, Mike, listen, as much as I despise this man for his intellectual pretentions and philistinism, I've got to give him high marks for the way he's managed to pull the wool over everybody's eyes. I mean, he's such a success! Don't knock it. Back at Michigan, he was Mr. God, but what did I know back then? I started writing for the campus paper, first letters to the editor, then I drew some cartoons, and I had all these professors mad at me. Like this one cartoon of a life-studies art class, showing this model wearing a coat that went all the way down to her ankles, and the art professor screamed at me! I couldn't figure it out. Weren't these the halls of learning? Weren't we all after some form of higher truth that didn't have anything to do with pasty-faced personal ambition? Then I started doing radio and television reviews of the university programs, and I guess I did review Bangor's show. He oozed such self-satisfaction, and he had this way about him, you know, he was able to put people down without seeming to just by inflecting his voice, and the show was such pompous garbage. You could listen for a whole hour and never know what you'd heard. Mike, think about it. Just because it's a campus station, does that give them the right to be boring and self-righteous? Doesn't the press, even the campus press, have the right to express an opinion? Demand something more discriminating?"

"Have you got copies of those reviews?"

"Sure. Somewhere here. I'll send them to you."

"So what was the upshot?"

"Huh?"

"Of the talk with Bangor and his lawyer?"

"Oh. Nothing. I mean he wanted an apology or something or they'd bring suit. His lawyer said he thought we could come to an understanding if I agreed to leave Bangor alone in the future, and I said fine, if he leaves me alone. Bangor says, 'What does that mean?' and I know what's going through his mind, and I say, 'You're a grown-up public figure, you figure it out. Don't I have the right to criticize?' And that ends the discussion. Mike, I talked to a lawyer friend of mine, and he said, 'Well, if he didn't sue you before, for other things you've written, how can he sue you now? It won't stand up.' He said there's something in the law about that. Would you please ask your lawyer? I don't want to get sued, Mike. Right now, I feel like I just want to go to sleep for a year or two."

I told her to take it easy and say nothing more about the case and get ready to meet with us in L.A., and she said, "Oh, my God, I feel as if I'm going to crack up. I'm not as young as I was, even a couple of years ago. And I've got a script revision that's due in three weeks—thank God you didn't offer me another assignment, although I am supposed to do one for *Esquire* about the new young comedians out here. I've got notes up to my tush but I can't even knock off the first paragraph."

"Trill," I said, "calm down. Get back to your Nepal state of mind. Think about it."

"You can't do it if you think about it, Mike. You have

to step ashore in a different world and realize you've been there all the time."

I remembered what Nels had said. I said, "Speaking of Nepal, the editor in chief thinks he might have met you there. Nels Barbidoux." I heard the bed squeak and she was quiet for about fifteen seconds. Then she said, "No, I don't think so. Maybe." And then, after another fifteen-second pause, "Mike, you know what I've been thinking? About those pictures Burley took for my California article. They were good, you know that? I didn't expect all that much, but I mean they were good!"

I said, "Good" and "Take care," and hung up. I put in a call to Struiker, but he was in court and wouldn't return until midafternoon. I wrote him a memo and took an early lunch.

Burley was Burley Moore—I guess originally it was Burleigh, but he changed it. He was that unpretentious, though he had quite a reputation as a photographer. He'd illustrated a lot of articles for us over the years, and he'd taken the photos for Nels's pieces for the *Geographic*. He and Trill seemed to know each other, so it had looked to me like a good matchup. I'd met Burley several times. An old-reliable image, with a shuffling gait and a face like a used tire, the fiftyish paunch dropping down over his belt. Bug eyes. Eyes so alert, it was said they'd never missed a shot, never missed a thing. Came to L.A. from Arkansas, and was always stopping in Manhattan on his way to someplace else. He'd had exhibits of his work on Madison Avenue, in the galleries. In fact, I'd bought one of his photographs the year before and hung it over my fake fireplace. It shows three little girls sitting in a doorway in a Third World country—Afghanistan, I decided. The walls of the house are redbrick. The girls are seven or eight years old, and two of them are looking at the camera and frowning, as if they're not sure what the photographer is doing there. The third has a leg up on one knee and is holding on to her foot, looking off and saying something or even singing. Their dark hair is pulled back tight, and there are metal bangles around their ankles and wrists.

At first when I looked at that photograph, I thought of my sister. Like the little girls, she's got a lot of spunk. Then, for a while, I thought about Mr. Kim and how he must be feeling, very much Third World. This happened whenever the full moon hung low over Manhattan, as it must over the somber lands of Vietnam and Afghanistan. Now, though, when I look at the photograph, I think of Trilla McGuffy, especially the third little girl, who's looking off singing, part of some celestial choir. I hear both their voices—the little girl's robust singsong one and Trill's softer one, less sure but still clear as a bell. Sometimes the sound of it seems to last the whole night long.

Four

By midweek, we still hadn't gotten a copy of Bangor's tape, and my conversation with Trill had lowered her still further in Struiker's esteem.

"You see what we're up against," he said on the phone. "She's a fuckup and has to be hobbled. I've been reading the correspondence you sent over, and you can see by her letters how weird she is. I wish I knew what she was doing that year in Nepal, but I can probably guess. Somebody like this, I'd think you'd have checked her out before giving her an assignment, asked what kind of reputation she had out there, or did she ever have anything to do with Bangor."

He put me on hold to take another call. He was particularly incensed over what she'd said in her early letters about working with Burley Moore, who was a favorite of Struiker's. Trill wrote that she had squeezed Burley into her 1967 cream-colored Mustang, open to the sky, and that as he shot roll after roll of the sights around L.A., she'd had to laugh, he was "such an old shoe."

"Burley's a nice-enough guy," she wrote, "but everything he shot was just so old-fashioned. Hackneyed, old hat, know what I mean? I don't say he's incompetent, but I wish you'd have let me team up with somebody who knew what he was doing."

Burley's own accounts of their adventures were more laconic: "More of the shots you wanted. We're staying with it. Let me know if it's not what you want." Or one comment that especially caught Struiker's eye: "Laudicek doesn't want his picture taken."

"Of course he didn't!" Struiker snapped. "Burley knew there was some difficulty between Bangor and Miss McGuffy, but he kept out of it, said no more than was necessary. And all she could see in him was an old shoe who was over the hill. Well, he *is* an old shoe, but he's worth ten of her."

Trill hadn't seen it then, how good he was. "He may be an experienced photographer," she had written, "but I still say he's no Steichen." At that point, she clearly wasn't going to have it said of her that she was in any way magnanimous.

Struiker came back on the line. He sounded downcast, almost petulant. "Mike, tell PBS to forget about the tape. Call Jim Provine on the coast and ask him if he can quietly lay hands on it, and let me know what he says."

I made both calls. I didn't know Jim Provine all that well. He was our West Coast advertising rep and a real go-getter, red in the face and built like a high school wrestler. He said sure, he'd look into it, he had friends at the public TV station. Anything for the company, he said, putting the stress on *company*. I knew he had no love for me, and I was sure he'd put in a quick call to ask Anton Black what was up. He had that just-below-the-threshold sneer in his voice that said, Who do you think you are, kid? and he wasn't going to do anything for me until he'd checked it out. And me out. "Who?" he'd said, picking up the phone. "Lindenthal? Oh. Yeah. Hi, Jack."

I reported back to Struiker, who was unavailable, and left a message: "Provine says okay." I was getting tired of being a message center. All these conversations going on all around me—what was Anton Black thinking? Where was Nels Barbidoux? It would never have occurred to me to send Jim Provine out on a job like this, yet I could see how he would be useful out there beyond selling advertising, as an extra set of eyes and ears. I was thinking about Bangor Laudicek and his outraged wife, and Trill and her almost involuntary pursuit of him, crowding him to the limit, and Harv Wallace pursuing her (wasn't he? hadn't he?). Why? What was going on? How deep was this going to get? It seemed like a tempest in a teapot, but if you're the teapot, you rattle and roll.

Jim Provine gave his all for the company all right. He postponed a trip with his wife to Catalina and stayed up two nights working on what he considered to be his assignment. He and three friends at the TV station secretly went through the place in the dead of night, two of them to make a search for the tape and one to stand by to copy it if it could be found . . . and then, for some reason, to erase the original! Because he didn't trust the first two any more than he trusted anyone else, he hid himself and watched their progress. He'd promised each of them two hundred bucks, but his friend on the tape machine wouldn't take any money, so he'd bought him dinner. They found nothing. After playing parts of dozens of shows, listening for the inimitable sound of Bangor's voice, the three friends gave up and went home. Provine stayed, going over the ground once more, checking for Bangor's name on labels. Finally, after a late dinner, he had gone back to his office to send me a report detailing all this.

> I don't mind giving up my vacation or going without sleep, but I guess I have to tell you, Mike, this isn't the job I signed on to do. I'm a great fan of the magazine, naturally, since it's my bread and butter—and what the hell, raspberry jam!! But I've spent years in magazine offices and I know what goes on there. Salespeople always meet editorial types coming in the

door. I mean when you're heading out at nine-thirty after the morning sales meeting to meet a customer, you can always count on an editor or two just getting to work. I know, I know, you guys and gals work hard and stay late. But you'll always get exemplary service from me because I believe in what *Beyond* stands for.

I often hear it complained that I'm sitting out here on my ass on the beach watching t. and a. (that's tuna and albacore, ha ha). 'Tain't so! We on the sales force are out pitching every single minute of the day. Now I don't want to complain about the article you ran. You never hear me mention editorial except to cheer. But as a longtime resident of Southern California I do take exception to some of the remarks of Trilla McGuffy, and as long as you have called my attention to the problem you are having I must say I don't think she had a call to put down Bangor Laudicek, who has the kind of reputation she'll never see as long as she lives.

You know, Mike, if you'd given me a call BEFORE you ran the story, I could have told you she was up to no good with one or two inquiries. Bangor Laudicek's reputation in this town is tops, Mike. He's A-number-one with his colleagues at the TV station, his ratings are among the best, and the people of the press and the other media are shocked by this attack on him. Trilla McGuffy's reputation, on the other hand, leaves something to be desired, and for months she has been telling everybody she could find, loudly and sometimes publicly, that she's been "out to get that bastard Laudicek" in some national publication. She has tried to do so locally but of course he would never sue a local publication, he's too big a supporter of L.A. She won't say why she's after him. One reason is that he may have spurned her romantically in the past. (Bangor was divorced a number of years ago and has only recently remarried.) In any case, this time Laudicek is determined to get her to cease her attacks on him and he will file a libel suit if necessary.

I've spent a good many hours on this project, but that's the kind of service you can expect from me, and in the old days that's the way it was always done, and they always asked before something happened, not afterward. But would you "new wave" types do it that way today? I guess not.

Mike, I've had a lot of complaints about what she wrote from nearly every customer I've called on. Even people who have nothing good to say about places like Hollywood and Vine found her article objectionable, that is in reference to So. Cal. And it brings to mind other instances of a peculiar lack of cooperation between editorial and advertising. Not nearly enough space is given to ideas for sales-oriented material, as would have been true in the old days just a few short years ago. Placement of ads, etc., etc., but I won't bore you with details about getting more advertising, without which there wouldn't be any editorial whatever, as I know you are not basically interested. I assume you will be forwarding this letter to Messrs. Barbidoux and Struiker. As I have a few other observations about the general lack of editorial cooperation, notably whatever happened to the idea I had for a special section on skiwear, and mentioning the cool reception to a section on the new swimsuits that *Newsweek* sells out with every year, I am sending them along with a copy

of this letter to Mr. Anton Black. Plus a couple
of other things not meant for your tender ears.
Yours sincerely.

Needless to say, etc., etc., my tender ears were burning. Since this was clearly an attack on editorial, I took the letter down the hall to Nels's office, hoping he'd be there, since he'd been away for the last three days. This was Friday, first thing in the morning. I expected him to be outraged, but when I showed him the letter, he waved it off with a "good old Jim" shake of the head and gave me a letter of his own.

It opened with "Dear Nels" and was signed, four typewritten sheets later, "Affectionately, Pamela Laudicek."

I looked up. "His wife?"

He nodded. "I told you we were old friends."

"It's been far too long since we've seen each other," the letter began. I said, "Are you sure you want me to read this?"

Again he nodded. "Take it with you and mull it over before you show it to Bob Struiker. But before you go, I want to tell you who she is." His voice dropped to a confidential level, even though the door was closed. "You know Burley."

I nodded.

"When Burley Moore moved out to L.A., he began taking pictures for the *Inquirer*'s ace gossip columnist, an old hand who started out covering the Hollywood scene for UPI. Harv Wallace, maybe you've heard of him."

I said I had. Didn't he remember it was Wallace who'd first suggested the story to me?

"Well," Nels went on, "Harv picked up on Burley's work right away and took him under his wing as what amounted to his personal photographer. What marvelous expense accounts they must have had! They did a lot of stuff together, some nice, some not so nice. Made a few careers, cut down others. You know Hollywood gossip. Then after a few years when Wallace started writing his books and getting his gossip on the air, Burley branched out, too, and started to build his reputation. My guess is that Harv's move gave him confidence that he could make it as a free-lance. Along the way, he did some fine work for me.

"Anyway, a few years ago, Wallace took on a new assistant, a bright young woman who wasn't getting acting jobs and anyway wanted to be a writer." He pointed to the letter. "That's her, Pamela Laudicek. She married the great man eighteen months ago. When I met her she was Pamela Bitterman, and her stage name was Pamela Winters. Between Off-Broadway auditions, she did some pieces for me at *Travel & Leisure.*" He gave me a quick smile and immediately looked abashed. "We had an affair. It went on for six months." He looked at the letter. "Anyway, read it. It won't cheer you up, but then that's not part of my job. Come to think of it, neither was Pamela." He picked up a sheaf of letters that needed his signature. "She sounds a little overwrought, more strident than she used to, but then you've got to consider who she's been living with."

The letter, once it got past the formalities, was completely hysterical. I don't mean funny, I mean sad. She could have sent a three-sentence fax: Bangor is too beautiful to be believed. Trilla McGuffy is a whore and a bitch. And unless *Beyond* puts this matter to rest, my dear beloved Bangor is going to do to you in court what I once did to you privately with your full cooperation.

Five

I called Struiker right away and gave him a summary of both letters. He expressed little interest in either. He said, "Go back to your guy at the PBS station and ask him to get us two copies of the tape. Have them sent back here. I don't want to take the time to listen to them in California."

"When are we leaving?"

"Monday. Be in my office at four o'clock and we'll go to the airport together. Tell McGuffy we're coming but nothing else."

"How long are we staying?"

"Two days. Maybe three."

"It's not the best time for me to be away," I said. "Nels will be in Washington, at an editors' conference."

There was a moment of quiet. "Never mind about that. Anton agrees that this is more important. I want to see all the people involved and reach an agreement if we can, get Bangor on our side. Otherwise, if we go into court, we can forget it."

"We don't have a chance in court?"

Struiker sighed. "Suppose Laudicek's lawyer wants to explore the question of whether there's anyone specifically at *Beyond* who doesn't like him."

"You mean besides McGuffy. And maybe Nels."

He said, "Yes, and you, for example."

I laughed. "Me?"

"Of course. You're the one who assigned the article and told the writer what you wanted and ordered around the photographer, so what might have motivated you? Suppose Bangor's lawyer puts you on the stand. He says, 'You're from L.A. When did you move to New York?' "

"After UCLA," I said.

" 'You like New York?' "

"Yes. I make my living there."

" 'Anything negative about New York in the article?' "

"Of course not. It wasn't about—"

" 'Just answer the question. Have you printed anything favorable about New York City in the past?' "

"Of course."

" 'So here we have an article assigned by a former Los Angeleno that goes out of its way to put it to one of the leading lights of New York's archrival, Los Angeles, and he specifically assigned it to a writer known by the magazine to have attacked said leading light several times before and eager to do it again in the national press.' "

I was still laughing. "Wait a minute," I said. "Objection. We didn't know that."

" 'How many articles has Burley Moore illustrated for you?' "

"I have no idea."

" 'How many times in the past year? The past two years?' "

"Ten or twelve. I don't know."

" 'Is he listed on your masthead?' "

"Contributing photographer."

" 'Practically a paid employee. Does he have a contract?' "

"A letter of agreement."

" 'Contractual employee knows the author had a hard-on for Bangor Laudicek and wanted to get him, expose him before the nation as the laughable jerk she thinks he is. How could Burley Moore not know? Bangor's wife works for Burley's best friend and colleague. Anyway, it's the Southern California entertainment industry, where everybody knows everything about everybody. How long has Jim Provine been sales rep for *Beyond?*' "

"I don't know. He was here when I came here."

" 'A long time? More than three years?' "

"*Beyond* isn't a lot older than that."

" 'And Provine, a contractual employee of the magazine—that makes two of them—knew all about McGuffy's blood lust.' "

"But that doesn't prove—"

" 'Just answer yes or no. How many people on the West Coast who might be knowledgeable did *Beyond* contact to establish McGuffy's reliability?' "

"Well . . ."

" 'Not one editor called anybody. Even after McGuffy comes up with this astonishing quotation, nobody calls to check it, not even the fact checkers, and nobody asks what is the relationship between McGuffy and Bangor Laudicek. Why not? Obviously, they already knew.' "

"So we lose the case," I said.

"Of course we do. Especially if it's a jury full of women and they all sit there drooling over Bangor, whose gray suit sets off his prematurely graying hair. So you see why we can't do this over the phone. Four o'clock Monday, all right?"

"Right. Two or three days?"

"Have a good weekend."

He hung up.

Then he called back and said, "Phone Burley and tell him to meet the plane, and tell him to bring along a tape recorder. We may need one. You'd better bring along some issues of your crappy magazine so we can impress the visiting firemen."

Things seemed to be speeding up, or else I was slowing down. I said, in some kind of daze, "Firemen?"

"Bangor. His lawyer. I know the expression is imprecise, but Jesus Christ, Mike, get with it."

I had a hard time finding Burley's number, and his wife seemed to be in as much of a fog as I was.

"*Now?*" she said, as if she couldn't believe it. "You want to talk to him *now?*"

But Burley came on the line. It sounded as if he had wrestled the phone away from her. "Yeah, Mike, what's up?" He's still in bed, I thought. Soft life.

I gave him the message. He said, "You know, they got those portable ones now." His voice was soft and flat. I couldn't tell whether he was kidding or not.

"Well," I said, "I've got a tape recorder in the office—"

"No, Mike, I'll bring it." He said something to his wife. "Mike, it's just a little joke Bob and I have between us. It goes back to the days when I was shooting portraits with a big old eight-by-ten view camera. Bob had some work for me in New York, so I asked him to rent one and have it waiting. He met me at the airport with one of the new little thirty-five-millimeter jobs. It was when they were first bringing them out. He said, 'You know, Burley, they got these portable ones now.' So now it's just a little joke." He paused. "Mike, is that all? What time you got?"

I looked at my watch. "Nine-forty," I said. Then I said, "My God, Burley, I'm sorry. It's six-forty in the morning out there!"

"That's okay, I know how it is," Burley said. "His master's voice. Have a good ride out, Mike." I heard the phone rattle around a bit before the connection was broken.

Ten minutes later, I got a call from Trill. "Hi," I said. "You always up this early?"

She groaned. "No! It's absurd! I'm sleepless and scared to death. Mike, what does this message mean?"

"What message?"

"You don't know? It was left with my answering service

and I didn't get it until about one o'clock this morning, telling me to meet you for lunch on Tuesday. Lunch? Do you know where my appetite will be?"

"Who's it from?"

"Some horrible legal-sounding—wait a minute. Robert Struiker's secretary, legal counsel for *Beyond*. She sounds absolutely cold-blooded."

I said, "They didn't tell me about lunch. We're flying out Monday."

"She didn't say where the lunch is. The message says to call you Tuesday morning at the Hollywood Plaza."

"Is that where we're staying?"

"You're asking me? Well, I'm glad you're going to be at the lunch. I've been hearing from some of Bangor's friends at the TV station, and I can't stand getting chewed over anymore."

"Relax." I started to tell her that Struiker had Bangor Laudicek in his pocket unless we got into court, but then I remembered I wasn't supposed to discuss the case with her. "I'll see you Tuesday. Take the weekend off."

"You bet I am. I'm cutting out. I'll try to be back, but I may just decide it's not worth it."

"Where you going?"

"Down the coast. I may not get past San Diego or I may wind up in Baja, maybe raped and pillaged by bandits. That might be preferable to dealing with the legal counsel for *Beyond*."

"I doubt it. I'll see you Tuesday, Trill."

"Oh, Mike! Are they going to take me away?" Her voice had risen to a quivering, high-wire sound, and the ensuing silence was startling.

"Trill," I said softly. I felt like I was talking to a child. "Be a good girl."

I could hardly hear her now. "Oh, God, Mike, please don't say that. That's what my daddy told me just before he walked into the ocean."

Merrilee, the production assistant, was standing in my

doorway with some final pasteup boards, waiting for an okay before they went to the plant. "I'm sorry, Trill, I didn't know. Trill, I've got to go now. We're on deadline."

"Okay, Mike," she said in that same small, faraway voice. "Don't worry. I'm okay."

She hung up. I turned and took the boards from Merrilee and sat staring at them without seeing them. It was a cool morning. They'd turned up the heat in the building, and the air was blowing through the ducts in the ceiling, sounding like a steady surf pounding the rocks. I thought, Her father walked into the ocean? Did I believe that? I'd told Struiker everything so far, but I decided not to tell him this. It turned out that over the next week I'd be keeping a number of things to myself, for one reason or another.

Six

Struiker's secretary was a small, dark-haired woman named Jeanne. Everything about her seemed neatly round and tidily efficient. She handed me the airline tickets and a three-by-five card noting the flight times—the return was for Wednesday—and said he'd be out as soon as he'd taken a call.

"Don't fuss over him," Struiker said sharply, coming into the paneled reception room and flashing me the grin that always startled me, the way it lit up his face so unexpectedly, and then startled me again, it was gone so fast, like a magical illusion. He stayed in motion, checking his pockets for slips of paper that he passed along to Jeanne and taking the dangerous-looking black briefcase she handed him.

"Was that Angie? Is she home?" she asked, and when he nodded, added, "She get homesick?"

Holding the door for me, he said to her, "Remind me I've got to put her on that plane when I get back, before they know she's gone." Going down in the elevator to the subbasement parking garage, he said, "Angie's my middle daughter. She's supposed to be in private school in England. I threatened her with banishment if she came home at Easter, so instead she comes home three weeks later."

"You have three daughters?"

"Just like the old 'Bonanza,' only different." He stared at me, examining my tie. "The oldest is at Harvard Law School, smart as a demon. Molly's in a Massachusetts prep school. Let me give you a word of advice about offspring. When they're fifteen, give them each twenty-five thousand dollars and tell them to get lost or you'll whip their ass." There was a glimmer of a smile. I didn't know what to say.

The elevator doors opened and I followed him across the concrete to a black Mercedes that showed neither scratches nor dust. He put my bag in the trunk and got in behind the wheel. "Well," he said, starting it up, although I could barely tell, "Pelham Manor and then JFK, and I hope you didn't forget your sunglasses and tanning lotion. I use number twenty-nine myself."

The house was a large, carefully ramshackle structure with an outdoor swimming pool built into the green slope behind it. Struiker hugged his errant daughter and then went off to finish packing. She scurried after him, trim and dark-eyed, with glasses rimmed in what looked like pink neon and a feminized drivenness that reminded me of him. Paula, his wife, surprised me. She looked nothing like her daughter. She was a tall, ample, even matronly blond. Her frequent smile, though, didn't have a lot of warmth behind it. The two of us sat down in the living room with drinks. She'd had one in her hand, I'd noticed, when we came in.

"So when will you be back?" Paula said, and I blinked. Didn't she know this?

"On Wednesday."

"Oh, really?" She said it as if she didn't care. "I was led to believe it might take longer than that."

"It could, I suppose." She seemed to be fishing. I wondered whether this was how she was used to getting her information. I changed the subject, not wanting to be in the middle. "Your daughter's very attractive."

"She hasn't seen her father for eight months." She sipped her drink. "I don't suppose you have children."

"I'm not married."

"Bob's a wonderful father, now that they're all gone." She looked around as her daughter came into the room.

Angie said, "He wants to know if you're ready to drive him to the airport." She glared. "He's sending me back Thursday!"

Paula got up and put an arm around her. "I'll want you to be ready when I get back. It's very informal, but they'll expect us to be on time."

Angie said, "Lawn parties, ugh! Nothing but adults and little brats." She sounded like a member of the Royal Family, even to the accent, and something of a brat herself.

Paula looked down at her and smiled. "The brats will be off to bed early, and you'll see some of your high school friends. Our friends want to get a look at you. They haven't seen you in ages." She kissed the top of her head, but Angie continued to pout. Paula sighed and sat down, picking up her drink. "Well, dear, it's two whole days till Thursday. You can party every night and sleep in late."

"Yeah, sure. They'll all have homework. It'll be like I was never even here." She looked over at me. "I wish I was going with you guys to L.A."

Her mother laughed. "You do not! You wouldn't even go with your father and me the last time."

"I do! That was years ago, and I hadn't been through an icky London winter." She picked up a small gold giraffe from a table and cupped it in her hands. Her mother suddenly got up and went down the hall.

I said, "I went to England once, about your age. About this time of year, too, with my mother and father. It was a cold spring."

"It's always cold. They don't have any idea about central heating, that's for sure." She sat down, still holding the gold giraffe as if warming her hands by it. "I suppose you went to the Tower?"

I nodded. She grinned and lowered her eyes, and started

swinging her legs like a much younger child. She didn't come out to the car.

The conversation on the expressway was businesslike, arrangements for this, arrangements for that, and especially for Angie's return to England.

Paula said, "You could let her stay through the weekend and we could drive up to Amherst and see Molly."

Struiker shook his head. "I'll be up to my neck when I get back. There's a long trial starting next Tuesday."

"You have more than enough help."

"John's in Bermuda until midweek. The rest are all kids, except Lorimer, and he's beginning to dodder." He grinned at her, the quick vanishing trick. "I'll be just like him someday, won't I, if I don't keep moving fast in a straight line. I keep telling you it's all in the pacing."

"It's a straight road to hell, too, you know."

He didn't reply to that, whatever it meant to them, and she said, "Will he sue?"

"No. Not if he's half the man I think he is."

"Meaning what? He's half a man?"

I thought that was pretty funny but didn't dare laugh. Struiker glanced at her, frowning. "And you know which half. He likes to have long intellectual but intimate conversations with young women who come to ask his advice about getting into television. Show them he cares. But it's not their intellect he's interested in." He pitched his voice back to me. "We're seeing Bangor at nine-thirty tomorrow, with his attorney."

"Oh?" I said.

He looked back at Paula. "I brought along the British tie Angie gave me for Christmas, the sincere one. I want Mike to wear it in the morning." To me he said, "We'll talk about it all on the plane. Some people like to sleep on airplanes. I don't." Fair warning.

There was no more talk in the car, and at the airport they didn't kiss good-bye. It was as if everything in their lives had been adjudicated and now they were merely executing the will of the court.

"I'll call you when I know for sure it's over," Struiker said to her, getting out of the car. "If I don't have time, Jeanne can fill you in." He shut the door, gestured to a skycap, and unlocked the trunk. "Tickets?" he said to me. I fumbled and found them and gave them to the skycap.

Paula called out from the driver's seat, "Call if you can."

"Don't count on it," he said, I guess trying to be helpful. I collected the tickets and we went inside. When I looked back, Paula was still there in the Mercedes, waiting for an airport bus to move out of her way.

Seven

We were seated directly behind the bulkhead in second class, on the left, flying over Pennsylvania in the dark.

"I always sit here," Struiker said. "You get the legroom of first class and it's the safest place in the plane. Egress up front, quieter, and you don't feel surrounded. You can't see the screen very well, but I never watch the movie."

He was droning, like the plane. It was the sound of someone who plans to talk indefinitely and is saving his energy for turbulent times, yet it was the way Struiker always talked: authoritatively, thoughtfully, with that latent threat of intimidation. A courtroom voice, on idle. Judges have voices like that. Like actors, of course, they vary them according to what they want to convey: command, contempt, reprimand, wit, boredom, impatience. Their delivery may rise or fall, accelerate or slow, but it's always measured and forceful. This is also the way of the teacher, the lecturer, and Struiker's tone was vaguely pedagogical right now, with the usual overlay of drollery or sarcasm. It was the sound of a man who didn't expect to be interrupted or disagreed with—who has no time for that—but who, if countered, was perfectly willing to wrestle an opponent to the ground. I began to think what Struiker really wanted was to put on a judge's robes and crack a gavel.

It was also the voice of someone who's a little tired at the end of the day. His head was back against the headrest, his eyes hooded, his mouth set. The smile lines in that taut gray face weren't getting much of a workout.

"Last week I tried to give you some idea of how easy it would be for us to lose this case," he said, "but we're not going to lose it because it's not coming to trial. I want you to help me on this. When we see Bangor tomorrow, you'll be this wise, all-knowing editor who only wants to do the right thing. All Bangor's looking for is some way to restore his reputation. He feels it's been besmirched by this screwball of a dame who won't leave him alone, but he doesn't know how to do that without a drawn-out court battle. You present a very reassuring picture that should put him at ease. You're young, but he should find you easy to talk to because you have this intellectual aura about you. Of course it would help if you were a female, and if there's another meeting between Bangor and McGuffy, I'm hoping she has big breasts. Just be sincere. I'll be showing him how we can get him everything he wants far more easily and inexpensively than he could do it himself. If he plays ball, we'll give him a retraction that makes it easy on everybody, and not only that, we'll give him Trilla McGuffy's head on the end of a pike. That's what he really wants. He feels so harassed, he can't stand it anymore. But he really doesn't want to spend the kind of money it takes to get her into court, especially since he has so many more agreeable things to do. You see that, don't you?"

I was beginning to see it, how Struiker was tuning up to play Bangor like a cello, the way he'd worked on me, getting me ready for the late Morton Brock. I was nervous this time, too. I didn't want to say the wrong thing. Would I be called upon to make some decisions? Was I experienced enough to play in this foursome? Bangor evidently was a sophisticated player in a high-powered industry. Would I come off sounding like a dummy? I began to wish Harv Wallace had never approached me with the story. I was feeling like a real screwup.

But I wasn't the only one who approved magazine assignments. Where had the editor in chief been? Nels hadn't said much either way, although he'd been all over me to do the Morton Brock series. Had he passively okayed the California story because he knew it would please Anton Black? Not likely. He'd shot down Black's ideas before, and he'd even been known to change jobs when a publisher tried to dictate editorial policy. But he'd sat back, abstracted and bemused, and let it happen.

And what was Trill's role in all this? She was a professional writer, with lots at stake. At first, she'd seemed to be that clear, unalloyed voice we wanted America to hear. Maybe if I'd kept my mouth shut and listened carefully to her, I'd have picked up some hint of impending disaster. But like all overbusy editors, I'd heard what I wanted to hear. In a way, Trill's voice had been the voice of the siren, the one that adventurers on dangerous seas have heard from time immemorial. It wasn't her fault that she wasn't exactly what we expected to get. I've always thought sirens have been misjudged. Sure, they may lure sailors to their deaths, but I've never thought of them as evil. Sailors in distress hear what they want to hear, too, and if they imagine these to be the voices of beautiful, compassionate creatures on whom they can utterly rely, then it's the sailors who are ultimately responsible for their own misfortune. Sirens are sirens, doing only what they were born to do, to be as alluring as possible. Trill was just being Trill. The blame fell on us for not making sure she was completely reliable.

Somewhere over the Midwest, perhaps within bombing range of La Grange, Illinois, they brought out the food. Struiker picked at a steak the size of a hockey puck and pushed it aside. Over coffee, I asked him where he was from.

"Encino."

"Really?" I said in surprise. Was that why he'd brought me along? Wasn't it more than a coincidence that two ex-Californians were flying out to do battle with what amounted to the L.A. chamber of commerce?

"When I was fourteen," he said idly, "my father died, and my mother and I went back east to live with relatives. Before that, I grew up the way you did, swimming in the ocean with the sharks and camping with the other kids in the desert, flicking up rattlers. And out in the orange groves, throwing black widows from the trees at each other. Kid stuff."

I wondered whether he knew how impressed I was. I'd never done those things. Maybe flicking up a few rattlers would have helped prepare me for the Struikers of this world. "So when did you decide to become a lawyer?"

"I don't remember," he said. "Pretty early. But I'll tell you when I knew I'd made the right choice. I'd just joined the firm, and there was a student sit-in at NYU. They'd been occupying the administration building for a couple of days, a bunch of real scumbags living like animals. It was the weekend and the university brass was getting desperate. Finally somebody in the president's office remembered Alex Jordan. You've heard of him. A founding partner of the firm. Died three years ago. And about the closest thing I've ever had to a personal hero."

He digressed on the subject of heroes. "People keep asking where all the heroes have gone. No more Charles Lindberghs, no more General Eisenhowers. I had a big advantage, growing up, in that my father never became an idol of mine. I suppose I was too young to appreciate him, and then he was gone. By college, I knew damn well there weren't any heroes in life, just clever men who lived at a time when it served the interests of their contemporaries to ennoble them. But certain people do certain things extremely well, and Alex was one of those. I stuck close and watched him.

"He was on the golf course when he got the call, and he stopped by the office and grabbed me because I was the only one there. We got a cab and went down to NYU and chatted for a while with the dean, then we climbed up the fire escape to the third floor, where these little shits were sitting around the faculty lounge with all their garbage. It smelled like the city dump, and I felt like we were going in there to shoot rats. Alex began talking. He said, 'Listen, you may hate what I stand for, but I want to tell you I represent the Establishment, and the Establishment knows how to get things done.'

"They yelled and cursed and spat on the floor, and when they finally calmed down, Alex said, 'Now, you can stay here and try to outthink and outfight the Establishment, but sooner or later it's going to win, because that's what it does best. Or you can leave here right now with your integrity intact, and we'll arrange a meeting between the dean and your leader, if you can find anybody like that among you. Otherwise, we're going to get an injunction and in about an hour you'll be going downstairs with an eighteen-inch police stick up your ass.' "

If Struiker's voice had a color, it was pitch-black with occasional shadings of gray. "Then Alex turned on his heel and left me standing there, and they were very quiet. Very quiet. So I explained to them how the injunction would work and what powers it would give us, and it became pretty clear to them that they'd lost control of the situation. So they left, and when I got back down the fire escape, the administration treated me like a fucking hero. Alex had already gone, of course, back to his golf game. And I said to myself, I can do that. That's the kind of lawyer I want to be, not standing there explaining how a legal mechanism works, but the guy who locks it into place by irresistible persuasion."

"An offer they can't refuse."

He turned his head and stared at me. "You don't get it, do you? It's not that; we don't have that kind of power. If we did, I wouldn't be in the game, because it wouldn't be a challenge anymore. If I'm trying to get you to do what I want you to do, I can point out all the terrible things I can do to you if you don't, and that may help you to see what a wonderful alternative I'm offering you. But it's coming up with the alternative that makes the game worth the candle. It's got to be irresistible."

"An offer they can't resist."

He grinned. "Now you've got it," he said, and put his head back.

Eight

But he didn't sleep. He fidgeted, yawned, glanced out the window at a trail of lights in the darkness below, went to the bathroom, and kept droning on as if that's what was keeping the plane in the air. He made a phone call home. "That cost the office the price of a long cab ride," he said. "There's nothing like checking in with the missus once in a while from forty thousand feet."

He told stories, all involving flight. The woman who'd told him she was so sick she thought she'd die, and he'd said, "Don't worry about a thing, I'm a lawyer, I can make you a will," and she'd vomited. How he had won seven hundred dollars in a game of blackjack at thirty-two thousand feet by splitting pairs and playing two hands, doubling his bet, then sticking with twelve because the dealer's up card was a five, a stiff hand that was sure to go bust and did. "Obviously, the object is to beat the dealer," he said, and I agreed, although my head was spinning. He told me how he had once spent a night in Abadan, Iran, on the Persian Gulf, riding around in a taxi with the wife of a low-level State Department official who thought her husband might have been taken hostage, but he was found at five o'clock in the morning sleeping in the men's room at the airport, victimized by some stray hashish. And when, at about nine o'clock L.A. time, we finally settled down over the City of Angels and came out of the terminal to Burley Moore's waiting Buick Electra, it was a relief to see the photographer's stolid, aging countenance and flat-footed stance.

Burley's baggy brown suit looked as if it was made out of cardboard, with a corrugated lining. But his hat was blue-green, a lake in the Alps, his tie a spattering waterfall in the vertical forest of his gray-green checked shirt. With his camera strap over one rounded shoulder, he made a small mountain of a man, though he wasn't much taller than average. I guess it was his weathered look of simple integrity. Strange. He gave that impression without even managing to look you in the eye. Maybe it was mostly in his voice, although it had no ringing timbre—it was soft and he took no pains to enunciate. Burley just seemed like the genuine article. I didn't really know him but I wanted to hug him.

"You've lost weight," Struiker observed as Burley took our bags and put them in the car.

He said, "Yeah, it comes of being woken up too early in the morning," and glanced impishly at me and fished in the pocket of his baggy jacket. He pulled out a small tape recorder and put it gently into Struiker's hand. "Something new on the market. They got portable ones now." Struiker grinned and we all got into the car.

As we left the airport, roaring jets sliced red-eyed into a thick leather sky. I'd forgotten how the buildings looked, so balsa-light, almost cellular, floating in rounded clusters or standing like tube-lighted matchboxes. The palms, tall and stubby, looked fake in the artificial glare. A pale green swath of night sky caught a flight of birds as they skimmed past a hotel and spread out, as if they streamed from a single window.

"So how's Helen?" Struiker asked Burley, referring to his wife.

"So-so. Her mother's out in Palm Springs, dying of cancer, and it's a long haul out there every weekend. But Helen doesn't want to change the geography on her at this stage. Things okay back east?"

"East is East. What do you know about McGuffy?"

"Well, I thought we had a pretty good shoot on the article," Burley said, swinging onto the freeway. "There we were, looking for beautiful people to photograph. I didn't know which ones they ought to be. Trill didn't know. We talked about it a while, and then I said, 'Well, I tell you what, let's pick out a few at random and have them drive by in their cars, and when they go by, we'll know that's them.' "

Then, as if to pass the time, he talked about Raphael. Raphael was a young man in Trill's story, anonymous really, a kind of free-floating character living in the Hollywood hills in a bare room with a view. He was loaded with academic degrees but had no apparent vocation except the one suggested by his computer and his endless cocaine supply. He represented the unrooted aimlessness of Southern California's shiftless educated class.

"We were taking all these pictures to illustrate the story, and I said, 'Raphael, that's a key shot. Who is he? Where do we find him?' Trill stalled for a couple of days, and then she said, 'Well, that's not his real name.' Gave me some other name—I forget what it was. Said he was a friend she just wanted to get into the story. We never did find him."

"Shows you," Struiker said.

I said, "Shows you what?"

"What a stinker she is." He said to Burley, "So did you know anything about McGuffy's vendetta against Bangor Laudicek?"

"No, I never heard of it back then," Burley said. "But I've been hearing about it every day since, from Harv Wallace. Pamela's been driving him crazy, complaining about it. Harv says, 'Let's get down to work now,' and she says, 'All right. But I'll kill her, I'll kill her!' He calms her down, gives her the rest of the day off, and she's back the next morning. Walks in the door shouting, 'She can't do this to my husband! Who does she think she is? God?' "

"How about Jim Provine?"

"Moody. Real moody. I tell him, 'Look, Jim, it's a corporation. You don't like 'em, don't work for 'em.' But he says, 'My whole life is built into this magazine.' It's like he's handcuffed to the place."

"Yeah, well," Struiker said, "it takes some people a long time to fall clear. You've been on your own all your life."

"I sure have." Burley laughed mirthlessly, then sobered. "Jim's an angry man. I don't see him much."

We left the freeway and took Pico Boulevard past the golf course and Twentieth Century–Fox to the Avenue of the Stars. The hotel was midway along the broad avenue. We gave the car to the beefeater doorman and went in past all kinds of glass and all kinds of help, some in Oriental jackets, and Burley sat down wearily in the lobby while I went with Struiker to the desk.

"Struiker," he said. "Hold for arrival."

The clerk looked, and then he looked some more. "I'm sorry, Mr. Struiker, I don't seem to have you here."

"Well, here I am," he said. "What are you going to do about it?"

"I'm sorry, sir. All we have left is the Presidential Suite. Otherwise, we're completely booked."

Struiker was silent, and I waited for the explosion. But after a moment, he reached for his wallet, saying calmly, "I think that will be all right, don't you, Mike?"

"What will?"

"The suite."

The clerk said, "It's on the top floor and completely private," and offered him the sign-in card.

Struiker signed, saying, "After all, we don't want it to appear to Bangor that we came all the way out here just to see him. Do we?" Which made absolutely no sense to me. If Anton Black was paying for our lodging, I had to admire

Struiker's nerve, why ever he was upping our bill by several hundred percent.

The bellhop got us into the elevator and shot us right to the top. "Private elevator," he explained, "for security reasons." When we got out, Struiker looked up and down the short hallway. There was another elevator at one end.

"What's that?" he asked.

The bellhop had the key card in the door. "Service elevator," he said, whisking the door open.

Struiker said, "So where's the security?"

The bellhop entered and flicked on the lights. "It serves only this floor, sir. And you need a key."

Burley took one look at the spacious living room and whistled. Then he looked down at his shoes, as if making sure he hadn't tracked any dirt in. "Nice rug," he said.

Struiker, tipping the bellhop, said to Burley, "I'll call you tomorrow morning after the meeting's over, may need your car or something. And thanks for the ride. It was nice of you."

"Anytime," Burley said, and followed the bellhop out.

I walked over to the bookcase, which was mainly filled with decorative objects and of the same wood as the walls and the furniture, pale but solid-looking and styled Italian Renaissance out of Cecil B. deMille. I leaned against it, soaking in the atmosphere. The room was huge, with a nonstop window wall full of balconies, a grand piano, a large bar, and a poker table. Behind me, past the bookcase, it seemed to go on forever.

Struiker lingered for a moment beside the piano, watching me with a faint smile. "You look as if you belong," he said. "I guess you'll do." Then he went past me toward the bedroom area. "I'm going to get some sleep. They'll be here at nine-thirty tomorrow." He turned. "Remember, be sincere. After all, it's the Presidential Suite."

I unpacked and returned with my address book, settling down beside the living room telephone. I hadn't told Struiker yet because I wanted to see how things went, but

I'd cleared it with Nels, staying through the weekend to see my folks and my sister, maybe some old friends, as well. I called my folks to let them know I'd arrived, then wandered around and forgot about bed, trying out the couches and ducking through the floor-to-ceiling drapes out onto narrow balconies overlooking the lighted guitar-shaped pool and ornamental fountain directly below—something to relieve the starkness of the parking area. Across the way on the Fox lot, a single-engine 1930s airplane painted silver sat alongside a rickety elevated structure from old Manhattan.

Struiker had taken the larger bedroom. It had a huge bed and a large sitting room with windows opening onto a balcony, and two of everything else: twin dressing rooms, twin baths, probably twin bars. Mine had two beds but one of everything else and no sitting room, no window, no balcony. Next to the bedrooms was a kitchen with a dining area. Along the window wall was a library with a couch and chairs where we'd sit down with Bangor and his lawyer in the morning.

Following Struiker's directives, I ordered continental breakfast for four for the next morning and decorated the library with copies of *Beyond*, then I moved restlessly from one end of the suite to the other, unable to unwind. The last thing I wanted was sleep. Finally I sat down with a book from the library, but I couldn't concentrate.

I was listening to the traffic, and I was even listening to the night air, frangible but cushioned, tropical but dry, when Struiker, in pajamas, robe, and slippers, came out to check on me. He seemed amused by my reading in the library, as if I'd already made it my own.

"It's nearly eleven," he said from the doorway. "That means it's nearly two in the morning back home. You going to get some shut-eye?"

I said I might, and he said, "Here's what I want you to think about when your head hits the pillow: McGuffy is an immature screwball who's shown herself to be undependable and undeserving of trust. She's a rat who's out to put it to Bangor, and in fact did put it to him not once but several times and didn't have the courage to tell us."

I stared, and I guess he sensed my reluctance to buy this completely. He came over and sat down in the armchair facing me. "Look," he said. "You remember the letter she wrote about Burley? She wouldn't have the nerve to say those things to his face. It was a mean letter, disguised as humor, and it could have gotten an old shoe fired. Sure he's old-fashioned, but he's steady as a rock. Suppose you'd decided not to use his work as a result of that letter, how would McGuffy feel? Sorry? How do you know that's what she'd feel?"

He got up, went to the window, and pulled back the drapes, leaving a floor-to-ceiling square of gauzy curtain spread over the night sky. "Burley knows what she is precisely. Remember what he said about Raphael, the drifter in her article? Raphael doesn't exist in real life. McGuffy either took a friend of hers and gave him phony attributes or else she made him up out of whole cloth because she needed him in her story. That means she mixed fiction with fact. A jury would say here's a young woman who doesn't know one from the other. And her vendetta is the key to the whole thing."

He turned and tipped over the heavy chair he'd just gotten out of. I pulled my feet out of the way and it went down with a great thump. I stared up at him. "It's like I deliberately kick you in the balls," he said. "It hurts. But if I'm just flinging myself around for my own pleasure and I inadvertently kick you, it hurts just as much. And that's exactly what she's done."

He went to the doorway, leaving the chair where it was. "The thing we've got to do tomorrow morning is get Bangor on our side, because he's merely a sideshow out here; I've told Anton that. We've got to soften him up, make him feel secure, and scare the shit out of his lawyer. You watch me. I have to win Bangor over even if I have to make our own people look bad. It's that important." He leaned against the wall. "I shouldn't even say this because feelings can be unreliable, but I have a feeling that everything depends on getting him to go along. Because in the end it hinges on our drawing up a retraction that everybody will find agreeable. It has to be a proper one—that's what so many lawyers forget. If it isn't, McGuffy can sue us for putting the kibosh on her career." He smiled. "Except remember, we do nothing final until we hear the tape." Then he turned and padded off.

I sat looking at the view. What had he said, Bangor was merely a sideshow? Then what the hell was the main act? And what about making our own people look bad? Did he mean Burley? Jim Provine? Me? Was he willing to sacrifice one of us if he had to? How much was going on here that I knew nothing about?

I went over it and over it, growing sleepier, half my attention on the book in my lap. It was *Twice-Told Tales* by Nathaniel Hawthorne. I'd taken it off the shelf because Hawthorne had been one of Professor Joliffe's specialties. Bernard Joliffe had been the American literature authority at UCLA, a wizened little man with a paralyzed arm permanently cocked for holding a book at the proper reading angle. His eyes seemed locked into place, too. Blue, very blue, they fixed on us as he labored to instill some understanding of how gifted writers went about their difficult task. Now I had been reading the same sentence again and again, and I knew it wasn't Hawthorne's fault: "This fated evening was an ugly one." The simplest sentence possible. Why couldn't I get past it? I knew that it was "the night between the last day of winter and the first of spring" and that it was ugly to Peter and Tabitha because there was a snowstorm. But try as I might, I couldn't get beyond that one sentence. Was it the word *fated* that stopped me? The prospect of something ugly? I went back to what Struiker had said, and I couldn't get anywhere with that, either.

I was thinking of a young woman going to the University of Michigan and taking an instant dislike to a distinguished teacher and subjecting him to painful treatment in the public prints every chance she got, then and later. Who had known about that? Everybody but us? At the time Trill's article was assigned, Bangor was angry and upset, already consulting with his lawyer. Pamela, his wife, was furious and beginning to scream in public. Harv Wallace, Pamela's boss, must have known about their state of mind, and maybe his friend Burley had, too, though Burley denied it. Jim Provine? Provine had said she'd been out to get Bangor for months, but where had he gotten his information? He didn't say in his letter. Had he really known all along, or was he simply insisting he could have found out to strengthen his case against editorial, particularly against me for not checking with him in advance?

So whom did Struiker plan to make look bad if he had to?

I decided Burley must have known about Trill's indiscretions. I decided Struiker thought so, too. But Struiker liked him, probably wanted to keep him out of it, and was able to precisely because Burley had himself been discreet, an attribute Struiker admired. That left Provine, and maybe me. Except Struiker needed me whole. He wanted me to help him put Bangor Laudicek at ease, so I had to be made to look good, at least for now. Provine?

I tried to turn it around. What was it that "our people" had done that could be made to look bad? Me, because I'd let it happen. But Nels had let it happen, too. Provine?

Well, Jim Provine had not demonstrated a whole lot of discretion.

It was now three o'clock in the morning, New York time. I'd left the book somewhere and was standing out on the balcony staring down at the shiny silver plane in the movie lot a block away and at the sparkling blue of the pool directly below. I was tired, all right, and my mind had gone ahead of me to bed, leaving my questions unanswered: Who was Struiker going to scapegoat? And what did he mean, Bangor was only a sideshow? I felt like a kid again, back in my hometown with my toy airplane and my backyard wading pool, wondering about the puzzling world of grown-ups and not having a clue.

When I did get to bed, sleep took a while. One nagging thought in particular: What had he meant by putting the kibosh on Trill's career? Was that what he intended to do?

Nine

With his magnificent head of graying hair, splendid brow, and father-of-his-country nose, Bangor Laudicek might have been Thomas Jefferson or George Washington or any other patriotic divinity sitting there, his legs casually crossed, his fingertips together, the great man, the wise man, the decent, caring, understanding man of vision and contemplation and influence. All he needed were the silk stockings and the satin knee britches and the ruffled blouse. And then, as he turned his all-encompassing gaze on me, it seemed to me that he was an actor playing his favorite role, and that outside his own personal theater of the mind, he probably didn't know what the hell he was doing.

He had all the right rhetorical phrases. He said "I am loath to" and "my direst, deepest feelings" and "ignorance closely analogous to danger" and even "the whole sum of human experience." His lower lip didn't move when he spoke, making his delivery starched and pompous. He said he regretted being drawn into this confrontation "through some strange, murky coincidence almost diabolical in nature." And when he tried to sum up what he'd said about drug users on the air, he nearly blew us away: "Taking the devious but exuberant path leading from desperation and desire, they carelessly approach nirvana." No wonder Trill had gotten it wrong.

Awash in his own rolling cadences, he seemed to hum internally, in tune with the universe. It was only when the talk turned to more practical considerations that his throbbing brain blinked and contracted. Then his eyes slid apart, suddenly unsure. His look of alertness vanished, and that open, generous facade of unending compassion and intellectual curiosity shrank to nothing, leaving him staring into a vacuum. And once or twice, when Struiker pointed out possible pitfalls in his intended course of action or mentioned the dollar cost, there was real terror in his eyes.

Bangor and I were seated across from each other in the library, the lawyers between us in the circle, the random little tables littered with coffee cups and rolls and magazines. Compared to Struiker, Bangor's attorney was a joke, the kind of man who has no choice but to be modest. He wore a fine thick collar and a flowing tie, but his face was flabby and blotched. He had no class. Struiker, lean and dark, his eyes flashing, not with fire, for he seemed to have ruled out emotion, but with plain comprehension, made a mockery of them both just by treating the conversation like a very ordinary meal or a thoroughly uneventful wine. He showed anger only once, at the first suggestion of a suit for damages. His eyes came around to stare at the other attorney, his jaw clamped as if he'd just bitten the man's head from his shoulders. He spoke to the lawyer, but his message was meant for Bangor.

"I don't think going into court would serve anybody very well," he said, his voice low and hard, almost a growl. He might have been addressing a neighbor caught dumping garbage on his lawn in the dead of night. "It's going to cost you plenty, and even if you win out here in California, by the time we take it through the appeals process, you'd wind up wishing you'd never thought of it. The publicity would be horrendous, and in the end there's no way you could come out a winner." He turned to look at Bangor, who was total attentiveness. "But the point is, a suit is completely unnecessary."

"A superfluous consideration," Bangor hummed eagerly.

"Exactly. And why mobilize a whole army when all you need to end the war are a couple of dedicated squads who know how to blow bridges and slit throats?"

I thought Struiker had gone too far. Wouldn't that offend Bangor's cultivated sensibilities? But the idea of devious violence apparently excited him. He smiled and said, "Get the job done incorruptibly. The elegant solution."

Struiker smiled, too, and turned back to the lawyer. "So if you want to sue for damages, go ahead, and I'll fight you right up to the Supreme Court, which is one of my favorite places in the world to win. And as Mr. Lindenthal here can tell you, *Beyond* is a magazine that has never hesitated to put all its resources behind what it believes."

The lawyer lifted his hand in what he meant to be a sweeping gesture, but it might just as well have been in supplication. "The magazine's resources are pretty impressive, judging by the size of this suite—"

"As I told you on the phone," Struiker said, "we're here for our annual publishing party. By nine o'clock tonight, this place will be crowded with writers and advertisers and salespeople."

Bangor said, "A gathering of the clan. The vernal tribal rite . . ."

"And since I'm preparing a case out here for one of our other clients, it seemed like a good time for us to meet and resolve this thing."

Bangor's lawyer sat up straight, yanking at the tail of his suit coat. "Well, on the other hand, the size of the magazine's coffers suggest that if we bring suit—"

But Struiker had obviously had enough of this guy. "Let's forget about that. We're here to resolve, not inflame, so let's just see what we have in common. I don't want to hear another word about the courts!"

The lawyer glanced at Bangor and said, in the mildest of tones, "Well, we must have absolute assurance of a binding agreement as far as the author is concerned. . . ."

"We're as eager as you are to put this author out of business." Struiker looked at me. "We feel we were misled and bamboozled, isn't that right, Mike?" He waited.

I didn't feel misled or bamboozled, but I figured my best course was to say nothing much in as many words as possible. I said, "We certainly weren't aware of anything in the piece that was unfair to you or anyone else or we wouldn't have printed it. Our writer had excellent credentials and we expected the quotations to be accurate. But of course we haven't heard the tape—"

"I can get you the tape," Bangor said quickly. "I'll send you a copy."

"Two copies," Struiker said, and Bangor nodded.

"We'll be reimbursed?" the lawyer asked, and Struiker shot him a withering look.

He said, "I think I can promise you that Trilla McGuffy will never write another word about your client if we can agree on a proper retraction. I'm assuming that even if our quotes were accurate word for word, the rest of the tape will show that you're not wandering around Los Angeles recommending drugs to kids on the street, and you consider using drugs unrealistic and cockeyed—"

"Foolhardy," Bangor boomed. "An impulse toward a reality that is at least ninety percent fantasy."

"Whatever. So we'll retract, and there'll be some kind of story in the magazine about the impact of your ideas on the environment, and I'll get a letter from McGuffy guaranteeing to forget you're alive, a Bangor-who letter—"

"Bangor what?" said the lawyer.

"Bangor-who. If you meet McGuffy on Sunset Boulevard a year from now and ask her if she's ever heard of Bangor Laudicek, she's going to say, 'Bangor who?' "

Everybody laughed pleasantly. We were now among friends.

The lawyer said, "And then there's the matter of recompense. I'm asking three thousand dollars for my services. That's fifteen hours at two hundred dollars an hour."

Bangor raised his eyebrows but his chin stayed firm.

"I'd say we could pay half of that," Struiker said, and the lawyer raised a hand in protest but said nothing.

Bangor fidgeted. Finally he looked directly at his attorney. "If you want the truth, I hate to pay anything. Even fifteen hundred dollars—"

The lawyer's hand went up again. "Doubtless," he said in a hushed tone, "I can arrange something. We'll talk about it."

"Well," Bangor said more cheerily, to Struiker, "I must confess I had no idea you'd be so sporting about all this, and I'll be utterly frank with you. It never occurred to me that there was any possible way to silence Miss McGuffy without taking her to court, and I'm positively delighted to have your help in this. It greatly relieves my mind."

Struiker stood up, and so did the lawyer and so did I. Bangor stayed where he was, looking up at Struiker as if lost in admiration before some mighty work of art.

"I'm glad we could get this settled quickly and move on to other things," Struiker said, and Bangor nodded. "Mike, why don't you tell housekeeping they can start setting up for the party. Gentlemen—" He held out his hand and Bangor, as if awakening, stood up slowly and took it. Then Struiker grasped the lawyer's arm and walked him from the room.

Bangor stood buttoning his jacket. He seemed dazed. I said, "Thank you for being so gracious about all this."

He suddenly saw me. "Yours," he said, "has been the truly gracious attitude. Full of light, full of . . ." He searched for words. "Full of extraordinary grace. I can't tell you how positively stupefied I've been over the last few weeks. The entire family, indeed the entire city, has been furiously upset."

We followed the others into the living room. "You have children?" I asked.

"Three. By a previous marriage that ended ten years ago." He smiled. "One of them is studying law and threatening to drag me by the heels into court to clear my name." He sighed. "But the most remarkable person in all this is Pamela. I would never have anticipated my wife's utter devotion and loyalty." He gave an odd chuckle. "Her anger has been almost Medea-like."

"I'm sorry she's been upset."

"Yes." He stopped beside the piano. I could see Struiker waiting impatiently at the door. "And the thing that truly boggles the mind is Trill." He shook his head.

"Trill?" I said, surprised.

"Miss McGuffy. You see, she was once a student of mine. I find her anger quite perplexing. Quite perplexing."

When he and the lawyer were finally gone, Struiker turned to me with a wide, triumphant grin. "Well, he bought it. Did you ever see such a pompous gasbag? And the lawyer, he's never seen two hundred dollars an hour in his life. If we pay him half his fee, he can charge Bangor nothing and still make out like a bandit. He hasn't spent anywhere near fifteen hours on this. What did he do, write a letter? Buy Miss McGuffy tea? Get up this morning and put on a tie?"

"Bangor didn't want to pay anything."

"Don't let his penuriousness fool you. He probably grew up in poor circumstances, but he's got plenty. He'll get a battery of lawyers if he has to. He's probably worth a few million."

"Really?"

"He lives a couple of miles up the street in Beverly Hills. Burley said his place looks like a sultan's grotto, or whatever it is sultans have besides harems. Burley grew up rich, did you know that? His father married Arkansas money, then lost it all when Burley was in college. Bangor's done a lot of commercial work, must be deep in residuals. The talk show's a front, to preserve his intellectual facade. He has investments all over the place, real estate and films. If he doesn't get what he wants from us, he'll probably buy out Anton Black and *Beyond*. You could be working for him by Christmas." I knew he was kidding but it sent chills up my spine.

"You, too?" I said.

He looked at me. "I'd still have to stay around to keep you out of trouble, wouldn't I?"

Ten

When the phone rang, Struiker clamped his lips together and stared at it, as if willing it to stop. It rang three times and he nodded. I picked it up. It was Trill, asking about lunch.

"I kept praying you wouldn't actually be there," she said, "like it was just a nightmare I had. Where do I meet you?"

I turned to Struiker. "It's Trill," I said. "Where?"

"Ask her to suggest something." He seemed distracted.

"You decide," I said into the phone.

"Oh," she moaned, "am I going to have to decide everything from now on?" But she picked a place in Santa Monica, and I asked Struiker when.

"One o'clock."

"One o'clock," I said.

Struiker said, "Tell her to get reservations and pick us up here."

I told her that.

"I knew this wasn't going to be my power-play day," she said. "Before this is over, you guys are going to have my car and my computer and everything."

I laughed. Struiker glanced suspiciously at me and said, "Hang up."

"See you, Trill," I said. I put down the phone and looked up. "What's the matter? Am I getting too friendly?"

He said, "No, that's all right, as long as she knows it's you and not me." He looked at his watch. "Okay, we have an hour and a half before she gets here." He loosened his tie. "So how did you think it went?"

I said, "Fine. I was kind of shook when you got so angry, when the lawyer mentioned going into court."

He took off his jacket and folded it carefully over the back of a chair. "I don't get angry. Nobody's important enough. I just wanted to throw the fear of God into him and show Bangor that anything might be better than getting into a courtroom with us. Power has to be dramatized, or what good is it?" He sat down and began cleaning his nails with a tiny knife on the end of a silver chain.

"We don't really have to run that story about Bangor, do we?"

"You have to do that to make him feel he's getting something substantial out of this. He can show the article to his friends, and we don't have to admit we were wrong."

"But when did Bangor Laudicek ever make an impact on the environment?"

"You'll think of something. He must have had talk shows about cleaner air or saving the redwoods. Just a couple of pages with his picture. You write the story."

"Me?"

"Call him up when you get back to the office. Interview him; he'll find the appropriate thing to say. He doesn't need convincing that he's God's gift to the ecology or anything else." He got to his feet. "I have to make some phone calls. If I'm not out in an hour, knock on my door."

He was in his bedroom for nearly that long, I supposed filling in Nels and Anton Black on the results of the morning's meeting and checking with his own office. I dragged a chair onto one of the narrow balconies and read Hawthorne, no longer worried about a fated, ugly evening, until I saw him come out and lean on the rail, looking down at the pool. The pool was purely decorative, I'd discovered, a shallow guitar shape with a small fountain at one end, a water sculpture meant for overhead viewing, something like a painting on the wall.

He said, "I want you to wait downstairs for McGuffy. This isn't the time for me to meet her."

"You're not going with us?"

He shook his head. "I'm having lunch up here with Provine and Burley Moore. We have various things to talk about that have nothing to do with the case. Take your time. Get to know her. Tell her how much experience you've had working with writers like herself. This is important. I want her to know that you have a high regard for writers. I want her to think of you as a father confessor—well, a brother confessor. And I want you to build me up as someone who's put in a lot of time with writers, admires the good ones, and would kick the shit out of any writers that cross me."

"The writer's nemesis."

He looked at me as if I was some bothersome stranger. "No, only the bad writer's nemesis. Listen, I want you to help me on this. You have to set her up for me. Say I'm a cold, ruthless son of a bitch who would murder his own grandmother for the magazine, which is true. Tell her I know all about writers, their self-conscious tricks, their worst fears and insecurities, their asshole dreams, their sentimentality, how pitiably ingrown and eccentric they are. How they think they're the only valuable commodity on earth and how unfair it is that everybody's against them, because how else can they explain to themselves why their unique talents go unrecognized and unrewarded? Just tell her I know more about writers than they know about themselves, so don't think she can get away with anything."

"Like what?"

"Like whatever. Look, this McGuffy is obviously weird. She's proved that she's capable of anything. What we have to do now is convince her that she has no choice but to do whatever I say. She has to abandon the right of independent thought and action. You think I want her running around like a loose cannon after we're gone? So when you've become her trusted adviser, make her see that she can't afford to fuck with me. Because I'm a mean SOB who stops at nothing. Which I am."

"Sounds like a great lunch."

He stared down at the pool, shining in the sun. "Well, you see how well we've done so far. The thing I didn't know for sure when we went into this meeting today was whether I could get Bangor on our side. I was surprised—it took me all of two minutes. Did you see how grateful he was when I told him we could actually help him get McGuffy? Amazing. Of course I'd have had a much harder time if his lawyer had been in working order. Or if they had the information we have."

"What information?"

Struiker straightened up and looked at his watch, then at me—or, rather, at my tie. It was the sincere gray silk job his daughter had given him, the one that looked like a memorial to the British Empire. "Take that off," he said, "and put on the crappy one you wore on the plane. Or better yet, don't wear a tie. Show her you're a plainspoken, open-collar editor who cares deeply about poor, bedraggled, suffering young female writers with big breasts." He turned and left the balcony, and I followed him, getting rid of the tie. "I have to call my office and dictate a memorandum. Go downstairs in about twenty minutes. And if you see Burley or Jim Provine, tell them to come on up but call first." He stood drumming his fingers on the poker table. "We should fly back today."

"Today?"

"My office is overloaded and everybody's out of town. If your lunch goes okay and Provine doesn't have any more surprises, we should be able to catch a late-afternoon plane."

"Then I guess I should tell you," I said. "Nels said I could stay on for a few days."

Struiker looked up sharply. "What for?"

I shrugged. "See the family. My sister's got a pad in Venice and is throwing a party. Then I thought I'd go out to my folks' in Laguna this weekend."

He looked around the room. "Well," he said, drumming again, "I guess there's no rush. I have a client in La Jolla. I could take a run down there tonight and still fly back in time to say good-bye to my daughter. I'll tell Jeanne to take you off tomorrow's flight, but give me a number where I can reach you tonight. And tell McGuffy to pick us up at two o'clock tomorrow."

"But if I'm not flying out—"

"I want you to ride along to the airport because that's when I'm going to sell her out. She's got to write Bangor that letter telling him she no longer knows him, and I don't want any hitches. Besides, I want to talk to you after she leaves, to make sure your head's on straight. I want you to stay clear of all these characters while you're out here, nothing more until we hear the tape next week. Right now, Bangor is exactly where we want him. The carrot has been dangled, but until we hear the tape, they get nothing in writing. They've got to trust us, baby."

"So all we have to do is scare the hell out of Trill."

He smiled. "You know, Mike, I forget how naïve and old-fashioned you are, like *Mr. Deeds Goes to Town*. Yeah, I use anger just like I use anything else. I got angry at the lawyer because he was heading for court, but I could be nice to Bangor because I could see he'd do anything if I held out a friendly hand. So what's it going to be with McGuffy? You don't know and I don't know, not yet. A lot of it's up to you, how well you motivate her."

I nodded. "All right, I'll do my best."

He was already heading for the bedroom. With his jacket slung over his shoulder, he looked lean and trim. Somebody had told me he'd done some serious boxing in college. I'm a few inches taller, but I decided I wouldn't want to mix it up with him. Or get in the way when he was flicking up rattlers.

Eleven

Trilla McGuffy, Trilla McGuffy. I hardly know whether she was a woman or a state of mind. Earlier I spoke of sirens, and she was one for me. Is there such a thing as being beguiled by sirens? I think so. And Trill made it seem true that sirens mean you no harm, you know. They aren't evil really, not deliberately villainous. They're merely powerless to help you, for they cannot help themselves. Although they are beautiful, beautiful.

She drove up to the entrance of the hotel on the curving white drive that circled the clustered fountains, and I knew it had to be her in the Mustang convertible but I wanted to see what she'd do. After about fifteen seconds, she called out, "Mike?" and I got up and went toward the car. My main impression was of all that long golden hair, because her eyes were hidden behind dark glasses. She smiled at me as I opened the door. I couldn't believe the radiance of her face. I'd expected a none-too-pleased expression on a set of furtive backwoods features. A certain charm, maybe, but not this outpouring of gold-tinged health and beauty.

"So you're Trill," I said, settling in beside her.

"Yes," she said, and looked away, her profile elfin. The

wheel was in large, capable-looking hands with very red nails. When she looked back at me, I knew she had a question.

"Do we wait or what?"

I'd forgotten to tell her. "No," I said. "He's not coming."

She shifted immediately and started down the drive, as if she was afraid Struiker might change his mind. "Couldn't he bear the thought of meeting me?"

I laughed. "No, things got jammed up. He's having lunch with a couple of people from the magazine, and tonight we're throwing a big party."

She was already in traffic, heading for Santa Monica Boulevard. "Whew! You have no idea how that relieves my mind. I thought you were out here just on account of me." So I'd made my first mistake of the day. I should never have mentioned the party. Struiker hadn't warned me not to, and it had just popped into my head. See how slowly I learn? The party was meant only for Bangor and his lawyer, a diversion to indicate how unimportant they were. But Struiker wanted to keep the pressure on Trill, and by mentioning the party, I'd lessened it.

Probably she was also relieved because Struiker wasn't coming, but it must have felt merely like danger delayed. "Will I meet him?" she said, no doubt hoping I'd say no. "Or is this the final test of strength?"

I decided to correct the balance. "You'll see him tomorrow. He wants you to pick us up at two. I think he wants to sharpen his fangs on you."

"Whatever do you mean?" she said in a soap-opera voice, but I could see her jaw tighten. "What's at two? A tour of Bel Air? Malibu?" She glanced at me. "I don't do Palm Springs."

"A ride to the airport. I guess he figures that's just about right for whatever he has in mind." I thought that would convey the right tone of menace, and I wasn't wrong. She jumped and looked both ways at traffic.

"That sounds super," she said. "So he's saving me for the very end. Dessert."

I watched her. She was a good driver. She wore avocado pants and a light sweater with red and avocado horizontal stripes. She glanced in the rearview mirror, then at me. "Looking over the victim? How's he going to do it?"

"I'm not Bob Struiker," I said, "so I don't know. But it depends on a couple of things. Either we go to court and he'll want to talk to you about your testimony, or else we settle out of court and he wants to advise you how to conduct yourself."

She nodded but said nothing more until we'd cleared the San Diego freeway overpass. "And how am I to conduct myself?"

I sighed. I was sorry I was doing this, because she didn't look nearly so radiant now. "Look," I said, "Bob Struiker is one of the toughest libel lawyers in Manhattan. He'll kill to win a case, and believe me, I don't take any joy in telling you this. I've seen him operate."

"Does he go for the jugular or directly for the brain?"

I began scratching the back of my neck, and perhaps sensing my discomfort, she said, "Have you met Bangor yet?"

"We talked this morning."

"I thought I detected a few Bangorisms."

I laughed. "God, what a lousy thing to say!"

She gave me an appreciative smile. "I'm sorry, Mike, if I got the magazine in trouble. I thought I was saying exactly what Bangor said. I might have known he'd scratch and spit." Was this the Trill I'd been talking to on the phone? She was being positively ladylike.

"Well," I said, "I should have questioned it in the manuscript. I'm usually good on red flags. I just assumed he was one of these weird Hollywood types who deliberately say outrageous things. I was wrong."

"You were mostly right."

"But I should have caught it."

"But that's what he said!"

Oh, oh. This wasn't going to be a cakewalk. "No, he didn't. He never said flat out that drugs are good for you."

"Not on the air he didn't."

I looked at her. "What do you mean? Did he say so anywhere? In the public record?" We were getting stuck in traffic, and she was looking for some way to go. "What we should have had was the tape. He says it'll show he said almost the exact opposite of that, if you put it in context."

"Sure, in three thousand mellifluous words." The traffic was piled up at a light. She looked past me, trying to edge into the right-hand lane.

"Well, I should have asked you for the transcript." I was trying to get Struiker's message across, but my own kept getting in the way. Now the car behind us was blasting its horn.

"Son of a bitch," Trill said, looking in the rearview mirror at the guy.

"Can't you let him go past?"

"How? It's too crowded to pull over. God, he'll probably get out and punch me." She was the old Trill now, the anxiety building, and when the light changed, we bucked ahead, taking off. She saw an opening in the next lane and took it, and the guy sped past, his horn going. "I can't believe they'd let that on the street," she said in disgust. "I mean, why don't they come and get him? He's going to do the very same thing to somebody else, and then somebody else."

I had a sudden inspiration, a lesson drawn from life. I said, "Maybe that's how Bangor feels about you."

She stared at me, then slowed for another light, then stared some more. "Oh," she said, sounding disappointed. "The moral of the story is."

"Right, the moral of the story is, if you're going to be reckless don't get caught."

"I wasn't reckless! And I didn't get caught, I was waylaid. Bangor was just waiting for a chance to get me. Can't I sue him for that? For setting up an ambush or something?" We were half a dozen blocks from the ocean now, and at the next light, she turned right. "I'm sorry, I get upset. We're almost there. Have you told me all you came to tell me?"

I decided to lay it on the line. "Well, you should know that Struiker has worked with a lot of writers in similar situations, and if you do exactly what he says to do, you've got nothing to worry about."

"I'll bet." She was looking for the restaurant now.

"Well, he's tough, but he really does know what you're going through. No, that's wrong. That sounds like he'll be a warm friend. He won't be. He'll be hard as hell on you as long as he thinks you're resisting his strategy or not being straight with him. If you set yourself against him, he'll do his damnedest to break you down."

"Yeah," she said, pulling swiftly into a parking lot, "I've heard all about Struiker and how he works."

"From whom?" I said, surprised.

"From friends in the business. They know what he is and how he operates." She braked and we got out. "Okay, I'll try not to make him so mad he'll kill me. Anything else?"

"No."

She was taking long strides, going a little ahead of me. She was strong, well proportioned, a little like those wonderful animals that always come in among the leaders at Santa Anita. In the restaurant, we got a table in the rear, on a brilliant green-sea terrace. That was from the translucent green roof and all the plants. There were lots of tables and lots of chatter.

She took off her dark glasses. Her eyes were green, too. No wonder she'd brought me here. "This is one of the best restaurants in town, whether my word is any good any longer or not."

"Your word is good with me," I said. "I'm impressed."

"Well, you're paying for it. Or are you? Should I begin dipping into my life savings?" She looked away, smiling uncertainly. "I'm sorry. You can see I'm uptight. I'll try to be more Girl Charming." She waved at a waiter.

"Don't, Trill."

"What?" She put the glasses back on and looked at me.

"Don't perform for me. I'm just your editor, okay?"

"I'm not performing." A flash of anger there, not just fear.

"I mean, you don't have to be self-conscious or defensive. Not on my account."

She took off the glasses and put them down on the table, and when she spoke, her voice was softer. "Okay."

The waiter came and gave us menus and rattled off some specials, and she said things like "Oh, that's nice!" and "Oh, how about that!" and when he was gone, she reached over and put three fingers on my wrist, just below my watch, and showed me something on the menu.

"Great," I said. "This is a great place," and she smiled and took the menu and her fingers away.

"God!" she said, and looked at me. It sounded like a breath of relief. "Pardon me, Mike, but I'm not used to relaxing in public in the middle of a lawsuit. If you want to know the truth, I'm not used to relaxing with much of anybody. I guess that means I don't trust anybody very much, doesn't it?" She took a sip of water. "I want to. It's just that every time I do—" She stared down at the slice of lemon floating in the glass.

"Trill," I said, "I'm not out here to hurt you, but I'm not here to make you feel better, either. I'm just doing my job. But I've worked with a lot of writers, and I respect what you do and I know how tough it is. I'll try to be absolutely straightforward with you, okay?"

She glanced up and said, "Okay." Then she took a deep breath and looked down at her menu and said, "God!"

She ordered a salad, mostly endive, I think. I did, too, mostly crab and shrimp and squid. Beer—a pitcher of ale.

"I'm a vegetarian, more or less," she explained. "Not a rigid one. I have to have red meat at least twice a year."

We laughed. "I guess I'm not a rigid anything, except when I get scared stiff by some New York legal thug." We were eating mostly with our fingers. She had chewed up all the squeezed lemon slices in sight.

"Where did you live in New York?" I asked her.

"In the Village, and then I wound up in Soho just before I joined the Peace Corps."

I looked at her, astonished. I was pouring ale and some splashed on the table.

"We landed in the Sudan," she said, mopping up ale with her napkin, "and were held for five days because they thought we were Israeli mercenaries. Can you imagine? So boring! I ran out of everything to read. We went to Zaire, Zambia, Angola. I got malaria. They shipped me home, to Illinois. I got out of there as fast as I could and went to India. I wound up in Nepal. That's where I finally got well from everything. Before I left, I was climbing mountains."

Naturally that rang a bell. I dug out a shrimp, saying, "Yeah, Nels is an expert, all right."

She said, "Who?" looking honestly puzzled, and then said, "Oh, your editor. I may have met him. There were an awful lot of guys out there. What's he look like?"

"Tall, blond. You'd remember the smile probably."

"I don't." She shook her head. The blond curls trembled. In the light, they looked pale green. A sea goddess, I thought, not thinking of sirens then. She was picking out the leaves of endive, white and pale green, even the white pale green. Holding them up as she talked and popping them into her mouth, little green boats going over the falls. "I just got me some Sherpas and up we went."

The word had a particularly funny sound when she said it. I said, "Sherpas?" and grinned at her.

She giggled and said, "Sherpas." I didn't know why she was giggling, or why I was smiling really, except her lips were wet with oil and her teeth were white and all I could think of was I wouldn't be seeing Struiker until tomorrow and there was that big, empty suite. I let myself dwell on that fantasy for about thirty seconds and then put it out of my mind. Thirty seconds more, and it was right back in.

The ale was cold but like drinking sunshine. She kept laughing at what we said. Her laughter was warm-blooded and provocative. I let my hand rest next to hers, and she looked away, smiling and enjoying it. After a while, I started feeding her crab with my fingers.

When she went to the rest room, I paid the tab and then leaned back, feeling oddly lost without her, and I guess I was aware of what she had done to me in the last hour, how her presence had begun to crowd everything else out of my head, all precaution, maybe all common sense. I didn't care. Struiker was out of my life for twenty-four hours and the case seemed far away, maybe in La Jolla or even Zaire. When she returned, I said, "Let's go to the beach," and she said, "All right," and turned away with a smile, her gold blond hair flashing, and I followed her out, watching her hips waver as if we were walking underwater. Ale is wonderful. So is sunshine, and somebody new, and a whole afternoon before you.

Across the street, I saw a swim shop, and I grabbed her arm, pulling her inside. I bought us suits. She held hers up in the three-way mirror, a crinkly elasticized orange and yellow job with spaghetti straps, and outside I turned her to me and kissed her. Ale and crab and oil and onions, like a sea breeze. In the park overlooking the ocean, she said, "Where shall we change?" We'd been walking dazed in the hot sun and the idea of something so practical stunned me, almost woke me. "Oh, of course," she said, remembering, "there are dressing rooms on the beach, or rest rooms or something."

I looked around and a sign caught my eye. Hell, it was a sign from God, a shining moment of religious ecstasy. "I've got a better idea," I said, and pulled her across the street into a bleached hotel with a central courtyard surrounded by white walkways and a room on the third floor, with a view. You won't believe me when I tell you it was called the Shangri-la. But I believed. I believed in everything.

She changed in the bathroom and came to the window I was looking out of and started drawing circles with one finger on my back—around and around. When I felt her finger move out of a circle and begin a figure eight that led up the back of my neck, I turned and kissed her, and then I began to fool with the spaghetti straps. She pulled away and put her head down, refusing to look at me. I hugged her and she hugged me back, but she was unbending. I put my face in her hair and said, "Okay, your ocean or mine?"

We went silently and slowly down to the beach. The water was fine. We came out and lay in the sand. I propped myself up on one elbow and looked at her, and she looked away, smiling. But it was a strained smile.

"Have I done something wrong?" I asked. She quickly shook her head. I said, "There's nothing more we need to do. I'll take you back to the car whenever you're ready. You can go home then. Whatever. It's not like I bought you a fur coat."

She looked down at her sassy little swimsuit and laughed. "Oh, Mike," she said. She said it sadly.

Twelve

When she didn't move to go, I lay back and dozed. I awoke feeling fried. The taste of beer and onions and crab wasn't so invigorating anymore, and she was gone. I found her in the room, dressed and sitting on the bed.

"Trill?" She didn't look around. I took a shower and got dressed, feeling worried. Coming into the room, buckling my belt, I said, "Trill? At least give me a clue. I don't want this to be the worst afternoon of my life without knowing why."

She looked up as if she might be trying to smile. Her hair was glorious. I sat down beside her and put my hand on the back of her neck, feeling the fine sculptural arc it made beneath the weightless foliage of her hair.

In a flat voice, she said, "I'm not at all what you think. I'm no golden girl. I have to watch myself. It got pretty awful in the car, when you tried to scare me because it was your job. I get scared easily."

"I get scared, too."

"No, you don't, not like that. Closeness doesn't seem to scare you, either." She reached up and took my hand away, holding it between her two hands. "I got well, mostly, in

Nepal, but then I had to deal with the fallout. It was hard, and it keeps coming back."

"You don't have to explain."

"I'm not talking about malaria or anything recent, but the real me, the one I brought along to college and then New York. I've had to go back and try to live with that person, and sometimes I feel like I never learned how."

I'd had a little therapy, back when I was working in books. Panky—Gisele—has had a lot. She's been in analysis for years, going way back to her childhood in Paris. Sometimes I don't think she's going to hang around with me much longer unless I get into it, too. "I was born to be in analysis," she jokes. "The French, you know, are so analytical." I didn't know what to say to Trill, though. I just couldn't see what she was trying to tell me. Sometimes you have to draw me a picture. I felt I was saying all the wrong things but I kept saying them, anyway. "I'm sorry you have this problem," things like that.

Gradually, she seemed to relax a little.

"You want to get the car?" I said. "We could go for a drive. I could drive."

She looked around at me. Her eyes seemed different—smaller somehow. Intense but soft. Focused but blank. She seemed to be looking at my chin, studying it. She put her hands on my face, her fingers touching my cheeks and mouth like a blind person's, and then she cupped my head in her hands and kissed me hard. Then there was a little whimper, almost inaudible, and she pulled me down on top of her and kissed me again, not hard but a long time. Since the kiss didn't seem to be ending soon, I rolled over on my side and took her along and held her. It wasn't actually one long kiss, but a series of shorter ones with no time in between, coming continually, as if she was trying out all the ways our lips could fit together. No open mouths or tongues, no great passionate episodes.

Well, only once, and it was my doing. I was hard, and our legs were locked together, and after a while I got pretty wild and she let me put my hands up under her silky sweater and unhook her brassiere and touch her breasts, which were full and soft and hard-tipped. I started thrashing around and went out of my head. I put my other hand down into her pants and found the wetness between her thighs, and she instantly pulled away and sat up. I looked at her, and I guess I must have seemed angry. I wasn't angry. I was astonished.

She found her shoes and slipped them on while I lay there frowning up at her, breathing hard, confused and wanting her. Then she turned and looked at me, and her lower lip trembled. Suddenly, she pulled her sweater up over her head. Her brassiere dangled from her shoulders, open at the front, and her breasts seemed to glow at me. Her chest was heaving. "I'm sorry," she said, and her voice broke. "If you want me, you can have me. I won't stop you."

I almost reached for her. But I looked in her eyes and I didn't see any invitation there.

"You don't want to," I said.

She put her head down. "No. I'm sorry."

We walked back to the car and I drove. We didn't say anything until the sun was all the way down, plopped sizzling in the ocean, with the sky yellow and red and blue. Then she leaned back, her hair flying in the wind, her head rocking from side to side, and she said, "God!"

We had started out on the freeway and driven up past Sunset and way up Mulholland Drive, and then all the long, winding way back down Coldwater Canyon through Beverly Hills, and through the UCLA campus, looking at everything, and then up through Bel Air. It was good being back home, good to sense the road beneath me, antennalike through the tires and the wheel in my hands, good to feel part of a place I knew and just roll with it, no end in sight. I hadn't done that in so long. The land had a raw smell, a wildness that couldn't be tamed by all this ambitious reordering of nature. Something about the bleak ungraded hillsides in the distance that kept the rolling green lawns only a hairbreadth away from danger, from upheaval, from death and damnation. Something indomitable just a finger's touch away, exactly the way a car might shoot through a guardrail and be instantly a tangle of hot metal. Only that far.

I kept glancing at Trill, wondering what to make of her. We were both windblown and she had that "life is just around the corner" look I'd seen when she'd first driven up to my hotel. Only then, it had seemed free, unrestrained. Now it was controlled, hopeful yet fragile. But otherwise she looked so damned healthy that I got to feeling if I could just drive long enough and far enough, I could make her strong. And could make me start to make sense.

We wound up at the Bel Air Hotel shortly after sunset. I just drove in. I was getting hungry. It was like a huge bower, and the swans were out on the mossy pond under the tall, endlessly branching trees. We went into the bar and had a drink. Fruit and whiskey. Me a maraschino cherry and slice of orange. Trill, a deep green wedge of lime.

"Better?" I said.

"Fine, thanks."

"I don't think I'll ever forget it," I said. "It's great to be back. It's been a great afternoon."

She said, "Only I didn't know you were born here, for Christ's sake." I'd told her in the car about my sister in Venice and my folks in Laguna and my brother in San Francisco, with aunts and uncles and cousins scattered through the valley and up the coast.

"Struiker, too."

"Struiker?" She looked surprised, as if that couldn't possibly be true.

"With sharks and rattlers and black widows for playmates."

"It fits," she said. "But it's revoltingly macho. He's obviously building a legend."

"He'd like to be a legend, I'm sure." Suddenly I thought, Politics. Maybe even a senator. Is that what he wanted?

I felt her hand on mine and turned to her. It got very quiet. She said, "I want to make love to you," and it looked as if she was holding her breath just the way I was. She looked away and moved closer. "I loved the ride. I like the way you drive. I loved watching you, your hands. It was wonderful to be high above everything else up there in the clouds, up on Mulholland. Am I starting to feel secure with you?" She took away her hand. "If I am, it won't last. It isn't security I want, anyway, it's knowledge. Do you think you could help me get to know what I need to know, help me be a better person? I want something from you. I wish I knew what it was."

She looked at me carefully. Didn't stare, just looked, but as if reading something written on my face. A movie there. A character video. Yet I felt she was using me just to keep her mind on track while she examined what was going on inside her.

She said, "If this had been three or four years ago, I'd probably be telling you I love you. I do want to go to bed with you, I know that. Only if you wanted to. And if my fears didn't get in the way. But this minute, I feel so safe with you. I don't think you'd cheat me. I have confidence in you." She stopped. Slowly she began to smile, and then she jerked her head away, but this time it wasn't as if she was nullifying my presence. "Well, you do have a certain charm. You're very handsome."

"Thank you," I said. Nobody had ever said that to me, not like that. I wanted to tell her how attractive I thought she was, but something held me back. I felt a shiver go up my spine and into my shoulders. They actually quivered.

"What's the matter?" she said, noticing.

"I don't know." I smiled. "Electricity, maybe."

She smiled, too. "I wasn't sure at first I liked you one bit."

"I had a few doubts myself."

"You better," she said. "I take a lot of getting used to."

It wasn't that we were falling in love, I didn't think. Not like Gisele. Gisele and I, if it's love, will always remain somewhat distant. There'll always be an aesthetic space between us, filled with something like awe, for me at least, an adoration that's partly mystical. But with Trill, it was more that we liked each other without qualification. We still had our objectivity. We were sitting in a pleasant, quiet place, with other people nearby and a fairly busy bartender in the corner. It was getting dark outside and the cool lights of the evening were illuminating the grounds, and there was dance music from somewhere. It was California, my hometown, where the air on a perfect night seems one substance with the darkness and both move indissolubly in a slow dance through the trees. It seemed to me that Trill and I were both experiencing this sensation outside and inside our bodies, but the feeling was too quiet and rapt to be heavy passion. More like being enamored of feeling young and alive. It didn't rule out sexuality, but we weren't in any hurry. Is that a perfect night or what?

So I couldn't stop smiling at her, and she looked pleased. When our table was ready, we got up and then just stood looking at each other, taking our time, as if we were wondering what we'd say next when it came time to talk again. Then we headed for the dining room.

Thirteen

I woke up in Trill's arms, bombed out on sex and fresh air and sunshine and sheer expanses of skin. It was something that had never happened to me before, sleeping all night long with bodies locked together, even our hands clasped, and my first thought was, Trill is fragile, Trill is unbreakable. Not unfeeling, far from it. But demanding, wanting what she was sure she deserved. And perhaps vulnerable because she asked so much.

We were in a plain double bed on a hillside overlooking Hollywood, city of the stars. In a carriage house high on a vertical acreage, with a big window and her bed against the opposite wall so you could lie there and see the dark sky and the twinkling lights on the far peripheral mountains, and, if you sat up, the grid of the city below and that more distant, even deeper darkness where the sea was and the monsters of the sea, and all the other creatures in it, down to the plankton rolling and bobbing and weaving there.

We had driven up after dinner, our headlights tracing the steep, uncoiling roadway that led through metal gates and around the main house, a Normandy château lighted up outside like Bastille Day. At the coach house, I'd carried her upstairs on my back. It was something I wanted to do, and she let me, her strong thighs tight around my waist and her small cries and long hair tingling my ears, and there wasn't any awkwardness or dopey shyness left by the time we'd closed the door. We didn't turn on the lights. We stood at the wall-size bedroom window, naked and touching lightly, our bodies, like the darkness out there, all unexplored and yet electric like the pinpoints of light. Then it was like a storm falling upon the city from the mountains, and I began to see how rigorous she was, how welcoming and how persevering.

I awoke before she did and showered, then put on my swim trunks and padded around looking at things. Her office cluttered with paper. A strong-backed office chair before the computer, and an elegant swan's-neck desk lamp. A kitchen sink stacked with days-old dishes. Persian rugs on the floors and Indian ones on two walls. Every room except the kitchen had a telephone, but there was only one TV set, a nineteen-inch Sony in the living room, with a long heavy-duty cord coiled up behind it—so it could be carried out onto the deck, I guessed.

The redwood deck was off the kitchen outside the windowed bedroom wall. It was turned away from the main house and cut off by trees from everything but the downhill view. I made coffee and went out there to drink it, and when she tapped on the window and then came out in a light blue robe, I went in and got her a cup and we sat gazing happily at each other in the morning light. She looked marvelous with all that blond hair, her eyes full of sleep, drinking caffeine and giving out waves of contentment. Then we went inside and made love, and she didn't seem demanding this time, just ardent. By then I wasn't sure which was her and which was me.

Getting dressed, I tried to get her ready for Struiker—or me ready. I knew he might be waiting at the hotel, and I hated knowing that. I thought about my plans to see my folks and wondered how I was going to do that now that there was Trill. While I was calling a cab so I'd reach the hotel ahead of her, I knew I'd miss her for the next few hours. What was I going to do about that feeling in the next four days, for Christ's sake?

But first there was the case to deal with, so I reminded her as accurately as I could of what Struiker expected and how he might apply this or that tactic to get it. "You made a mistake," I told her. "You had this hard-on for Bangor and didn't tell us."

"Hard-on?" She gave me a puzzled frown.

"This fascination, whatever it was," I said, keeping to the past tense, "you know, like being mesmerized by a deadly snake. You brought us into your personal game with Bangor and didn't use common sense or ordinary caution. We're out here because you didn't behave responsibly or professionally. You made a mistake. I should have caught it and I didn't, because I trusted you as a professional. You let me down. Well, maybe in a way we let each other down." I wanted to say she hadn't let me down last night, but I didn't. I wanted her to be thoroughly alarmed and on guard, the only way I knew to protect her.

"Anyway," I said, "now we have to do some things we don't want to do, to wrap this up, and Struiker is going to want you to do your part. If he feels any uncertainty about that, he's going to apply heavy pressure, and he'll go just as far as he thinks he has to, to relieve his nagging doubts. You can handle that, can't you?" Christ, if Struiker had heard me counseling her like this, he would have killed me. Or maybe not. Maybe I was doing just what he wanted me to. In any case, I tried to stick to the essentials.

"Trill, I won't be on your side when we see him this afternoon. Don't look to me for help. I respect your ability and I'm still your editor. I'm not going to attack you. But Struiker will, if he thinks he has to. That's all I'm going to say, because I'm not inside his head. Just try to be ready for anything."

Looking at her, I couldn't help it. I reached out and grabbed her and kissed her.

She giggled. "Anything?"

"Anything." I stepped away and let cool reason return.

She saw my look and sobered, nodding up at me. "I'm sorry you missed your party last night."

I stared at her. "Party?" I hesitated, then I thought, What the hell. "Trill, there wasn't any party. The party was just part of Struiker's strategy."

I saw the fear in her eyes. "Then you're really just out here for me and Bangor? It's serious?"

"It's serious, Trill."

The taxi came, and I rode down into the city wondering whether Struiker would know instantly that I wasn't the same as I'd been the day before and whether, when we saw Trill, he'd know why. I decided it didn't matter. I just wanted him to leave town and let me get on with this new thing in my life. I didn't have a clue as to how to handle it.

He came in shortly after noon, low-key and uncommunicative, and went into his bedroom to make some phone calls and pack. My suitcase was already at the door and I was back in my own tie. My sister's party was tonight. Afterward, I'd stay with her or drive down to my folks' in a rental car I was picking up at the airport. Or maybe I'd invite Trill to the party and then take her along to Laguna Beach. Who knew what I was going to do?

About one-thirty, while I was reading in the library, the phone rang. I was surprised to hear Struiker pick it up in the living room and, after a series of curt questions, invite the caller up. From the questions, it wasn't Trill, and she wasn't due for a while. My guess was that it was someone he hadn't been expecting but couldn't turn away. Bangor? He appeared in the doorway and stood looking thoughtfully across the room at a bust of Beethoven, and then he said, "It was a mistake not to leave yesterday. You do what has to be done and get out while you're ahead."

"A surgical strike," I said. "Hit and run."

"Well, we dawdled and meanwhile Bangor's wife has been burning."

I put the book in my lap. "She's on her way up?"

"So far it's just Bangor. He's waiting for her downstairs. He'll try to dissuade her. If he can't, we'll just try to get them out the door without taking too much damage." He sat down where Bangor had sat the day before. He looked completely relaxed, which made me think the fires of hell must be seething inside him. I was getting to know Bob Struiker pretty well. "This is not the worst thing that could happen, not yet. He says she's on her way over here to give me a piece of her mind. That could be unpleasant. On the other hand, it could give us an opportunity to show Bangor how much we care about him, how sympathetic we are. It depends on how hysterical she is."

"Hysterical? What does she want?"

"She's incensed. She wanted revenge and now she's afraid we've talked her husband into letting McGuffy off the hook. She wants to rattle my cage, shake me up. She wants too much. Here we have a case of *A Midsummer Night's Dream* and she's playing it like Lady Macbeth. She's upset out of all proportion to the deed."

"Well, what can she do?"

"She'll threaten, cajole, try to intimidate. I'll bring her down gradually. Don't let her panic bother you; it won't last long. If she's completely unreasonable, we'll just leave and close the door, tell her we'll see her in court. Time passes, she comes to her senses, and all is forgotten. My guess is that Bangor fears going to court more than he fears his wife. Of course if I'm wrong, if she has some hold over him that makes him decide to sue after all, or if she's coming here to present new evidence, we could have wasted our time out here."

I started to ask him what new evidence when there was a soft rapping at the door. As I followed him into the living room, he said, "After the preliminaries, offer them something refreshing. Whatever she drinks, make it a double." Then he opened the door and Pamela Laudicek came in.

She was overwhelmingly attractive, a dark-skinned black woman in her thirties, all in black. Black hair, of course, and a black jumpsuit clinging to a tall, sleek model's body, her chest layered with strands of glittering black beads. Large dark eyes, liberally lined and lashed. High cheekbones, an aquiline nose, a generous, sensitive mouth. One moment, she stood framed against the blurred silver-gray form of her husband, like a black Stealth bomber banking off the clouds, and in the next, she brushed past Struiker and swept into the room. She was halfway across it when she stopped abruptly, as if she'd crashed into a mountain. She turned, her eyes wide. Like the drink I was about to offer her, her look was just this side of lethal.

"I'm sorry, I didn't know," Bangor said from the doorway, sounding like Banquo's ghost. He came in, all in gray, with that great gray head. His face was gray, too, but not hard like Struiker's. It looked like a marshmallow that had rolled into the ashes. "This is Mr. Struiker, my dear. Mr. Lindenthal. Pamela Laudicek."

She said, "Sorry! He's sorry!" and stomped her foot. The beads jangled softly. The eyes flashed.

Struiker closed the door and gestured toward a chair, saying, "We're leaving for the airport, Mrs. Laudicek. Please sit down and tell us what's on your mind." We all settled down, but she stayed on the edge of her chair, looking ready to spring. Two hours at the health club every day without fail was my guess. Her eyes popped. I thought I had seen something of her in Bangor yesterday, something she brought to him that otherwise would not have been there: a touch of nerve, an extra energy, a borrowed daring that were not there now. Right now, he looked positively stunned.

"I guess I'm the last thing you expected to see," she said. I thought how right she was. Did she know we'd pictured her with snowy skin pristine as the peak of the Jungfrau?

Did she imagine Nels would tell us she was black? Not that it mattered, but why hadn't he?

Struiker said, "Obviously you have an interest in this, Mrs. Laudicek. However—"

"Yes, I shouldn't have come," she said. "It's Bangor's problem." Then she sat up even straighter and cried, "But how could I let you leave town after what you've done to him? A letter! A letter and an article in a magazine! And nobody pays. Nobody pays!" Her husband covered his forehead with one large, powerless-looking hand.

Struiker stared at her calmly. "Somebody always pays, Mrs. Laudicek, and don't you forget that. I won't."

The lashes went down momentarily. It had not been a good beginning and she knew it. Her chest began to heave, and she held on to the arms of the chair as if she feared she might fall out of it.

Except for a flickering glance at Bangor, who was now massaging his right temple, Struiker didn't stir. "Would you like something to drink, Mrs. Laudicek? We have some time. I want to hear what you have to say." He looked at me, and I got unsteadily to my feet.

She said, "Gin and bitters." Then she looked up. "It's warm. It's warm in here."

Bangor showed a vague alarm. "Are you all right, my dear?"

She said impatiently, "Yes. Yes," and got up and walked across the room and out onto the balcony. I looked at Bangor, and when he finally saw me, he said, "No, nothing," and then, "Yes, a little brandy, please."

I got busy at the bar. Nobody said anything. Struiker was staring at the woman in black standing out there with her back to us. I picked up her drink and looked at him and he nodded. I took it out to her and said, "Gin and bitters, what the doctor ordered."

She gave me a formal smile, but I had the impression that she hadn't heard me. There were tears in her eyes and what I took to be loathing. I held the drink out to her, not knowing what else to do, and all at once she leapt past me. The glass flew out of my hand and smashed on the concrete floor of the balcony. I turned to look at her flying across the room, screaming at Bangor.

"You've got to do something! You've got to stop this charade! You won't listen, and you've got to be made to listen. You've gone down into some perfect hiding place where this man put you, and your fucking lawyer won't lift a hand to stop him. Don't you see what he's done to you? Don't you care?"

She was crying now, and Bangor had put his head back and shut his eyes. Then Struiker was coming toward her, speaking so quietly I couldn't hear what he said. I turned away and started picking up pieces of broken glass, some of which were missing and probably in the pool. The pool wasn't for people, and maybe this was one reason why.

I carried the glass inside, cutting through the library toward the kitchen. She was standing at the piano, her head in her hands, and Struiker was leaning back against the bar, talking slowly and steadily. I took my time getting rid of the glass and washing up, and then I heard her frantic cries again. She was telling Struiker he was a shark who took advantage of desperate people, bought them off cheap, opened the jails and freed the criminals. "You don't know what she's done," I heard her say, "and now she'll never let him go!"

She was sobbing and snarling, and then she started to wail. I waited until it was quiet again. I figured Struiker would call me if he wanted me. I told myself he was getting paid for this and I wasn't. But then I got edgy. I wanted to see what was going on, but I wanted to be able to disappear if I didn't like what I saw. I went into Struiker's bedroom. His luggage was still there. I picked up the bag and the briefcase, and the phone rang. I put the bags down and stared at it, the hair on my neck bristling like I'd just awakened from a nightmare. The whole place looked strange, as if somebody had rearranged the furniture of a dank Transylvanian castle to make it look like Southern California, but hysterical women in black were smashing glasses and screaming and falling into the arms of Dracula-like attorneys. I grabbed the phone, expecting the accents of Bela Lugosi, and it was Trill. I thought, Trill, my God, are you real? Are you alive?

"Hello," she said. "I'm downstairs."

I said, "Stay there." I wanted to say, Run!

"What's the matter?"

"Nothing. We'll be down in a minute. If we're not down in a minute, call back. It's nothing—a piece of business. Something came up. Trill?"

"Yes? My God, what?"

"You're all right?"

"Of course. What is it? Is anything wrong?"

"Don't worry. Nothing's wrong." I hesitated, wondering what was going on in the living room.

"You're scaring me," she said. "Mike, am I in big trouble?"

"You're not. Don't worry. I'll see you." I hung up. I stood looking at the room, as if somebody had just died there of bat bites and the bat was still hovering. I wanted one thing: to keep breathing. Men faint, too, did you know that? I fainted once, when I was twelve. My mother roused me, helped me up, and sent me off to school. I haven't fainted since—not yet, anyway.

I picked up the bag and the briefcase and carried them into the living room, putting them down alongside my suitcase near the door. Bangor looked drugged, sitting back in his chair, and the other two were talking near the balcony. As I turned to go, her voice rose as if somebody had plugged in a PA system.

"She has! She's been after him all along! Oh, I know what happened at Michigan, and I know exactly what's happening here. She's such a perfect bitch!" She glanced at me, and her arms clawed the air. She screamed, "Bitch, bitch, bitch! You hear that? Bitch! And everybody says, 'Oh, yes, isn't it a shame how she's out to get poor Bangor,' but he won't stop her. He thinks he can save her. Well, I'm going to stop her! I'm going to see her pilloried. And we're not going to settle for a picture in a magazine and a letter of apology. I'm going to tear out her hair and braid a noose. She's going to swing for what she's done!"

She began to wail again. Bangor heaved himself out of his chair and went past me to the bar. He found the brandy I'd poured for him and gulped it down. Then he poured himself another. Struiker was moving Pamela Laudicek out onto the balcony, and Bangor's back was to them. I could see his face working, experiencing the effects of the brandy. His eyes were blinking rapidly, and he seemed to be feeling better. He saw me, I think. But he really didn't look at me. He might have been there all alone, or he might have been part of a crowd, but either way he seemed to be in a solitary world of his own, making it up as he went along, sampling it the way he continued to sample the liquor.

Then Pamela Laudicek strode quickly into the library, heading for the bedroom area, and Struiker was saying to Bangor, "She'll be all right. I've explained our position, the one you and I agreed on. I'll leave you here now. I've got a plane to catch. But take your time. I'll tell the desk you're not to be disturbed. I'll be in touch with your attorney, so go home and forget this. It will all work out."

Bangor nodded and cleared his throat but didn't speak. They shook hands solemnly. Then Struiker was opening the door and picking up his bags and we were going down the hall.

"That was Trill on the phone," I said, my mind still lagging.

He pushed the elevator button, his jaw tight. "Jim Provine has been hearing this woman scream about McGuffy for months. Burley has, too. They both knew we were planning a piece on Los Angeles, and that McGuffy was writing it. Why didn't anybody tell us we were walking into a brushfire? Burley knew Bangor was mentioned in the piece. He saw the manuscript at the photo shoot. None of this lets you off the hook. You should have checked. But that was merely a delinquency, laziness or inefficiency or both. For Burley not to have told us is inexcusable."

He shut himself down, perhaps regretting having said so much, and the elevator arrived. On the way down, he said, "Not a word to McGuffy. Nobody's upstairs. Remember your role in this. She's got to write that letter. It's more important now than ever. Don't flinch if I get rough. Remember I've got daughters, and you haven't. This is for her own good. If she continues down this path, somebody's going to get badly hurt, and it could be her. Just keep Pamela Laudicek's fury in mind if you don't believe that."

When the door opened, he stepped out and said, "Give me your key card." He put his bags down and took it, then made for the front desk. I'd never seen him move that fast before. But then I'd never seen him come so close to losing his cool, either.

Fourteen

Trill jumped out of her chair and came toward me like a beautiful boat under full sail, going before the wind. She was wearing some kind of meaningless dark blue frock that reached to her knees but was almost entirely obscured by an oversize free-form white jacket that almost reached her knees, too. With her hair cascading, the jacket looked buoyant and unwieldy and almost comic, but it was cut with a certain style, expensively. We stood looking at each other, and slowly the elfin mouth turned up. The blue of the dress, I could see now, was deepened by black polka dots. The teeth were pearly.

"Hi," she said.

I said, "Hi."

"A ferret."

"What?"

She giggled. "He looks like a ferret darting for cover. What took you so long?"

"Last-minute arrangements," I said. "Where's the car?"

"I had them take it around to the lot. I wasn't sure how much longer you'd be."

I looked around for an exit to the parking lot. "How do we get out there?"

"Out the side. Why are you so nervous? Is it me? Have I done something? Shouldn't I have said *ferret?*"

"No, nothing." I glanced at Struiker. He was still busy. I wanted to make some arrangement to see her again but I didn't know what. I felt too uptight to smile, but I tried it, anyway. "Nice jacket."

"Thanks. I was afraid it might be too outlandish."

I stepped closer. "Trill, you're going to leave us at the airport."

"Yes." It was almost a moan.

"Can you meet me later? Around five o'clock?"

"Yes!" Her eyes glowed.

"Park in front of the Shangri-la."

"Not the airport? I can wait."

"No. I'll be driving. I'm picking up a car at the airport after he leaves." Struiker was on his way back. I reached for my bag. "Five o'clock." I turned and waited for him. He didn't look at Trill. I said to him, "The car's out in back. We can go out the side door."

He nodded, picked up his luggage, and said, "Coming, Miss McGuffy? I'm Bob Struiker."

"I know," she said. "I've heard about you," but he was already on the move. She glanced at me and winced, and I smiled, nudging her along.

He did look something like a ferret, I thought, darting along ahead of us lean and pinstriped, except the ferrets I'd seen at the zoo were brown, a solid, warm brown, and if that's what he was, it was a ferret without much natural grace, because he held himself stiffly erect, everything contained and under control again. I once watched a ferret move along a transparent tube only a little larger than it was and then change directions halfway through, bending its furry body like a soft rubber hose. Struiker was capable of doing that, I thought, and probably, like a small, agile carnivore, before you knew it.

I wasn't wrong. As we headed down Pico Boulevard toward the freeway, he relaxed, jollying Trill along, one arm draped over the back of the seat, while I sat behind them wondering whether Bangor and his fiery Pamela were on their way home yet. Struiker was behaving like a favorite uncle, the one who should be listened to and heeded above everybody else if you want to grow up and make people proud of you. Maybe he did know how to deal with daughters, I thought. Having a sister wasn't the same.

But then I began to see what he was doing beneath the fatherly guise. His manner was open and friendly, but instead of building her confidence, he was going right down the line point by point in his usual air-hammer fashion, knocking little chunks off it, questioning her judgment and her assumptions, leaving her no way to turn but his way. I was feeling protective again, but then I thought, It's for her own good, maybe for everybody's. She was a big girl. She could take care of herself.

It was starting to rain lightly. Trill had put the top up, and Struiker's voice was as lulling as the play of the windshield wipers, and just as persistent. He was saying, "There's a terrible hangover, you know, from the days when you were just a tiny tot back in La Grange"—she glanced at him and grinned, probably startled at his knowing that—"and I was a kid carousing on street corners in beautiful downtown Encino, and all over the country flower children were blooming like goldenrod." I almost blushed at the figure of speech. Was he overdoing it, trying to show her he wasn't entirely bereft of literary instinct? "Tell her I understand writers," he'd told me. "Tell her she can't get away with anything."

He droned on, his way of soothing mad tigers in the breast, hers or Pamela's. "Young people have finally come to realize that building a career and a credit rating are more important than leftist pranks and wild-ass haircuts. The punkest cuts you see now at Hollywood and Vine are strictly for commercial purposes, but the carryover from the sixties is there, and it's indefensible. Kids who still feel that people are old at twenty-five. Kids who ridicule responsibility and a sense of purpose. When will they learn that a little mild happiness is better than their kind of illusory excitement? Don't they know that the cry of the eighties, 'I've got mine,' wasn't just pure selfishness? If I have a philosophy like that, it doesn't mean you can't get yours, too." Insidious, I thought. Trill, like me, was about twenty-five. He was taking a chance, trying to turn her off on antisocial types, trying to ally her with the likes of me, the serious young editor, and even with himself, a sober-sided forty-five. But maybe he could do it. He'd undoubtedly done it before.

"I don't mean rockers," he went on. "The music and the lifestyle are both getting easier to take. It's all business, anyway. What the younger generation always comes up against eventually is the established one, and I was a young Establishment lawyer in the late sixties, in the days when push came to shove. I learned pretty fast how to handle punks and demonstrators."

Trill said sharply, "Dogs and hoses. Flamethrowers."

I winced, but Struiker grinned. "Oh, you do remember! Good. Well, there are ways and there are ways. Flamethrowers? You're talking Vietnam, and I don't want to get into that. But hoses and dogs? Why not? Sooner or later, rebels have to learn to respect authority, and it's whatever it takes to get their attention. A prisoner at Attica or Alcatraz, the best way to rehabilitate him was with a five-pound truncheon. Brain him. Reform through persuasion. Like those Chicago bayonets. The kids in Chicago at the 'sixty-eight convention complained a lot about that, but you notice how comparatively quiet things were by 'seventy-two."

Trill was taking us down the freeway now, the palm trees and red-roofed houses soaked with mild rainfall. I could see her eyes in the rearview mirror, and I wondered what exactly was going through her mind.

Struiker said, "Business. Sooner or later, it all comes down to the legitimate needs of conducting business. Sometimes people have to be brained to get them in line. Sometimes people have to be fired. At the *New York Blade*, there are a few hundred male employees and at least twice that many females. Apart from the cuts that have to be made during recessions, people get fired all the time. Attitude problems. If you're responsible for the bottom line, you can't afford to think twice about it. Inefficiency, alcohol, drugs, inner-office sex are disruptive. They have to be dealt with."

"They still fire people for falling in love?" Trill asked.

"Sure. Last week at the *Blade*, they fired them both. They presented a particular problem, and the problem stopped"—Struiker snapped his fingers—"just like that."

Trill drove silently for a while, the wipers beating back and forth. She didn't look at him, and her eyes in the rearview mirror had stopped looking at me, too.

Struiker asked casually, "What does it cost a month for someone like yourself to live in L.A., Miss McGuffy? A thousand dollars? Two thousand? I mean if you're just getting by, paying the rent and eating lots of lettuce and peanut-butter sandwiches?"

"I suppose if you're down on your luck, you could live on that," Trill said. "I've lived on less."

"But not lately," he said. "Maybe in Nepal, but not lately, not with four movie credits and more to come." She glanced at him, stiff-lipped but obviously impressed that he'd done his homework. She had to be wondering whether there was anything about her he didn't know, so no flashing teeth, no elfin smile. She was driving very carefully now—no passing, no fancy moves. I wondered whether I should risk saying something to lighten things up. But what? This was all between them now, Struiker taking her without pause down his list, punching out his message. "And so what would happen if it suddenly fell off, this free-lancing for magazines and a film script now and then? What if it just stopped?"

She said nothing.

"Like Burley," he said.

She looked at him and said harshly, "What about Burley?"

"You had fun with him in your letters to the magazine during the photo shoot. Burley was a clod, Burley was an old shoe. All through the letters you seemed to be questioning his competence, pointing it out."

"I've got nothing against Burley. He's a good photographer. I was just entertaining the editors."

"You were being clever at his expense. But what if Burley never got another assignment with *Beyond* magazine because of those letters?" In the mirror, I saw her eyes tighten up, looking at me. "See, you've got to live in the real world, where people get brained occasionally and often fired. You have to be aware of the consequences of what you do. You have to deal with hard facts."

She looked at him and nodded. Oh, how she must be praying he'd stop, I thought. But we still had several minutes before the turnoff to the airport. The rain was letting up. Trill shut down the wipers and began driving faster, passing again.

"Maybe you should stop writing for the magazines and stick to movie scripts," Struiker was saying. "Fiction. Fiction doesn't hurt anyone."

"I never intended to hurt anyone," she said. It was taking an effort to keep her voice steady.

"You were just having a good time, but it stings just as much." He looked back at me. "Mike here has a great regard for your talent, and he's one of the best young editors in New York. That's why I keep *Beyond* as a client. Editors like Lindenthal and Barbidoux have a lot more than success going for them. They care. They treat their writers with the warmth and regard they deserve. It's clear to me that they value your work and want to keep you writing. They'd like to see you have another chance. So would I."

Her eyes flashed at me in the mirror again, and she said evenly, "That's certainly nice of all of you." She was taking the turnoff. The surfaces of the city had begun to sparkle in the returning sunlight and we were almost there. Still Struiker kept pressing, but he seemed to be in no hurry.

"I wonder if you know, Miss McGuffy, how things start to come out once you're in court. Things you think will never be known. Personal matters. Things you never figured would ever see the light of day."

She said, and now her voice was getting out of control, "We're going to court?"

"I didn't say that. I hope it won't happen. Because there's talk out here that might make getting up on the stand an ordeal for you."

"What talk?"

He let his eyes rest on her, on her face, on the voluminous white jacket, on the capable hands on the wheel. "It's been suggested to me that there's more between you and Bangor Laudicek than I'd been led to believe."

She had started around the car ahead, but now she braked and swung back into the following lane.

"In other words," he went on smoothly, "a hostile lawyer questioning you on the stand might make it sound worse than it is. He might suggest you had a stronger motive to go after this man with such a vengeance, so that the jury feels it's a clear case of vendetta. Now, this line of reasoning would argue that you weren't just irritated by thinking he's such an intellectual fraud, but that you had some deeply personal reason to want to punish him through public ridicule."

"I don't see what you mean."

"Maybe you don't. See, unless Bangor Laudicek specifically urged drug use, he has a case on the face of it, a clear case of vendetta, especially since you've attacked him before. He might very well win. And if his lawyer could show that there was some other, more personal involvement between you . . ." He let that trail off, just let it lie. My God, I was thinking, is this what Pamela had come to the hotel to tell him? Was it hysteria or had she known exactly what she was doing?

Trill said, "There's nothing. He's lying."

"Good," Struiker said. "I was hoping you'd say that." He seemed to have finished, and precisely as we pulled alongside the terminal and stopped. But he made no move to get out of the car.

Trill looked at him and said, "So what do I do now? Burn all my belongings and head for Tahiti?"

He turned to her. "Stay put and Mike will be in touch with you. We may want you to write us a letter. He'll advise you on that. Keep in touch, don't talk to anyone about the case and don't forget what I said about the power of the established order. The thing is, as long as you keep your ideas to yourself and don't hurt anybody, you can think anything you like. I don't care and neither does anyone else. Intellectually or sexually or any other way, in the privacy of your room, within the boundaries of the law and good taste, nobody can touch you. You can espouse any cause, underwrite whatever approach to life you please, any drive for moral justice that seems right to you. You can think anything and feel anything or do anything, and you can feel absolutely certain of your own rightness vis-à-vis the rest of the world. But when you step outside those boundaries and inflict pain on someone, then you've got problems, Miss McGuffy, and I stop envying you for your intelligence and your insight and your memory for details and your talent, all those things that Mike admires in you as your editor, because what you've got then is trouble with the established order."

He watched a 747 taking off into the blue. "I understand why you've done what you've done, I think. I understand the message you tried to give the rest of the world about a pompous public figure you considered asinine. But he happens to be part of the Establishment, and the Establishment understands your message but rejects it because you've made trouble, and the Establishment doesn't need trouble. At the moment, Miss McGuffy, it considers you undependable and, in fact, dangerous. And because it's got all the power, that makes it right and you wrong."

We sat there in the sunshine in the open car, all three of us, like doomed desperadoes waiting to be taken away. After a while, Struiker gave her a grin. It wasn't much of a grin, though, and you couldn't hear it in his voice. "You'd just better pray that Bangor Laudicek is so eager to be rid of you that he decides to accept your guarantee that you'll forget he's alive, rather than go into court, where he just might come out with a barrelful of money along with your scalp. You don't want that to happen, do you, Miss McGuffy?"

She sat still, giving no indication that she'd heard the question. Then, very slowly, she shook her head several times. That didn't bother me as much as the fact that her head was down, and I could no longer see her eyes in the mirror.

Fifteen

Struiker got out and took his bags toward the terminal, the ferret, having struck. I said to her, "Five o'clock." She didn't look up. "Trill," I said, "we'll get your letter and it'll be fine. We had a talk with Bangor and his wife at the hotel. They're probably still up there, sorting it out, but everything's calm. Trill?" She didn't move.

Struiker was waiting impatiently at the door. I got out and grabbed my bag. "Five o'clock, okay?" Her head came up and she nodded, still not looking at me. Then she roared out of there like a rocket.

We sat in an out-of-the-way section of the passenger lounge. Half an hour before flight time, two hours before I was to meet Trill in front of the Shangri-la, and four days before I had to be back in my office, Struiker was unloading the last of what was on his mind. The last foul measure of obscenity, I thought. I knew I was reacting like an adolescent. He was a decent man with an enviable record, he had three daughters, all younger than Trill, and he was probably even capable of compassion. But I was angry, and everything he was telling me tasted of bile.

"It's what I was afraid of when we came out here," he

said. "I was hoping we could get out while this was still a simple matter of McGuffy's bad judgment."

I said, "So what else was between them?" I wanted to know and I didn't want to know.

His eyes searched my face, no feeling in them that I could see. He said, "She and Bangor were lovers, of course."

"When?"

"Way back at Michigan, the wide-eyed student and the brilliant, sought-after communications professor. What curdles Pamela is not so much the sexual part of it as the intellectual tie, a meeting of minds that went off to the moon. Very European, out of Goethe or Wagner. Grand passion, seated in the brain. Father and daughter. Genius and child."

"He's no goddamned genius."

"Well, the trappings of it. His enormous popularity, which he plays for all it's worth. You saw that."

I nodded. I could see that, all right, could even see how a very young woman might succumb to it, briefly anyway.

"What it does is make it easier for Bangor in court. His lawyer doesn't have to draw a jury a picture anymore. Her vendetta is no longer even faintly mysterious. It's all the old movies any juror has ever seen. Frantic love spurned. Hatred. Revenge."

"Just like Provine said."

"Provine knew, and he was able to embellish at the luncheon yesterday. Burley had some idea, but even now he's reluctant to say so. That would all come out if there's a trial—the fact that they knew, making it general knowledge. Making it appear that we must have known, too."

"So that's why you went for the settlement, before they knew we knew."

"It's why we had to come out here, to silence our own people."

"Where did Provine get it, from Pamela?"

"Not initially. He doesn't run with that crowd. But when you contacted him, he checked it out. Pamela was happy to talk about it. She'd been hysterically phoning McGuffy for days and had been bending Harv Wallace's ear around the office for months. That's how long ago Burley began to get wind of it. She accused her husband of it a long time ago, and he admitted it freely, not a love affair exactly, but a deep involvement, probably bragged to her about it, in his way. He's a hollow man, a certified charlatan dazzled by the idea of his own personality and incapable of deep engagement with anyone but himself. I don't know what Pamela is besides being a failed actress and aspiring author. He married her because she's exotic goods, but she turned out to be more than the bizarre toy he thought he was getting. She embraced the man, squeezed him dry. Imagine his surprise. Imagine hers, when she discovered there was nothing inside him." He recrossed his legs, as if he was tired of speculating in that vein and intended to change direction.

I said, "But Trill denied it in the car."

"Yes, but she wouldn't be able to deny it to a jury. She might plead extenuating circumstances, but those could be even more damaging in the end. Intensify her motive in wanting to hurt Bangor."

"What circumstances?"

He looked at me again. He clearly didn't want to say. "Oh, her youth, her susceptibility." He began again. "Bangor was showboating with McGuffy at Michigan, of course, just what he's always done, getting his kicks from the unqualified admiration of trusting, naïve young people, puffing himself up like a balloon."

"Using her," I said. The words tasted bitter.

He stared hard at me. "It wasn't just at Michigan, Mike. Then and later, there were drugs. There was free-floating panic. And it hasn't gone away."

I couldn't stand it. I said, "Excuse me for a minute," and got up and walked up through the long corridor full of hurrying travelers and bright informational signs to the main terminal. I bought a *New York Times* and read it while

I got a shoe shine. When I came back, he was reading the *Wall Street Journal.* He put it aside as I sat down.

"You don't want to hear this again," he said, as if I hadn't been gone, "but I want you to remember it. There were bad indications in McGuffy's letters. Why didn't we check on her? Jim Provine made it clear—"

"Jim Provine can go fuck himself."

Struiker folded his arms. "Exactly his feeling about you. He thinks you're a young jagoff who's helping Nels run the magazine into the ground. He feels cut off from his old friend Anton, outflanked by flashy newcomers."

I said, "He saw a chance to take a shot at me and took it. What did he write to Anton, anyway?"

He ignored the question. "Bangor could go into court and get a bundle if he knew what we know. Provine's the cause of it all, shooting off his mouth. I told him and Burley yesterday that if they're called to testify, they may be forced to say some things that will disturb the people back home."

"Such as?"

"Provine's letters would come into it. I told him his burglary of the TV station was unwarranted. The risk wasn't worth it. And putting the gory details into a letter that might be produced in court was foolish or worse. But that's not all his letter would show. It would show a working relationship with the magazine, and so would your earlier letters to Burley, ordering him around on that photo assignment. The odd thing is, Provine knows better. Yesterday he tried to get me to tell Anton to send out a memo advising the magazine staff not to write memos to each other when there's trouble, and blaming you for suggesting he do so."

"I didn't."

"He thinks you did."

"If he knew better, then why did he write it? As a textbook example of what not to do? Or just so he could dump on me?"

Struiker didn't answer. "The point is, never write anyone but me—I'm privileged. Always phone. If I want something in writing, I'll ask for it." He was studying the ceiling. "Provine made one valid point in his letter. He knew all about the flap and could have told us if we'd asked him. But it's also what's most damning. Just imagine their lawyer talking to the jury. Here's a major American magazine, he'd say, with writers and sources all over the world and two longtime employees right here in Hollywood. You'd think an editor would call and ask, 'Who's McGuffy? Has she ever written about Bangor Laudicek before?' They knew, he'd say. They were helping McGuffy besmirch the reputation of this man because of the magazine's antipathy toward L.A."

I was shaking my head. "I just can't believe a jury would go for that. It's absurd."

"Follow me through it, Mike. One, L.A.'s antagonism toward New York. Two, if it's a jury of women, they'll be outraged at our magazine having fun at this marvelous man's expense. Three, McGuffy as a witness is unprepossessing. She appears to be unsteady and unreliable at the least, and could be made to seem not only vindictive but out of control. Four, Bangor has respected friends and supporters in high places—colleagues and newspapermen, politicians and judges. Five, a question of fact: What did Bangor actually say on television? Six, Provine's letters and the McGuffy correspondence, all damning. Seven, the Laudiceks are attractive people, well placed in the community. Eight, Bangor could show hurt. He could stay home, lose his job, get his friends to say he'd lost weight. He could point to his wife's increasingly unstable state. Build the damages. Nine, Provine rifling that TV station. Ten, if we'd checked with Burley or Provine, they could have told us McGuffy was no good. Suppose they had to say that on the stand?"

I said, "Eleven, Nels and Pamela."

Struiker looked at his watch. "Ten is all I have time for. So now we need that letter from McGuffy, Bangor's story and picture in the next issue, and the check for the lawyer's fee, phone calls, and the tapes. Make it a small front-of-the-book story, Mike. Something like, 'Bangor Laudicek, well-known asshole, when queried for his views on drugs, said I don't have time to comment. I'm too busy having sexual relationships with starry-eyed young things like the once-nubile Trilla McGuffy.' " I looked at him in astonishment. He grinned back. "He's a cocksman, Mike, can't you see that?"

And she'd let him get to her. I didn't know whether I wanted to meet her at five o'clock or ever.

"Two thank-you notes I want you to write," Struiker went on. "One to the PBS guy in New York for trying to get the tape for us, the other to Jim Provine."

"Provine? You're kidding!"

He was still grinning. " 'Dear Jim,' " he said. " 'Thank you for your letter about breaking into the TV station. I always knew you were a friend, but I didn't realize how valuable until I read your letter. I was also filled with admiration at your prose style. Jim, if you can write as objective an analysis of Ronald Reagan's contributions to society as you wrote about mine, we'd like to run it in an early issue.' "

"Jesus Christ," I said.

"Well, tell him you appreciate his strenuous efforts to help the magazine. You never know when you might need him."

I said, "What about Trill? Can we use her again?"

"Don't give her any assignments for six months."

"Then it's okay?"

"If she's carefully watched. But don't tell her that, not till this is settled. You may decide she's not worth it. Remember, private feelings of rightness are wrong when they get the established order into trouble, and when that happens, talent and insight go right out the window. Even a psychopath may appear to think straight most of the time."

What did that mean? Did he believe she was a psychopath? Maybe he did. He'd reduced Bangor Laudicek to a cocksman, Jim Provine to a fuckup, Bangor's lawyer to a hack. So what did that make me?

He looked at his watch again. "There's a little more you should know. If Bangor's peccadilloes had ended when he left Michigan, we wouldn't have seen Pamela Laudicek today. He came out here because he was afraid of a campus scandal. That was when a very distraught Trilla McGuffy left for New York, then Nepal, and eventually California. Whether she was trailing Bangor or not, they met and got into it all over again."

"As lovers?"

He nodded. "Briefly. And later, when she mocked him in the alternative newspaper, that's when Pamela got into it. Bangor didn't tell her all of it at first. What he'd encountered at Michigan, he told her—and what was still trailing him around the country—was a strange young woman obsessed with punishing him, even ruining him, because he'd selflessly tried to help her kick a drug habit."

"She was really on drugs?"

"In her first year at Michigan."

"Jesus Christ."

"That was the mid-eighties and the fashionable thing to do especially if you desperately wanted to appear sophisticated. Don't forget, she was enamored of an eligible older man who was king of the campus and cock of the walk."

"And they were really lovers?" Why couldn't I just accept it?

"That came out later, when it no longer mattered. All Pamela knew at first was that Bangor was this Good Samaritan caught up in a student's drug problem, and that he'd been attacked by her in print when he refused her sexual advances."

"Is she still on drugs?"

"She apparently thought she'd kicked the habit in Nepal, but out here she fell into it again. Bangor said he was trying to break free of her, and that's why she was out to get him in the public press. Pamela had already gone around the bend emotionally, and now she was beside herself with jealousy and pain. She saw no end to McGuffy's vendetta. She still doesn't. She could still convince her husband to sue. He may not be able to resist her."

I sat back, trying to picture a Trilla McGuffy obsessed by drugs and by Bangor, and I couldn't. It was far too much to absorb. "No wonder she went after him," I said. "No wonder she hated his guts."

Struiker nodded. "But it wasn't rational."

"Can you imagine what she felt when she heard him babbling about drugs on TV?"

"One other thing," he said. "I want you to call Jeanne at my office tomorrow and tell her where you'll be while you're out here. If anything goes wrong—"

He looked up. The public-address system was saying, "Passenger Struiker, please report to the check-in desk. Passenger Robert Struiker—" He reached for his briefcase and got to his feet. "You'd better come along," he said. "I may need you to hold my hand." I picked up my bag and followed him.

Sixteen

The two men in business suits at the crowded airline counter looked as if they were used to dining on raw meat but didn't quite know what to make of Struiker. Too gristly, said Papa Bear?

"Robert Struiker?" the beefier one said, and flipped out a leather flap with a badge on it. My heart sank. I thought, Trill. Had she been in an accident?

Struiker said, "Gentlemen, what can I do for you?"

"I'm Detective Bannister, Homicide. This is my partner, Detective Braun. You just check out of the Hollywood Plaza, top floor?"

Struiker looked at his watch. "Two o'clock, yes. I'm catching the four o'clock to Manhattan. This is Michael Lindenthal of *Beyond* magazine, also New York."

"We're going to need statements from both of you," Bannister said. He was big and rock-solid, but he had very mild eyes, as if he bore nobody any ill will. "We have a questionable death at the hotel. You have some visitors who were still there when you checked out?"

"Sort of," Struiker said. "Who's dead?"

I got an ache in my throat, but I knew it couldn't be Trill. So why did I feel panicky?

"Television performer named Laudicek. His body was found in the pool downstairs."

I put my bag down. The second cop was looking at me. He had sharp dark eyes in a face that was otherwise expressionless. He said to me, "Anything you want to tell us?"

Struiker looked at me, too, and I shook my head. He said, "When we checked out, the Laudiceks were having a drink." He thought for a moment. "They were unexpected guests, so I didn't feel obligated to look after them. In fact, as a lawyer in contention on a legal matter, I had no business talking to them at all. Are we going someplace?"

"Headquarters, to get your statements," Bannister said. "We'll stop off at the hotel to have a look if you don't mind."

"I'll need to change my reservation and call my office."

The big cop nodded. "You shouldn't be delayed more than an hour or so."

They went past the line of passengers waiting at the desk. Braun glanced at me, then took out a cigarette and lighted it. "How are things in New York?"

"Fine. Listen, I'm supposed to meet someone at five, and I don't have any way to reach them. Do you think we'll be through by then?"

"Probably," he said. "You're not catching the plane?"

"No. I'm staying on to visit my family. I'm from out here originally."

"You don't say. When did you get into town?"

"Monday night."

He glanced over at Struiker, who was telling a wide-eyed reservations clerk what he wanted. "You out here on a lawsuit of some kind?"

I grinned at him. "I think I'd better let my lawyer answer that."

He nodded. "He a hotshot?"

"The best."

"I have to hand it to you. Traveling with your lawyer is the only way to go."

Now Struiker and Bannister were moving off toward a bank of telephones. I asked, "What's going to happen to Mrs. Laudicek?"

He threw me a look. "She's being held pending the investigation. Why? You have any reason to think it wasn't an accident?"

"Well, you said homicide. I just thought—"

"We haven't been to the scene yet. What time did you get here?"

"About two-thirty." He took out a memo pad and wrote it down. Still looking at the pad, he frowned and said, "Trilla McGuffy."

I wondered how he knew her name. "A writer. She drove us here."

"You know where she is now?"

"Maybe at home. Hollywood Hills, in a coach house. She writes for the magazine. She's a well-known screenwriter." I took out my address book and gave him her address and phone number, and while I was at it, I gave him my card. "When did it happen?"

He consulted his notes. "We got the call sometime after three." He looked up as Struiker and Bannister came toward us.

On the way to the hotel, Bannister looked back and said, "Mrs. Laudicek was all strung out. She's receiving medical attention downtown, and there's supposed to be a lawyer coming over to spring her."

Struiker said, "I hope for her sake it's not her husband's lawyer."

"They were suing you?"

"He was talking about it, before the settlement."

"You settled?"

Struiker nodded. "That's why I was on my way home."

"They came over unexpectedly, you said."

"She was upset. He tried to head her off at the pass, but she came up, anyway. She was calm when we left. Nothing had changed."

Bannister glanced at his partner, who was behind the wheel. "Well, she wasn't so calm downtown, I understand. She says it's murder."

"She killed him?"

Instead of answering, Bannister hunched closer over the back of the seat. "This young woman who drove you to the airport, Trilla McGuffy, what would she be doing, going back there?"

Struiker's jaw tightened, but he took his time. "To the hotel?" I was starting to panic again, but now I knew why.

"She got back there a little before three."

Struiker said, "Naturally I have no way of knowing that." He glanced grimly at me. "Mrs. Laudicek says Miss McGuffy killed her husband?"

Bannister glanced at me, too. "All I know is, if she's your client, you'd better see she surrenders."

When he said that, I nearly flew out onto the freeway. If only I hadn't told her they were there—

"She's missing?"

"Right now she's a fugitive."

"How does Mrs. Laudicek say it happened?"

"Says this Trilla McGuffy came in, fought with him, tipped him over the railing, then ran out. Says she has a history of making threats and taking drugs, in fact looked strung out at the time."

"Not unless she shot up on the way back to the hotel," Struiker said. "We've had several meetings with her out here and she looked clean."

"Well, she ran. We've got an all-points out on her." He glanced down at his notes. "Five foot six, hundred thirty pounds, blond hair, white jacket, white Mustang convertible. That check out?"

"Perfect," Struiker said dryly. "By the way, she's not my client." He looked at me. "This young man here is, at least for the time being."

Up in the suite, Struiker took the detectives through the afternoon's events, the Laudiceks' arrival, Pamela's hysteria, and the drive to the airport. It was a beautiful day. The late-afternoon sunlight was beating down on the now-empty pool as if nothing had happened, but the TV trucks with their satellite dishes were reminder enough. And upstairs and down, the crime lab was going over the suite and the landscape below. I was wondering whether Trill would be at the Shangri-la at five, and beginning to realize I'd never make it by then. I still hadn't told anybody about that, I don't know why. Wanting to protect her, wanting her to be out of everybody's reach, if only for a little while. No, it wasn't rational. I never said I was a rational human being.

Struiker had called Burley's wife and asked her to try to locate him. Trill wasn't answering her phone and he wanted Burley to find her and stay with her. "If he finds her, tell him to get her downtown and ask for Detective Bannister or Detective Braun," he said to Helen. His primary interest wasn't Trill. He was more concerned about Burley and Provine. "I want to be sure our people are completely clear of this mess," he told me. But still, he had a seven o'clock plane and he meant to catch it.

"Whether it was an accident or she pushed him," he said, "there's nothing to keep me here. They'll take our statements and we'll be free to go."

"You think she did it?"

"Well, the prosecution could show motive. Of course, she might plead insanity. In that case, we might both become star witnesses for the defense."

I looked at him and kept it light. "At least Trill doesn't have to write her letter, and I don't have to write that phony article."

"I may suggest to Anton that he send Pamela the money to pay her lawyer. We can say it's a gift in Bangor's memory. I think a gesture like that would appeal to Anton, don't you?" He was watching the two detectives talking with some gold braid across the room. "On the other hand, maybe it's not necessary, since the Laudiceks aren't being charged anything for the use of the suite."

I couldn't think of anything to lighten that. He was talking about a woman who right now was probably half out of her mind with grief.

Half an hour later, while they were taking our statements downtown, Burley phoned, asking for Bannister, and Struiker took the call. Burley said he was still looking for Trill. She hadn't come home, he said. He'd phoned a couple of the studios but they'd been no help at all. Struiker told him to go home and let the police handle it.

"Detective Bannister will be in touch with you when they find her," he said. "When they do, get down here and stay with her as long as you need to. Can you do that, Burley?" He gave him a phone number. "She'll need a good lawyer. Ask for Whitley."

When we were through, Struiker got a cab for the airport. I found a phone and called my sister. I told her what had happened and explained that I'd probably be late getting to the party, if I made it at all. Then I took a cab and drove past the Shangri-la. If Trill had waited, she'd been waiting for an hour and a half. But there was no Mustang convertible in sight.

"You want to cruise up and down a while, it shouldn't take you too long to find something nice," the cabdriver said. "They'll be coming off the beach in droves from now till after dark."

"Thanks," I said. I got out at the next corner and walked back, carrying my bag. The Shangri-la was the same pleasant looking place, white concrete surfaces and large windows overlooking the sea. I went in and asked for Miss McGuffy. Third floor, the clerk said. I got her on the phone. It was the same room.

"Come on up," she said. "I'm not going anyplace."

She sat in a heap on the bed, her eyes puffy and red, her legs crossed like a Camp Fire Girl, her dark blue dress riding up high, her blond hair straggling down over the turned-up collar of her jacket. "I thought if I stayed here maybe you'd find me," she said, keeping her eyes on me as if otherwise I'd run. "I'm so scared."

I sat down and held her. "What happened? Tell me. Take your time."

"I don't know." She was all quivering shoulder blades. "He was alive when I left him, not dead." She began sobbing, and talking through the sobs. "The way Pamela looked at me. You'd never know . . . you'd never know we were friends."

I didn't know what that meant. "Friends, Trill?"

Her head went up and down. "We were friends once, back in New York."

I hadn't known that. "Was Pamela on the balcony?"

She drew away and blew her nose. "We never went out on the balcony. He was lying down, back in the bedroom, when I got there. He was drunk, I think. He wouldn't even look at me."

"Was there a struggle, or what?"

"He got up and I hit him to make him look at me. But not on the balcony, in the room. I just let him have it." She shivered. "I was so mad." She looked at me in surprise. "You think I pushed him? Me?"

"No," I said.

She tossed her head. Her hair flew and settled. "I don't want to go home, not ever. It's so lonely there after dark. Could we go away? Oh, Michael, could I go back to New York with you? I wouldn't bother you. I wouldn't dream of imposing on your life. I just don't want to be here. I feel so isolated. I've always been comfortable in older cities. I liked New York. I liked Paris. And London. And Istanbul. I liked Kathmandu. God! I should never have come out here. I wouldn't have, either, if it hadn't been for Pamela."

"You came out here to see Pamela?"

"We were friends. I didn't know she'd married him. I didn't know she hated me. She was screaming, 'Leave him alone,' and looking at me as if she hated me."

Where had Trill been? I wondered. Pamela must have

hated her for at least a year, or whenever it was that Bangor had confessed they'd been lovers. I said, "Pamela's jealous. You were lovers."

"Is that what it was? Maybe that's why she was so unfriendly when I came out here! I flew all the way from Nepal, hoping to stay with her, but she wasn't at her old address. I began work on a film. I got very busy, and then one day I heard she was working for Harv Wallace. I called her that afternoon. She sounded different, very distant. She said she was married. I said who? She said Bangor Laudicek. I'd told her about him back in New York, years before. I didn't tell her everything. I guess I must have made him sound attractive. I guess I wasn't over him yet. Obviously I wasn't. I ran into him out here at a studio party. By then, I knew they were married, but it didn't matter. I can't believe he's dead, can you?" She looked around the room, her hair flying. She was talking a mile a minute. "Where's Burley? He was at the hotel, did I tell you? I was getting into my car and he came running up."

"Burley was at the hotel?"

"Um-hmm. We went to have a drink. I told him I was meeting someone. Then we saw it on TV, that he was dead and they were looking for me. He made some phone calls, then we left. He told me to leave my car in a parking lot, on Wilshire I think it was. I've got the stub here someplace." She went scrabbling through her bag. "Then he brought me here. I told him I was coming to see you."

"What was he doing there? At the hotel?"

She looked up. "I don't know. I didn't think to ask him. Burley's always turning up. He's that way." She held up the parking receipt. "See, here it is."

"Trill," I said, "Pamela says you pushed him."

She let the parking stub fall to the bed. I picked it up and put it in my pocket.

"She's lying. What does Struiker say?"

"What?" I was astonished. Why did she want to know that?

"He's a lawyer, isn't he? He knows about these things."

"He's not here. He's gone back to New York."

"Oh." She sounded disappointed. "He went back to New York, just like that?"

"He asked Burley to keep an eye on you."

She frowned. "Burley's not my keeper." Then she sighed. "Actually, he's been very helpful. He called Struiker from here, and he called a lawyer, and he's seeing the lawyer right now, and then we're all going down to see the police. He doesn't think they'll hold me, or charge me with anything, at least not now. But we have to do it, he says. They'll want me to make a statement. I will, too. She killed him; she must have." She put her head against my shoulder. "Oh, God, I'm so tired. Rub my back, will you?"

I went to work on her spine, between her shoulder blades, and she seemed to go to sleep, except whenever I hit a certain spot, she said, "God!" Finally she sat up and smiled, her hair falling over her face. I brushed it away and kissed her.

I said, "Why didn't Burley tell Struiker he'd found you?"

She opened her bag and started putting on lipstick. "That's Burley. He has his own style. If he cares for you, he'll go out of his way to look out for you. He's very surprising that way." That's for sure, I thought. "But he's like all the rest. All you men get possessive, you know, controlling. He doesn't like Raphael. He thinks Raphael's my secret lover. He thinks he takes advantage of me."

"Wait a minute. Hold it. You're saying he knows Raphael?"

"Sure," she said cheerfully. "Once he threatened to break his arm."

Burley Moore had said Raphael didn't exist. What was going on here? I got up off the bed, my head whirling. I wasn't even surprised by the knocking at the door. Or that when I opened it, Burley himself was standing there, looking like a Buddha in an old brown suit.

Seventeen

He looked different, bigger than I remembered. Then I realized it was the bright Hawaiian shirt. It flowed down over his belt like a tropical landscape. Otherwise, he was the same stolid servant of mankind. He didn't look alarmed or angry or distressed or pleased. He didn't look anything.

"Hi, Burley," I said, and glanced around at the bed. It was empty. Trill wasn't anywhere. I said, "Come in." I heard water running in the bathroom. Of course. She was taking a shower. What did I expect?

Burley didn't look at me. He went directly to the chair in front of the window and sat down. "She told me to come back about eight o'clock," he said. "I've been to see the lawyer, the one Bob said to call. He's meeting us at Homicide in an hour. How is she?"

"Okay, I guess."

"How are you?"

"Fine."

"Bob said I should look after her," he said, "so that's what I'm doing. You can take over if you want." He stood up and began patting down the chair he had been sitting in, as if to make it habitable for the next occupant. "Listen,

Mike, I don't know what you're up to with her and I don't care." He turned toward me and put his hands in his pockets. "I just know Bob Struiker, and I know he likes things all tidy and zipped up. Since I talked to the lawyer, maybe I ought to be the one to go with her."

"Well," I said, "I'm supposed to drop in at my sister's, in Venice. Maybe you could call me when it's over." I wrote the number on a slip of paper and gave it to him. "If I'm not there, I'll be here."

Burley said, "I told her to stash her car for the time being. It seemed like the only thing to do."

"Thanks for not telling Struiker where she was."

"I did it for her, not for you. Bob's all right. He just doesn't have much patience for the foibles of humankind." He shrugged.

"What were you doing at the hotel?" I said.

"Harv Wallace. He said Pamela had gone off in a fury to beard Struiker in his den. He'd already called Bangor to tell him that. I went over to see if there was anything I could do. Bangor looks like a Greek god but he folds fast. I mean, that's how he was." He looked at the bathroom door. "How long's she going to be in there?"

I heard the water shut off, and said, "Not very long."

He said, "I was working in the photo lab. I've got a lab over on Pico where I keep all my files. I guess I've got a negative or slide of every shot I ever made, going back to the old portrait camera. The last month or so, I've been shooting some celebrity parties for Harv. You know him?"

"I've met him."

"He's a wonderful fella. Columnist. Books. Knows all the stars, knows lots that are gone now, Marilyn Monroe, that kind. George Burns, well, he's still around, but you know. I called Harv this afternoon about the party shots, Debra Winger, for instance, Jack Nicholson, Shirley MacLaine. They were in that picture together years ago, can't remember the name. Lots of people like that. Looking at the photographs, it seemed to me like I'd been to a lot of parties with people who worked in the same movies, and I thought maybe Harv would like that idea, doing a photo spread on these people getting together again at parties, that kind of thing. Call it 'Cast Parties.' He didn't want to talk about that. He said Pamela'd been so upset, he was afraid she'd do something crazy at the hotel. I told him, 'Don't worry about Pamela.' I've seen Pamela when she's upset, and people worry about her, but underneath she's very steady, even when she's yelling around. Even everyday occasions, she gets pretty hyper sometimes."

He moved over and sat down heavily on the bed. I was surprised to see him smiling. Not a happy smile—it had something malicious in it. I wondered whether he'd hidden the instincts of an ordinary gossip all these years.

"You know, there are people like her all over," he said. "They love to control other people the way she does, I mean did, Bangor, just by the force of their personality. They can be very persuasive, and when they're provoked, they get their way just by flying off the handle. Lots of actresses do that. Actors, too. Even some agents are that way. I guess they learn it from the talent they handle. Pamela knew all about it. That's how she kept Bangor in line."

The bathroom door opened, and Trill came out in her dark blue dress with a towel wrapped around her head. Her face lit up when she saw Burley sitting on the bed. "I thought I heard voices!" she said. "Burley, I was beginning to think you weren't coming back." She crossed to the dressing table, sat down, and began busily buffing her nails.

"You said eight o'clock. We have about half an hour to get to the police station."

"Fine," she said, "I'm almost ready."

"The lawyer wants to go over the statement beforehand. For instance, what you'll say about leaving the hotel."

"I'd done what I'd come to do, tell him what I thought of him, that should be obvious." Her gaze rested on Burley while she took two or three deep breaths. "Burley understands all this better than any of us, although he's pretending not to. I don't understand why I should be considered guilty of anything." She seemed to be taunting him. There was some kind of tension between them I couldn't figure out. She went back to her nails, buffing away.

I said to Burley, "It's a good thing you were there. You can tell them she wasn't panicky or anything. Not heading madly for the border." He just looked at me.

I went over and sat down in the chair by the window. I was beginning to feel the strain in my shoulders. I said to Trill, "Burley's going with you to the station. I'll take a run over to my sister's and meet you later. Or if you feel like going on home, I can call you in the morning." I didn't want her to feel she had to do anything she didn't want to do. Burley seemed to be pressuring her in some way I didn't understand. Or maybe I did. If Burley was jealous of Raphael, he'd be jealous of me. But I couldn't get it through my head. Burley Moore, the old shoe, jealous? What had gone on between them? Was it going on right now?

Trill, examining her nails, said, "Burley, you've been very nice. Thank you for taking me downtown." She sighed. "God, I have such a lot to do this week. I have to get started on that article for *Esquire*, I just have to. Every time I start, something keeps getting in the way. Well, I'll just sit down in the morning and work on it until I finish it; that's the only way." She said to me, "I don't suppose I'll ever get another assignment from *Beyond*."

I said, "I don't know, Trill. I'm not the editor in chief. But I'll talk to Nels when I get back."

"He won't. I know he won't." She said to Burley, "What did you do today?"

He said, "Worked in the lab, mainly. Called some book editors I know."

What kind of conversation was this, just before you go to see the police about a murder? She was looking straight at him, as if she almost didn't dare to meet his gaze but was determined to. I could have sworn there was fear in her eyes. Of Burley? Or going to jail?

He got up suddenly and went to the door. "I'll be out in the car. It's around the corner, half a block up." Then he was gone. Trill put her head down, her nails forgotten. Her hair shimmered in the light from the lamp. Her blue dress was getting a little crumpled.

"You don't mind going with Burley?" I said. "He's met with your lawyer. He's going to call me when it's over."

"No, not at all," she said, but she didn't sound quite certain of that. After a moment, she looked up. "I'm glad there's just the two of us right now. You're a wonderful man, Michael."

"Trill," I said, "I've never met anyone like you, not ever."

She sat for a while, apparently thinking that over. Then she nodded her head, turned around, and began brushing her hair. I leaned back in the chair, listening to the swishing the brush made and watching all that thick blond hair fly. When she was through, she came over and sat on my lap and kissed me, putting her tongue deep in my mouth. Then, before I could get my bearings, she was up and out the door, jacket and handbag and all. When I caught up with her, she was going down the courtyard stairs. She looked back and said, "I'm not scared. Why should I be? I didn't kill anybody." I walked her to the car and then went back upstairs and opened my bag and put on the scruffiest clothes I could find. Then I went to the party. It was just about the last thing in the world I felt like doing, except staying in that room all by myself.

Becky's apartment, which she was sharing with two girls who went to USC, was in a long green frame building that looked like a military barracks on some godforsaken coast, except there were curtains in the windows. Inside it was clearly a pad of some importance, with shag carpeting, oversize pottery bearing pampas grass, and wall hangings and posters of every description. Most of the two dozen kids in the place were women. A surprising number of the men were distinguishable only by the hair on their arms and faces. Everybody tended to look vaguely alike, that loosely draped, shoulder-padded look, lots of belt buckles just missing the groin. Two rooms that more or less ran together were being used for dancing, to a small but loud band of Afro-Americans who looked to me as Rastafarian as they sounded. The dope was being used sparingly, perhaps for my benefit—they surely placed me in the adult category though some of them looked older than I did. Even Becky probably thought of me now as a stuffy person, gone east.

She was glad to see me though. She threw her arms around me for all to see, crying, "Michael! Here's my brother, everybody!" and then introduced me around. She looked both older and younger than I remembered her from Christmas, older, I suppose, because she was in her own setting, younger because of the eyeliner smudged above her eyes with what seemed to me childish abandon.

"My older brother, from Manhattan," she said, hanging on to my arm and turning me like a display of hors d'oeuvres. "Not my younger older brother but my older older brother, and not Manhattan, Kansas, but the real thing, like Murder, Incorporated, and the first thing that happens is the guy he's out here to see takes a dive in the pool—yes! The one on the six o'clock news! The TV guy with the gorgeous wife, at the hotel in Century City. Michael, meet Maisie, my roommate, and—where's Deb? Oh, she's in the kitchen." She pulled me onto the crowded dance floor, where we boogied our way past several more introductions toward the back of the apartment. Maisie was round-hipped and red-haired, and Deborah, at the kitchen counter, was dark and somber and dead set on constructing abstract designs on small seafood pizzas. Leaning against the kitchen wall was a tall, unsmiling, sunburned kid without a trace of hair on his head, in buff jeans and a pale yellow T-shirt. The shirt had a cartoon foot on it and read PLEASE KICK ME OUT BEFORE I DO IT AGAIN, and Becky was saying, "Mike, meet Derrick, my beloved." He said, "Glad to meet you, Mr. Lindenthal." Becky, having wrapped his other arm around her shoulders, was smiling up at me proudly. She gets by mainly on her teeth and eyes and figure, which is a little long-waisted but trim and tall. And on her brains, of course.

"You at USC, Derrick?" I asked him, and he shook his head as he let Becky go in response to a cry from Deb, who was running out of pesto and hot peppers. "University of Alaska," he said. "I'm down here for a semester, surveying the fishing industry along the coast. Independent studies."

"The language of the whales?" I asked.

He grinned. "More the curses of the fishermen." The grin pulled his eyes tight. It turned out that he'd already met Bill, my brother, and my folks. He'd grown up around Los Angeles, then his parents had split up and now his father owned several fish canneries along the upper Pacific. Becky had met him when she was in school in Oregon, but now she was taking a year off, and then what?

Eventually, I wound up in one of the rear bedrooms talking with Carla, a Scandanavian-looking USC senior from Albuquerque who was avoiding her boyfriend, a tireless, devilishly handsome Filipino who kept looking in the door, asking her to dance. "I've been dancing all night," she kept saying. "I'm exhausted, Squash!" And he would shrug, grin, and go back to the music.

"You don't look exhausted," I said. She had marvelous full red lips like tropical flowers.

"Well, I am. We go dancing every weekend. He likes dancing and he likes films. He's seen *Dirty Dancing* seven times, all of them in movie houses and most of them with me. When I go home, I ride into the hills and sit in the sun. I like the beach better than movie houses. I'm afraid of the water, though. It's so immense. It's like the New Mexican desert at night. Endless. I hate the city. I can't imagine living in New York; I'd strangle." She laughed. She put her hands around her throat and sang "New York, New York" while making strangling noises, and then stopped suddenly. "Oh. Sorry. I forgot you're a murder celebrity. Did you know him very well?"

"I hardly knew him at all."

"Well," she said, "I'm not afraid to die, but later."

I laughed. She held up her empty glass and said she was going for a drink. I watched her go. In her jeans, she had very slim hips that made her look like a cowhand. It takes me a long time before a face becomes unforgettable, but I knew I'd remember those tight jeans, the way they fit her.

I had a couple more drinks myself and talked to a few more random people, then wandered around until I found Becky taking pizzas out of the oven. "I have to go soon," I said. "Will I see you at the folks?"

"Oh, you're not staying?" She puckered her lips in disapproval. "I thought a little later we could walk down to the water and talk, the three of us. I told Derrick I'd go with him to Monterey this weekend."

"I'm sorry. I'll be back, maybe in a couple of months. Maybe sooner." I grinned at her. "How long has this been going on?"

"Since January tenth. He came to Oregon on his research project, and I sat behind him at a college basketball game, admiring his bare skull. I told him he was lucky he hadn't been dunked. He gave me his phone number and said the ball was in my court. He's really serious about his life. He's a very hard worker."

"What happens when he goes back to Alaska?"

"Well, I think he lets his hair grow out." She laughed, then grabbed my wrist and looked at me intently. "Relax. Come say good-bye to him and have a pizza or Deb will be mad. She made one especially for you. I might spend the summer in Fairbanks, but that's all, then back to Oregon. He's graduating, and I don't want to get married and wind up without an occupation, like Mother. Now, come on."

Becky wanted to be a laboratory technician. She wanted to make the world a safe place for people and for animals, and most of all, right now, for fish.

I walked for a while on the way back to the Shangri-la, remembering other nights, other parties, other girls in jeans, thinking specifically of Panky Janvier in her DKNYs. I thought for sure now I'd ask Trill to go down to Laguna with me if she was allowed to leave the city. I remembered the rental car that was waiting for me at the airport and made a mental note to cancel it in the morning. It was nearly midnight when I hailed a cab, wondering why I hadn't heard from Burley.

Eighteen

Just twenty-four hours before, I remembered, Trill and I had turned opposite ways when we said good night, but later we'd wound up tight together. She'd slept soundly, hardly stirring, holding on to me as if I was rescuing her from drowning. Ordinarily, it's not easy for me to be that close to someone so attractive without getting all hot and bothered, but for some reason this was different. We had been like an old married couple who knew all about each other, cared for each other, and had all the time in the world for doing all the things we wanted to do. But now I lay alone in the midst of strange shadows and the sounds of the ocean, and then I was listening to the traffic begin—a waterfall, a roaring, misty river of it, a steady surf, a rapids. I didn't feel as if I'd slept at all.

Outside, the day rose like a chill fog from the ground, making the air heavy and lusterless. I phoned Trill and she said, "Oh? Michael? Where were you last night? Just come and crawl into bed; don't wake me. I'm exhausted, but they haven't charged me with anything yet. My lawyer is wonderful."

I found the stub from the parking garage in my pocket

and checked out. I took my time, letting her sleep, read the papers over breakfast, then took a taxi to the garage, picked up her convertible, and drove it up the winding road to her place. Along the curved approach to her driveway were four parked cars and small clumps of newspeople and photographers, looking bored. A couple of them ran up and asked me who I was as I waited for the wrought-iron gates to swing open. I'd already given my name to the people in the main house, on the intercom. I told the reporters I was a real estate agent. That amused them, anyway.

The redwood coach house, or guest house, or whatever it was, became visible only after you passed a stand of trees and came abreast of the main house. It sat at the far end of a gently sloping rough-cut lawn, seventy or eighty yards away. The trees ran all the way along one edge of the field and then up behind the coach house, framing it, and the other side of the field was all panorama: the long drop to the ocean, the city, the sky, the sunsets. The ground floor of the house was set into the slope and was all garage. The outside stairway rose to the second level like the gangway of a big dark houseboat that was about to shove off, the way biblical illustrations of Noah's ark show the endless procession of animals entering two by two, to escape the deluge. The flat, wide-eaved roof angled upward in the direction of the deck, then stopped abruptly just short of the steep downward plunge into more trees. Seeing it for the first time, you might almost think it was a mountain ski ramp waiting for the first snows.

I left the car at the foot of the stairs and went up through the long living room, glancing in at Trill's workroom, where she'd been getting ready to work on the *Esquire* article about the new West Coast comedians. There were lots of them, from the look of the small mountain of folders and spiral notebooks next to her computer. Next door, she was still asleep, so I sat down at her desk and the phone rang. I let her service pick it up. Then I called my folks, telling them I'd probably be down the next day but would let them know. I called the rental-car people, and then I called Struiker's office to give Jeanne my folks' number.

"Wait a minute," she said, "he wants to talk to you."

Struiker came on in an exceptionally dreary monotone that suggested I'd get no colorful chatter from him until I told him everything he wanted to know, the implication being that I was either a dullard or deliberately withholding information. I don't know how he managed to convey all that just by saying, "How are you?" but he did.

I wondered what range of items that might possibly include, then decided it probably included everything except how I really was. I couldn't imagine he really cared, as long as I could talk. "Well," I said, "it's in the *L.A. Times*. Pictures of the whole cast. They're playing the story pretty big, and I'd guess for the Sunday editions they're planning one of those long recaps like you see in *Texas Monthly*, how the oil heiress got the hired hand to kill her whole family—"

"How's Burley?" he said.

"He found Trill. He'll be calling you."

"He called me a little while ago. I mean how is he? How's he reacting?"

"His usual self. The dependable old shoe."

"How is she taking it?"

I glanced at the folders stacked up on her worktable. "She was asleep when I called. She hasn't been charged with anything."

"Well, she can say anything she wants about him now. You can't libel the dead. She's got a good lawyer. If she cooperates, she may only do ten years for manslaughter. You'll be at your folks' the rest of the week?"

"Yes, I'll be going down to Laguna tomorrow."

"I want you to have dinner tonight with Jim Provine."

"Provine? Why?"

"He's nervous. Anton is worried about him. Feels he's been upset by all this and won't sell his usual quota of advertising. I want you to calm him down, make him feel wanted. Ask his advice about editorial. Get personal, convince him that you're interested in him as a human being. He's got a daughter who's a multiple sclerosis victim, did you know that? She's in a special-care home and he goes out to see her every Sunday. He's a very responsible person, in fact he's anal compulsive. His wife is not doing very well, either. She drinks, and so does Jim, more than he should at his age. It's the nature of the business, but family problems are also getting to him. Try to find some way to bring it up. I don't think he has anybody to talk to."

"Does it have to be dinner?"

"Lunch or dinner, I don't care. It can be a cruise to Catalina, or fly to Hong Kong for the weekend, just so you're back at work Monday. Make it a good restaurant. Salvatore's is nice. And if you can get through, put in a call to Pamela. Convey our sorrow."

"Call Pamela?"

"I'll leave it to you to decide how upset we are over her husband's death. You'll sense her mood. Don't overdo it. If she starts demanding money, hang up. Tell her you have to leave town and regrettably can't attend the funeral. Mention that we're sending a small token of our sorrow to pay off the lawyer. Tell her that's all he deserves. She shouldn't feel she has to pay him any more than that. Tell her I said so."

Something moved in the doorway and then Trill, full of sleep, settled herself on my lap, smelling of hay or straw flowers. She was wearing a shorty flannel nightgown of faded daisies. She fairly exuded the warmth of the morning sun.

"If I'm going to do all this, I have to rent a car," I said. "Tell Nels I might need another day or so out here."

"You ought to tell him yourself, but he hasn't come into the office yet. I'll mention it to Anton. Nels has been at this editors' convention since Monday. Anton's afraid he might be jumping ship. He hates it when you editors get together at meetings. He thinks you plot against publishers and devise ways to create havoc. Nels should get married. Never tell him I said that."

"Did you get your daughter on a plane?"

"We made a deal. I said if she's not gone by Monday I'd cut her out of my will. She said wills were old-fashioned, a plot device from old British novels. Let me know how your lunch with Provine goes. Say hello for me. Tell him Anton sends his regards."

"I will."

He grunted and hung up.

I said to Trill, "I may never get down to Laguna, with you or without you."

"Fine," she said, and yawned. "You can sun out on the deck while I put the coffee on and go to the bathroom."

"I can't do that, either. I've got to find our sales rep out here, then see if I can talk to Pamela Laudicek."

"I'd hate having to do that. I mean even if I were you."

I thought about the hateful things in her life now, all the things we weren't talking about. "I hate doing it," I said. "I've never talked to a brand-new widow before, especially one I don't think wants to hear from me. She's probably incommunicado, anyway. The press must be all over the place."

"Then that lets you off the hook."

"But I have to try. Maybe I should call Harv Wallace and let him deliver the message."

"He'll put it in his column, then he'll put it in a book. He's probably already writing a book about this. *Death in Hollywood.* Or *Tragedy in Tinseltown.*"

I looked at her, breathing her in. "Did Harv Wallace ever hit on you?"

She nodded. "He even offered me a job once. I knew he wasn't serious. He couldn't possibly have hired me with Pamela around. He just wanted some young thing to screw."

"So he's really like that? Like his books?"

She sighed. "Oh, Michael, I don't think he knows anymore. He's been pretending so long to be like his image, the Hollywood smartass who fucks the great ones and tells, I think he's forgotten what's real and what isn't." She kissed me on the forehead, then got up and began riffling through an open file drawer. I liked the way her thighs looked, pink and rounded and strong. "He's not a bad man. Kind of pathetic, but bright and funny and very good at what he does. I would have liked working for him for a while. I could have learned a lot."

"And screwed a lot."

She looked around at me and slammed the file drawer shut.

"I'm sorry," I said. "I was talking about him, not you." I picked up the telephone directory and flipped to the *B*'s, for *Beyond.* Then I remembered I had Provine's number in my address book. I looked it up and dialed.

"Let me talk to Jim Provine," I said.

Trill was glaring at me from the doorway. "You look like a New York magazine editor," she said. "Impatient. Demanding. Cruel." She made a thin line of her lips. "You hurt my feelings."

"I'm sorry." His voice came on the line. "Jim? This is Mike Lindenthal. I'm still in town, and in view of everything that's happening out here, I'd very much like to take you to lunch. I think we need to talk, for the good of the organization. I think you have a lot to tell me and I'm ready to listen. How's today?"

It took him a while, but I could hear him gradually warm to the idea. The final stumbling block was a previous appointment. "Change it," I said. "I'd really be grateful."

When I hung up, Trill was gone. I called Harv Wallace's office and left a message that I needed Pamela's home phone number. I left my sister's number, thinking she'd get a kick out of this. Then I went out into the kitchen and figured out how to get the coffee going. Trill came out of the bathroom and was rolling a blank sheet of paper into her typewriter when I brought her coffee. I put my face next to hers.

"Forgive me," I said. "If there's one thing I know, it's you don't screw lightly."

"I didn't screw you," she said. "I don't screw people I care about. Harv Wallace screws. I make love. I care about you."

"Then let me borrow your car. I'll have it back by three. Will you be all right?"

She sat without moving for a while, and then she finished reeling up the sheet of paper and began typing. "Yes, you may borrow my car," she typed. "Yes, I will be all right. And fuck you." She tore the piece of paper out of the machine and let it fall to the floor. "I don't mean that," she said. "I just don't want you to go. I like having you here."

I kissed her. "I'll be back."

"You want to?"

"Yes, I do."

"I don't know whether I believe you."

I said, "We're new at this. Let's not let it get too heavy at the start."

She nodded. I had to smile, she looked so marvelous.

Nineteen

Jim Provine was a sunburst of a salesman, his smiling fiery red face rising out of broad, well-tailored shoulders. He wasn't much over medium height, but he sat tall across the table, checking the ash on his cigarette.

The smog had burned off and we were in the spacious courtyard of one of Beverly Hills' finest, all sun and glass and lush, perfect plants, a place buzzing with conversations as well turned out as the bodies of luxuriant women everywhere around us. The food had been superb and the drinks plentiful, and we had been over the mandatory ground: the expectations for the magazine's advertising sales in the western third of the country, our editorial plans for the rest of the year, and the mutual admiration between Provine and Anton Black, Provine and Nels, and now, at long last, Provine and Lindenthal. I had delivered the regards I had to deliver and collected his for distribution back in New York. We had avoided all talk of what was uppermost in our minds, and now I raised the remaining thimbleful of Armagnac in its great glass globe and said, "Jim, here's to you. You've done a marvelous job in a very difficult situation. I know I'm just a novice in this business and have a lot to learn. I just hope when the time comes, I have half the savvy and the balls you have."

His smile gleamed with gratitude, but I was thinking perhaps I should restate my toast. Did I really want only half the balls he had? But he was too fired-up to notice, and I let it go when he said, "Go for the savvy, kid, and you can do without the rest." We drank. Then he plunged ahead, accepting my unstated apology for having underestimated him. I let him ramble, watching yet another supersophisticated lady cross the dazzling courtyard.

"The way you and Bob Struiker handled that girl, that McGuffy person, out here confirms everything I've always expected from an Anton Black operation," he said briskly, sounding a little like the old film clips of General Eisenhower. "I used to run across Anton out here when he was trying to get up a West Coast publishing association back in the seventies, and he had Bob Struiker at his heels then, helping him with the legal end, and they were going great guns, even if it didn't work out. Only the best, only the brightest. You did good out here. You were tough, uncompromising. I'm going to spread the word. Of course what Trilla McGuffy did to Bangor in life is academic now, but the whole town was upset by it, and he had a million friends in high places. Poor guy. It's tragic, just tragic what she did to him, let alone what she did to him on that balcony."

"I take it you think she did it," I said.

He looked at me, puzzled.

I said, "Well, it could have been someone else. It could have been an accident. It doesn't have to be murder. It could even have been suicide."

He shook his head. "Not suicide, naw. A terrible accident, maybe, but it looks like murder to me. I'm just worried about what will happen now to Pamela. Well, she's got her foot in the door out here. She'll do all right." He ordered a refill from a passing waiter.

I said, "Struiker wants me to call her and express our regrets."

"Sure, sure," he said. "Struiker's a class act. He gets onto something, he moves. Listen, they say life just flows out here. We're all coasting along, everybody's happy, nothing matters, every day's a nice day, the women are beautiful, the dope grows on the trees and it's a free and easy life, and we go through it half bombed out of our minds. But you can cut more deals out here in an afternoon around the pool than there are crazies in Arabia. So when people see a class act like Struiker operate, or Anton operate, they can appreciate it. It helps me, it helps you. It's a shame your visit out here went for naught, though. It takes away the taste of victory. But we didn't lose, that's what's important. The word gets around."

So far, I hadn't seen the Provine that Black was worried about. Was he just on a momentary upswing?

"But you're right—what *does* Pamela do now?" I said. "She was going for the whole shot, you know. She was determined to get him to sue."

"Well, sure, the McGuffy girl wouldn't leave him alone. I can see Pamela's beef. I'll bet she had Bangor on the ropes, too. Another day or two, she might have gotten him into court, who knows? When I talked to her, she was like a wild woman. She said a lot of things I'm not at liberty to repeat, just out of human feeling. It's all over anyway, what's the good of going over the ground? Let him rest in peace. Get on with it." He shrugged. "Isn't that the way you feel?"

"Yes, except I've got to talk to her, so I wish I knew what was going through her mind exactly."

"She's a bereaved widow, for Christ's sake, that's all. Tell her you're sorry. Tell her I'm sorry. Tell her we're all sorry. Christ, it's a damn shame. Life is hard enough."

"How's it going with you?" I said. "I mean personally?"

He gave me a look, wondering what I was getting at. "First-rate, never felt better. Twentieth wedding anniversary next week. Little trip to Hawaii we've been planning for months. Twenty years! You know how many guys out here I know who've stayed the course that long? Not a lot. It takes doing."

"Bangor told me he had three kids from his first marriage, one in law school."

"I saw that in the papers." He sat silent, and when he went on, his delivery had slowed a notch. "I'm going to the funeral. I always go to funerals if I halfway know anybody. I think public ceremonies help keep a country going. Times to consider what life is all about, what business is all about."

Death was on his mind, all right. Death and business. And hardship. "You'll see his kids then, at the funeral," I said. "When is it?"

"Saturday afternoon, up in Forest Lawn, the best place in the world to be buried. You coming?"

"I don't think I can. I'll be down at my folks, in Laguna."

"Oh. Well. I hear Nels might be coming."

"You heard from him?"

"Anton said he might."

That surprised me, but then I remembered Nels's old tie to Pamela. Of course he'd want to be there, and Anton, with his penchant for protocol, would want to show the flag. "You have any kids, Jim?"

"A daughter." He looked straight at me, his eyes suddenly empty tunnels. "She's under care. MS." His voice cracked on that one.

"I'm sorry, Jim." I wished I hadn't asked. He was crumbling fast, and trying like hell not to.

"So am I. She's a beautiful person. It's just one of the things that can happen in this cruddy life." He took out his cigarettes, and now there were tears in his eyes. "I'd love to be able to take her to Hawaii with us. I'd love to be able to do things with her. But I can't."

"How old is she?"

"Fourteen." He turned abruptly sidewise in his chair, crossed his legs, and worked his lighter, blowing the smoke away from the table and fanning the air with his hand. "I'll tell you this," he said, his voice shaking, "I don't regret we had her, not for a minute. I do regret her suffering. It's so bad sometimes, I get to feeling like it's something I did. I know that's futile, the guilt, but I can't help it. But not to have had her, that would have been worse."

The air filled with smoke, one puff, two puffs, three puffs, like a steam engine that had a lot of freight to pull. "I think I know what you mean," I said, knowing I didn't. "I feel sorry for guys like Burley Moore, not having kids."

"Burley." He gave a short laugh, then a short cough. "Burley's a character. He doesn't look like somebody who could get gallery shows, does he? Yes, I see Burley as a man who's missed out on a lot that way, but still, he's one of the few who's stayed the course. I imagine they've been married all of twenty years, maybe more. And he's poured himself into his work. You've got to give him credit. What a guy."

He blew more smoke and fanned it away. He was starting to go for the ashtray when I saw him freeze, the cigarette in midflight. "My Lord," he said, and then he finished the motion and stubbed it out, turning back to me. "Don't look. She just came in with Harv Wallace. I don't believe it."

"You mean Pamela?" I asked, looking anyway but not finding. Then I saw the media. The maître d' and two waiters were holding them off like offensive linemen resisting the sack. Then I saw a flash of shiny black satin and, beside it, what had to be the owner, Salvatore's pockmarked, angry profile.

Provine had turned pale. His elbows were on the table and a few beads of sweat had formed on his brow. It was warm, all right—we'd touched on some emotional matters and now I could see Pamela making her way through the crowd. But his reaction seemed all out of proportion to the deed. What else would Struiker have said? We were doing *Hello, Dolly!* and he was playing Willy Loman?

He said, "They're going to the far side of the restaurant.

Less conspicuous back there, as if that's what he wants. Jesus Christ, I should have expected it. Harv Wallace always shows up with whoever's in the public eye, whoever's being talked about at the time. Guess who was in here with Steven Spielberg a week before the Academy Awards, when it looked like they were going to honor everybody but Spielberg. Wallace has an instinct—he attaches himself to whoever's hot. He doesn't even have to think about it, he just does it. He's got no feelings. He doesn't care who he hurts."

I was watching Provine carefully now. He was staring at my tie, which was Struiker's tie, the sincere one, and he seemed to be bearing down, like a pitcher at three-and-two and two outs, and he can't believe the signal he's getting for the next pitch, and maybe the next one he throws will bean the batter.

"He acts like this happy old Saint Nick, full of jollies and good humor, but he's always cooking up something for his column," Provine went on. "You hear the laugh, but you look in the eyes and they're so cold, they don't even glitter."

He looked down at the table and I thought maybe he was going to be sick. I reached over and put my hand on his arm and said, "What's the matter, Jim?"

He looked up. "Nothing," he said. "I just hate the son of a bitch."

So I asked him why.

He sat up, his elbows still on the table, talking into tightly balled hands. But he was looking at me and seemed steadier. "It's an old story and not very interesting. Sylvia, that's Mrs. Provine, hasn't had an easy time of it these last few years. There was one year I wasn't home much. In effect, we were separated, but it was nothing we even talked about particularly. I just was away on the road a lot and wound up sleeping more at my club and in the office than at home. We agreed we'd try to work on our problems independently for a while, since whenever we were together they just seemed to get worse. I should have stayed home. It was the first year my daughter was out of the house, in the medical facility. I spent most of my free time there, with my daughter, to tell you the truth. Sylvia stayed home and suffered alone. She started drinking more. Nothing new exactly, just a whole lot more. But hell, she had to break out once in a while. Now, I'm not very big in this town, I'm no celebrity. But Wallace caught Sylvia out on the town a few times with a notorious director and made an item of it—not once but twice. The second time I went to see him and threatened to punch him out, and then I went home for good. That's all. Not a big thing. Maybe he even saved my marriage. But I can never forgive him for making something out of nothing, the son of a bitch, at a time we were heaving our guts out."

He sat back now, his arms dangling at his sides, and looked over in the direction Pamela and Harv Wallace had taken. "They'll be sitting over there, and everybody in the place will know they're there, and he'll be Mr. Bighearted. Maybe Salvatore, who owns this place, will sit with them a while, and his staff will try to give them some privacy from the few sharks that always swim by. The press will be baying at the door, of course, but the rest of the people will leave them alone, either because they respect the dead or maybe because they never warmed up to Pamela in the first place. But nobody will know that the biggest shark of all is sitting right at the table, because he has a nose for blood."

He leaned toward me. "Now, what you want is to have a few words with her." He held up his hand when I started to protest. "No, no, let's see what we can do. We'll send over a note with the waiter saying you have a brief message to deliver, an expression of sympathy. Let's see what happens. If she says yes, you can join them for a few minutes. If she says no, at least you'll have gotten your message across."

"Struiker wanted me to tell her not to give her lawyer anything. We're paying his fee."

Provine looked at me as if he didn't believe me. "I'll be damned," he said. "All right, we'll say you have a brief message to deliver from Bob Struiker. We'll say it's personal, for her ears alone. That will get Harv's attention. He'll insist that she see you."

"He'll leave the table?"

"Like hell he will. He'll have his notepad out, waiting for you." He took out a loose-leaf notebook of his own, wrote something down, tore out the page, and handed it to me. "That all right with you?"

I read it. It was about what he'd said. "Okay," I said, and gave it back to him along with my card. He signaled the waiter, gave him the delivery instructions, and told him to wait for a reply.

"You can see what an effect they've had already," Provine said, looking around. Heads here and there had been turning, and the volume of the conversation had gone down. The talk was more subdued. There was more whispering. On the other hand, the clinking of silverware and glasses seemed to have accelerated. "Pamela has always been a topic of discussion in this town. Bangor was one phenomenon, and then she seemed to be another. Even people who didn't know he existed knew Pamela. Different. Attractive and ambitious and always on the job. A hustler."

"Why did Bangor marry her? I would have thought he'd have gone for somebody on the quiet side."

"The Queen of England?" Provine grinned, more like his old beaming self. "Bangor always had this showman in him, I guess. I really think he expected to be a national television celebrity someday, and she probably thought so, too. I'll tell you what I really think. I think he loved her. She's a knockout, and I don't think he ever expected to latch on to anything like that. I've got this feeling he would have done anything for her."

"And she apparently felt that way about him. I mean she was so upset over Trill. Trilla McGuffy."

"Well, maybe it was just pride of territory. Miss McGuffy kept moving in. Moving in and trying to make Bangor look ridiculous. Either she was threatening to damage Pamela's property or take it away entirely. I told you Pamela's ambitious."

"She wouldn't kill rather than become a loser, though, would she?"

Provine frowned at me. "You saying she might have done it? That's the most ridiculous thing I've ever heard!"

I feared we were losing our newfound accommodation. But the waiter was approaching our table and I said, "You sure you don't want to go with me?"

He shook his head. "Not on your life."

"Excuse me," the waiter said, bending over Provine. "The party you asked about will see you now."

I got up. So did Provine. "Mike," he said, putting out his hand, "I've enjoyed our lunch and I hope we can do it more often."

"You're leaving?"

"I've got a pitch to make for *Beyond*. I'd better be on my way. I'll take the check."

"No. It's my lunch."

He shrugged. "All comes from the same pot." He grinned. "Good luck, old sport. Be seeing you."

Old sport? I watched him hurry out past the bar, and then I followed the waiter toward the back of the restaurant. It was all closed in back there and not quite so elegant, but it would do. It had a feeling of the original California, Spanish bell towers and adobe haciendas.

Pamela Laudicek and Harv Wallace were sitting just beyond a low half wall that was giving them some privacy, but not too much. I could see his white wispy hair and large pink dome and jowls burrowing in like an Irish politician deep in some deal. Pamela sat straight and composed beneath a painting of a Spanish mission. In the black frock, she might have been Hispanic herself, a young widow of the territory going over the sad details of her inheritance.

Wallace stood up when he saw me and stuck out his hand. He was wearing a light gray business suit that covered him like a tent. He must have weighed two fifty, and he was not tall. "Sit down, young man," he said, smiling broadly. "Always glad to see an editor from the big town. Pamela, this is the young man who edited my third book. Did a hell of a job. What'll you drink?"

"Nothing, thanks." I shook hands with him and then looked down at her. "Mrs. Laudicek, I want to express my deepest sympathy."

She looked up at me and nodded. Her face was drawn, but not a hair was out of place. She turned to Wallace. "Actually," she said, "we've met before."

"That's right, that's right," he said. He sat down. I kept standing. I wanted her to invite me to sit at her table. Or not, as she wished.

She turned back to me. "Well," she said, and suddenly gave me a dazzling smile, "what does Mr. Bob Struiker have to tell me?"

I sat down. To tell you the truth, I felt as if she had willed me to.

Twenty

"I have a very simple message, Mrs. Laudicek," I told her, keeping my eyes on her and ignoring Wallace. If he was making notes, I didn't want to know about it. "Just that we're sorry."

"Condolences," she said. She said it airily, but the eyes were opaque with what could have been pain. Something about her seemed to have bloomed overnight, like a flower that flourishes in a graveyard. I thought, death and resurrection. Her dark skin had a pampered, untouched look, as if the sun never fell on her, let alone wind and rain.

I said, "We met under difficult circumstances, but I could see how it was between you. He was a fine man. I have to return to New York and won't be able to attend the funeral, but you have our deepest sympathy. Anton Black, our publisher. Nels. Bob Struiker."

"Thank you."

"One other thing and then I'll leave you alone." I glanced at Wallace. He was quivering with concentration. "Mr. Struiker wanted you to know that we'll be sending the money we agreed to pay the lawyer. Don't feel that you need to pay him anything more. I'm sorry even to have to mention this, but Mr. Struiker felt you should have that information."

"Thank you," she said.

I got up to go. She said, "Won't you stay while we finish our drinks? We're not planning to order for a while."

I looked at Wallace. He was watching me with a little smile on his face, and now he lifted one hand, a gesture of either invitation or resignation. I looked back at her. "Coffee? You're sure you don't mind?"

She shook her head and smiled. There was a waiter hovering six feet away, and she said to him, "One coffee, please. For the gentleman." She said to me, "Everything up to now has been very regrettable, and sad. Your Mr. Struiker was a perfect gentleman to me when I was . . . out of it." She paused. "I really was out of it, you know."

"I know."

"It's just that I was terribly worried about my husband." She glanced at Wallace. "I was afraid he was being taken advantage of. Now that it no longer matters, I can see that you and Mr. Struiker were being as generous as you felt you could be."

"I'll let him know that."

"We were adversaries, and I'd had a couple of bad days. He calmed me down, otherwise—" She shrugged. Her eyes were glistening with tears.

The waiter brought my coffee. I said to him, "Will you tell my waiter I'll stop by and take care of the bill?" He said he would. I said to Pamela, "I was having lunch with our ad rep out here, Jim Provine."

She nodded. I glanced at Wallace. He cleared his throat.

"He sends his best," I said.

Again she nodded.

I said, "I hope the police investigation is over as far as you're concerned. You have enough to deal with." I took a sip of coffee.

Her eyes went blank and she looked at Wallace. He cleared his throat again and said, "There are a few matters to be cleared up, according to the police. I'm afraid we aren't permitted to talk about it."

"I just hope for your sake it ends quickly."

"That's kind of you," she said, and looked away. "I suppose they want to eliminate any doubts about anything." She looked back. "You left the hotel so quickly. I was afraid I'd made you miss your plane. If only we'd left, too, but my husband wasn't feeling well. I made him lie down. We weren't expecting . . . visitors." She wasn't asking questions and yet she was.

I said, "The police found us just before boarding. They told us what had happened." Nonanswers to nonquestions.

Wallace said, "She just dropped you at the airport and left. You had no idea." More nonquestions.

Pamela had finished her drink. She said, "It all comes back to me like a bad dream. Bits and pieces." She smiled. This time, it was an effort. "It's terrible, trying to remember and trying not to. If only I'd been quicker, maybe I could have prevented it."

I said, "You're not sure what happened?"

"She didn't say that," Wallace snapped. I looked over at him. He was angry. His face had grown redder, and the red went right up into the roots of his white hair. Was he angry at her, for talking about it? At me, for intruding on them?

"No, I didn't say that at all," Pamela said. "I remember perfectly. But the shock—I feel guilt, too, that I let it happen. And for going there in the first place, but I had no choice. This may sound strange to you, Mr. Lindenthal, but I feel like someone back in the Middle Ages accused of witchcraft. Like Joan of Arc. She was just doing what her voices told her to do. So was I. I was following my conscience."

"Well, fortunately," I said, "that's no longer a burnable offense," and then regretted saying it because Wallace barked, "What do you mean by that?"

I looked from one to the other. "Nothing."

He said, "Listen, young fella—" But she put a hand on his arm. They were both looking at me as if I'd brought up something unspeakable.

Then Pamela's eyes softened and she reached down and picked up my card. "Mr. Lindenthal," she said, "you may as well know, and you can tell this to Mr. Struiker but I hope to no one else, because of my vague and faulty memory of events, the police are still questioning me. Apparently, they're not at all sure I didn't murder my husband."

"Pamela," Wallace said urgently, "get a grip on yourself."

"I need an attorney, Mr. Lindenthal," she said.

"You don't have one?" I said in surprise.

"It's slowly dawning on me that someone more capable might be in order, and perhaps your being here has helped me see that. Someone like Mr. Struiker."

I was dumbfounded. "Well, you know, he's not a criminal lawyer."

"I don't care what he is. Would he help me?"

Wallace growled, "Pamela, I've given you the names of a dozen lawyers who'd take your case in a second."

"Well?" she said to me. "Will you ask him?"

"Of course. I'll give him a call right now if you want me to. But I don't think he'll be able to help you."

She sat very still, looking at me. Wallace said to me, "Look, why don't you forget you even heard all this? What she needs now is a first-class guy out here who can take the ball and run with it. She's just very upset and very worried. Thanks for stopping by."

As if she hadn't heard him, she said, "Yes, I think I'd like you to."

"For God's sake, Pamela, this is going to be all over town. You think he's going to keep it to himself?"

She turned to him and said, "Shut up, Harvey." She kept looking at him until he knew she meant it. Then she said to me, "Call Mr. Struiker. We'll get a telephone." She glanced around for a waiter.

I said, "If you don't mind, I think I'd better speak to him privately." I got up, smiled down at her, and shrugged. "That's the way he likes it. I'll be right back."

I found a phone in the anteroom to the men's room and reached him just as he was going into a meeting. "Make it fast," he said.

"Pamela's asking you to represent her. She's afraid she may be charged with murder. Can you do it?"

There was a lengthy silence. "Call me back at seven, my time," Struiker said, and hung up.

Going back to the table, I wondered what to say to Pamela, but Harv Wallace was sitting there alone, smiling at me like the cat that had eaten the canary. A very fat cat, so the canary could have been any size at all. I sat down, figuring she'd be right back. "So," he said, "how did it go?"

"He wasn't in."

"I didn't think so. I doubt whether Bob Struiker will be very interested. There's also the matter of the previous association. Is it good ethics, according to the American Bar, to represent someone close to a guy who was suing you and maybe got killed for it? What do you think?"

"I don't know."

"Neither do I, but it's certainly a pretty tangle, isn't it?

"If you say so."

"Now, look, young fella, I've been covering this beat for thirty years and nothing surprises me anymore. Nobody bugs me, nothing upsets me. So why don't you stop acting as if I'm some kind of piranha and talk to me like an ordinary guy?"

I couldn't help smiling. "Shouldn't that be pariah?"

"Piranha, pariah, what's the difference? You some kind of copy checker or what? Listen, talk in some way I can understand. I don't need to be quibbled to death."

"Okay. How's your new book going?"

"That's better. It's going fine. It'll be out in the fall. You don't look like an editor, do you know that? Too young, too much hair. My editor at Random House had worked for eight different publishers in twenty years. Everyplace he went, he left a hank of hair. He was as bald as a fan dancer's ass by the time I got him."

"Genes," I said. "My father's fifty-two and he has all his hair."

"But he isn't an editor, am I right?"

"He's in charge of sales for a type house. He lives out in Laguna."

"You from out here?"

I nodded. "I grew up reading your column."

"Why?"

"I was interested. I thought I might go into journalism."

"So it wasn't the wonderful world of Hollywood that interested you. Good. You'll probably do all right. Though I must say if you publish any more articles like that one on Bangor, you won't last long."

"You didn't like it?" I looked around for Pamela, wondering whether she knew he'd offered Trill a job once. "But you suggested the writer."

"Yeah, I know, I'm sorry about that. I just didn't think her piece turned out to be very interesting. Of course, I don't find your magazine very interesting. The outdoors stuff, for example. As far as I'm concerned, fresh air is something to escape from. I hardly go outside except to get a cab or go on location or ogle bodies around a pool. But you can see I'm no exercise addict. I'm only addicted to one thing: sex and money and gossip, listening to people. You probably never knew they were all the same thing. Suppose you tell me your life story."

I laughed. "I should be going. Is Pamela—"

"She's gone. We're skipping lunch, which doesn't hurt my avoirdupois. Also we had a shouting match, which is not abnormal for us about this time of day, and she asked Salvatore to put her in a cab. She doesn't act like she's on my payroll, does she? She acts like I'm on hers. Well, that's okay, especially right now, while she's suffering. Right now I'm glad to hear her shouting—it's better than the lugubrious Pamela. It's healthier. We were shouting about you. I told her to send you and Bob Struiker packing, and she accused me of not loving her anymore. I said she was almost right. I love her dearly but sometimes I can't stand her. The way we fight, we might as well be divorced."

"She's gone home?"

He nodded. "She expects you to call her, though, and let her know about Struiker. I got your phone message. Here's her number." He gave me his card with her number written on it. "Let her have a couple of hours to rest up. She hasn't slept much in the last few days."

"Do you think Trilla McGuffy killed her husband?"

"I don't think. I take notes from conversations with people who are supposedly thinking something. Or doing something, like me, without thinking. The police think they're on to something. They think Bangor may not have walked into that apartment and tripped over the balcony railing. They see him as a man about six feet tall, in good health, with most of his wits about him and in disgustingly okay physical condition. Hell, he used to run six miles a day. He had reasonably good reflexes and eyesight. He wanted to live a long time, like his daddy and his granddaddy. Moreover, he was a very careful man, a tidy man, even a cautious man. The only rash thing he ever did was allowing Trilla McGuffy to come within ten thousand miles of him. Oh, his marriage may have seemed rash, but on the whole you'd have to say he picked a marvelous person. Certainly he didn't pick someone who would push him off a balcony someday. Pamela wouldn't do that. She might have creamed him with a poker, but she wouldn't have shoved him—it's not her way. Still, the police surmise that maybe she did it. But hell, there hasn't even been an autopsy yet. He may actually have been killed with a poker and then tossed over. In that case, she might have done it. Or he might have died of booze. He liked his liquor. Anyway, the cops are sorting out the possibilities. So she can use a good lawyer, and I suppose if Struiker will oblige, there's nothing I can say. I have nothing against Struiker. I don't know the man. But I'd rather she'd get one of ten other guys I know who've been up to their steel-trap minds in criminal law for a couple of decades. I don't even know if this Struiker ever goes near a courtroom."

"He does. He wins."

"But not criminal cases. Oh, well." He stood up, shoving back his chair, and so did I. "I won't keep you, since you say you have to go. But I'd like to meet this guy if he decides to take the case. I'd appreciate it if you'd call me when there's an opportunity to do so. You have my card."

"All right, I will." I put out my hand. "Nice seeing you."

He shook hands. "Jim Provine had a problem a few years ago and I didn't help him any. As I told you, I'm not paid to think on the job, so sometimes I do something I regret later. I may be entirely wrong about Struiker. It's just that I don't want anything to happen to Pamela if I can help it. You understand?"

I nodded.

"Pamela has a lot of friends," he said. "Like your editor. What's his name—Barbidoux?"

I nodded, surprised.

"I met him last—Wednesday it was. Hell, that was yesterday, wasn't it, the day Bangor—Yes, he flew in and then right out the same night. But then you knew that. I met him at Pamela's. Nice fella." He patted my arm a couple of times. "Well, best to be going. You're a good lad. If you ever do want to get into the newspaper business, come see me. It isn't worth a damn these days. But then, what is?"

He waved and walked away. I followed, then sidetracked to the telephone. I thought, Nels in L.A.? Flying in while Struiker was flying out? Did Struiker know? I called Trill and said I'd finished my errands, killed two flies with one blow, and would take her up on using the sun deck. Her voice sounded faint, and for a moment I wasn't sure she knew who I was. Then she said she'd been sleeping.

"On the deck?" I said.

"On my bed, I think."

"Well, go back to sleep. I'll just go out and get started sunning without you."

She laughed. She had a breathless laugh that stirred my loins. "Oh, I love you," she said.

I said, "Trill?" but she didn't answer. I kept repeating her name but got no response at all. I pictured her dozing, with the receiver dangling off the bed. Probably, I thought, she didn't even know she'd said it.

I bought a paper, the *Inquirer* this time, and turned to Harv Wallace's column. Sure enough, there it was. "Dear friends of the deceased closed ranks around a sorrowing widow." There followed a list of movieland luminaries, political and otherwise. Then: "*Beyond* magazine genius Nels Barbidoux left a Washington, D.C., editors conclave to fly in at midnight, then red-eye it back to Manhattan. . . ." And there Nels was on page five, getting out of a cab, his face pasty white with camera flash and fatigue, but still a tired smile. The caption called him an "editor-mountaineer" and a longtime friend of Bangor's.

There were only two cars outside Trill's gate. When I'd left, there had been three. Apparently, the focus was still on Pamela. I was hoping it stayed there.

Twenty-One

Trill didn't come out on deck. She was awake, though, and had moved over to her word processor. I hoped they were good words, because she seemed determined to put every single one of her notes into the thing. I pulled a book off her shelves and lay back in the sun with my shirt off and read and slept on an old plastic folding lounge chair that reminded me of one of her new Hollywood comedians. It seemed to be doing a comic impression of the kind of thirties farm furniture Pa Joad tied on top of his Okie car in *The Grapes of Wrath*. But it was all she had for sunning except for a set of faded leather pillows.

At four, I plugged a phone in out there so as not to bother her at work and called Struiker. He said it was the consensus among his partners that he not represent Pamela Laudicek in view of the previous adversarial relationship, but that since it was possible that our own people might get involved, he was flying to L.A. the next day to check things out and do what he could in Pamela's behalf, should her fears be realized. Again, he had other business to attend to as well.

"I'll call Pamela and tell her," he said. "Get me a room

at the Beverly Wilshire for the night. And one for yourself, as long as it's not a suite."

I told him that after I picked him up at the airport and got him stowed away, I'd head for my sister's.

"That's very commendable," he said, "saving the company's money."

"You might mention that to Anton," I said. "By the way, did Nels come in?"

"Yes, he called."

"Did you know he was out here last night, at Pamela's?"

He said, "He told me that. I said he was on his own. He's aghast that the police are still dithering over whether to bring charges against Pamela. He's convinced McGuffy's guilty, and he's probably right, though like me he's biased. McGuffy's the one with the motive, and as in most murders, she was acting precipitously, driving back to that hotel on impulse, charging in without a thought. McGuffy's a lost cause. They'll charge her tomorrow, in time for the Sunday papers."

I swallowed. "You think so?"

"Police departments and prosecutors don't have PR people for nothing."

I hung up feeling that I'd just completed my last phone call and was sitting at the brink waiting for the fireball. Trill's computer was still softly clicking away. I went in and offered to take her out for something to eat, but she said she didn't have time. She sat in that green blur of a room with these odd little beeps sounding like Jiminy Cricket was giving her a helping hand. Leg. It doesn't matter.

So for dinner, I found some eggs in the refrigerator and asked her how she liked them. Any way at all, she said, but no yolks. She'd had two yolks on Sunday, and two yolks a week were all she allowed herself. She said there was a recipe for a yolkless omelet in a spiral notebook on a shelf over the stove, and I found it, and found the instructions in among the recipes for Eggless Mayonnaise and Make-Your-Own Granola, and sure enough, there in the refrigerator were the onions and shallots and fresh parsley and fresh dill and fresh chives, and she told me where I'd find the dried tarragon and cayenne pepper and the can of smoked yeast, for God's sake, and I cracked the six eggs and threw away all the yolks, splat, splat, splat, splat, splat, splat, and whipped up something that looked like a bleached, scorched lily pad wrenched from a subterranean cave. She didn't look up from her computer. "Put it over there. Thanks a heap," she said. I ate my omelet out on deck. It tasted pretty good. I found most of hers in her office the next morning under an old film script, its back cover stained and corrugated, the world's first yolkless movie.

I carried the television set with its mile-long cable out onto the deck (I could hear Burley saying, "They make portable ones now") and watched a rerun of the old "Cheers" on cable and then read a bit more. I was well into Kafka's umpteenth interview with one or more characters I just didn't dig, they were so shadowy and spectral, when Trill finally came out. She sat down on the stack of leather pillows and looked out over the city that went down to the sea, into which a red sun was slowly dropping. "Tired?" I said.

She grimaced and shook out her hair.

"Article shaping up?"

She looked at me. "I can't lie to you," she said. "Raphael was here today, when you were at lunch." Her voice sounded harsh, unequivocal. "I love you," she had said into the phone. Maybe not to me.

"You don't have to explain," I said. I closed the book and put it down on the deck. I leaned back and closed my eyes. Today she was with Raphael, I was thinking, tomorrow she'll be charged with murder. How'm I doing? Did I pick the right girl, or what? Let Raphael look after her. Or Burley. "You had a life of your own when I showed up out here. Anyway, I'll be taking off soon."

"That's why I'm telling you," she said, "while you're still here and we can talk about it."

"I don't want to talk about it." I felt like doing something crazy. I laughed. "Struiker thinks you made Raphael up, did you know that?"

"Struiker doesn't know everything."

I opened my eyes wide and spoke in an accent that was shadowy and spectral and Kafkaesque. "Trill, nobody knows everything." She was looking at the sun dancing on the rim of the ocean. She didn't hear Kafka, she just heard the words.

"You do," she said. "Everything that matters. Everything that's important to me."

That brought me back to earth fast. She sounded so trusting, so naïve. But not like a child this time. "Do you love him?"

She sighed. "I thought I did. But sometimes he's so quiet, I don't know he's around, and then I wonder. You were quiet out here today, but I knew you were here every second." She got up and came over and lay down next to me on the lounge chair. There almost wasn't enough chair for that. It groaned, and so did I. She found a way to get close, her head on my shoulder. "I don't want to hurt him. He's a genius, you know. You can tell by the look in his eyes. He's wonderful with computers."

"Does he live around here?"

"Down the road. Up, actually. You can see everything from his window."

"What is he, some kind of computer genius? Or just an all-around whiz?"

"He's plugged into the university, and some businesses in the Valley, and he does some work for a couple of the studios."

"Sounds like he's plugged in everywhere, kind of like God. You meet him at some studio?"

"He found me, actually. He was doing some work for a manufacturer who lives around here, and he came out to see him and thought this might be the place. Nobody was home at the main house, and I buzzed him in so he could try finding him in the phone book. He came up here and we got to talking. He just stayed."

"Stayed?"

"A couple of days, for God's sake. That's the kind of man he is. He's just Raphael."

I worked myself around so I could look at her. "Well, so Bangor didn't have all your attention."

She laughed harshly and sat up. The chair groaned and creaked. "Bangor? Attention? Fascinated, wasn't that what you said? Yes, I was fascinated. I didn't know how I was ever going to make him pay for what he did. But it wasn't like Raphael." She shivered. I put my hand on her shoulder, inviting her down, but she wouldn't come. She shook her head and said, "Aren't you the faintest bit jealous? Doesn't it mean anything to you?" She bit her lip, looking down at me.

"I'm still trying to figure it out, Trill," I said. "We've had this thing going for a couple of days." Like Raphael, I thought. Two days. "I don't know where it's going. Yeah, it bothers me, Raphael turning up. Someone who's important to you, and I knew nothing about it. Like I didn't know you and Bangor were lovers. Or that you knew Burley that well. It seems like more things keep happening before I have time to get the first thing straight. What was it Bangor did to you? I mean back at Michigan. I was told there was some kind of scandal. What?"

She looked away. "I was just a kid from his hometown. I thought he was wonderful. I didn't see the age difference, I didn't see a lot of things."

"Trill," I said, "I know about the drugs."

She turned and stared at me. I was sorry I'd said it just then. She seemed shocked, and hurt, offended that I'd known and hadn't told her. "He gave them to me, you know. I took them because I didn't think he'd ever do anything that wasn't good for me. I didn't have the faintest notion where they'd take me. It was just something we did together, that nobody else had. It was ours." She turned back to the sunset, and the lights that were coming on all over the hills. "Everybody knew Bangor. Everybody thought he was wonderful. But nobody else did cocaine with Bangor—I mean I knew that, I knew he just couldn't go around the campus doing cocaine with just anybody. You have no idea what knowing that did for me. I was in heaven." She shivered again. "It was when I discovered that he was doing it with a couple of others that I went out of my mind that first time. I wanted to get his attention, mostly. I wanted to hurt him, too, but just enough. I'd been reviewing some of the campus broadcasts. That's how I'd got his attention in the first place. He said I had a—" She choked, a sob. I hadn't realized she was near tears. I sat up and put my arms around her, and soon she went on. "He said I had a wonderful mind and he wanted to share everything with me." She was shivering steadily now, and her hands were playing off each other, little gestures that seemed to emphasize their emptiness. "Well, he wasn't married, for God's sake, and my folks knew him from back home, and it seemed just perfect. But then when I found out I wasn't the only one and wrote this review, he got so angry, I knew I'd lost him. I had one last shot. I told him I was going to the dean about the drugs." Her eyes were full of tears, like Provine, like Pamela. "I wasn't really going to do it. I just wanted him back." She held her head in her hands and began to cry.

"Trill," I said, "don't talk about it now."

"Yes, yes, I want to! I haven't talked about it in so long."

"Not with Raphael?"

"No. We don't talk about things like this." She slowly calmed down. "Anyway," she said, wiping her eyes, "it did scare him, what I said, but it didn't get him back. He left. He just packed all his things and left!" She put her face in the hollow of my throat, and her face was wet. "I didn't know what to do. I couldn't stay there. So I left, too." She wiped her eyes some more. "I never should have gone to that hotel. But I had to, I felt positively caged. Here I was supposed to write him a letter that I'd leave him alone, but he was the one. He was always there, everyplace I turned. I screamed at him. I said, 'Leave me alone, you fucking bastard!' He wouldn't look at me, so I hit him. I only wanted to get his attention. I didn't push him. I didn't want him dead. You believe me, don't you, Michael?"

She reached up to put an arm around my neck, and just about then the old lounge chair packed it in. The legs buckled and we went sprawling. Laughing and clinging to each other, we lay there with the sky going dark and last light of the sun sending out wide streamers of orange and pink. I bent over her and kissed her.

"I'm worried about you," I said. "There's not enough time."

"Yes." She pulled my head down and kissed me back, her tongue working like the last colorful streamers of light in the sky. We held each other until it was completely dark, and then we went in to bed. I forgot about Bangor, and about Raphael. For the first time, I was feeling a real need for her, a real desire. It scared me a little, it seemed so indestructible, like the sun that was still there on the other side of the world and would always be there, no matter what. I'd never wanted anyone before, not like that.

We had breakfast on the deck under an almost cloudless sky, and then Trill walked me down below to show me her garden. It was where she grew the herbs I'd found in her refrigerator, a whole forest of parsley and battalions of chives, and sweet basil and dill and thyme, and she started to pick some for lunch and I told her that Struiker was arriving at six o'clock and I planned to drive down to Laguna Beach for the day. She pouted. She said she couldn't go. She wasn't up to taking the risk, meeting someone so important to me when she felt so unnerved by events, and besides, there was the article to be done.

I didn't want to go. I wanted to be there if Struiker was right, but how could he know what the authorities were thinking? I figured I'd see my folks and pick him up and be back before dark, and then we'd have the whole weekend to ourselves.

Trill drove me down the canyon to the rental-car agency. The media presence had vanished from the roadway. Or perhaps it was just too early in the day. I kissed her goodbye and watched her drive away toward the hills, the white convertible getting smaller and smaller and faster and faster.

My folks lived in an oversized brick ranch house on a slope overlooking the ocean from half a mile away. I had never lived there myself, but Becky had, in her last years in high school. Dad had chosen the place with an eye to retirement. The wood floors and the compact, orderly groupings of chrome and glass and dark brown leather seemed cold, far different from the warm, casual surroundings I'd grown up in, but this seemed to be Dad's house, not Mom's. He'd started out as a designer for an agency, and he thought in terms of uncluttered, careful arrangements that wouldn't require changes. Make a plan, construct it come hell or high water, and hold out against the revisionists, that seemed to be his view.

We picnicked on his boat. I could hear Mom saying it since the beginning of time: "Why don't we pack a lunch and go down to your father's boat?" It was a twenty-seven-footer, trim and sturdy, named the *Shoo-In.* He'd always had it but hadn't done much sailing until the last few years, when they were finally able to live within a mile of the water. We came in a little early when a row of scudding gray clouds and a brisk wind made rain seem likely, maybe even a severe blow. He made a fire; he wanted to show off his fireplace. He was a tall man with wide shoulders, a quiet Scandanavian given to outbursts of pleasure and occasional bouts of mild depression. The boat, the house, the fire—these were among his treasures. Mother had always been his opposite, dark-haired and cheery and small, self-contained but outgoing, a mix of German and Irish. But lately, she seemed to have grown more dependent. He was eight years older. Was she worried about losing him? Whatever it was, she was doing her best to please him.

"Gosh, Mike," he said, sitting back in the sleek chrome and leather couch, his legs outstretched, his long arms behind his head, "that was a dandy sail. If you come back on Sunday, we'll do it again."

"I don't know, Dad. It depends on what happens in town."

He shook his head. "A sorry case. It shows you how uncertain life can be. I never heard of the man, but apparently he had a lot to live for."

"He did."

"I was hoping for a long trial," my mother said. "I thought we might have you with us all summer."

"Be glad you have him while you have him," my father said, and she said, "Well, he got us out on the boat. That'll keep you from grumbling for a while." She laughed and got up to bring in the coffee and rhubarb pie.

I heard it on the radio, on the way to the airport in the rain. Trill had been charged with Bangor Laudicek's murder and released on bail. I was glad I wasn't seeing it on television. I pictured her frightened face as she was hurried past the camera into a waiting automobile by Detective Braun or Bannister, and I cursed myself for not being there. I stopped at a roadside restaurant and called her. No, she said, Raphael wasn't there; nobody was there except all the reporters and TV trucks outside the gate. She told me to come up when I was through with Struiker. "I've got a good lawyer. I need one. Pamela's lying. Why is she lying? We were friends once."

I told her I loved her. I didn't know whether I loved her, but I wanted her to believe someone did. If Raphael really cared about her, he'd be there, wouldn't he?

I nearly missed the turnoff to L.A. International, and I still hadn't collected my thoughts by the time Struiker came off the plane, said something surly about my new tan, and led the way toward the parking lot. That bothered me. How did he know I was driving instead of cabbing? How did he know I'd parked it where I parked it? He just assumed things would be there, right where he needed them to be. Hadn't the rain stopped the moment he got off the plane?

"Well," I said, catching up as he went out the door, "I guess you've heard the news." I was pretty sure he hadn't.

He said, "Is it official?"

"Is what official?" I was outraged.

"McGuffy." He stopped and looked at me and grinned.

"Yes, all right. She's out on bail." I was damned if I'd ask him how he knew. I wanted to say, "Okay, smartass, where's the car?" If I didn't point it out, I thought, he'd be standing there all night. I could see by the way he was grinning that he knew I was furious, but I didn't care. I had the feeling he'd failed me, failed Trill. By throwing the fear of God into her and leaving her feeling trapped and desperate, then letting her be charged with the responsibility for poor old Bangor's mighty fall, forced to walk the plank after the old heave-ho as if her guilt wasn't open to question.

"I talked to Braun by phone yesterday," he said, explaining. "He told me there was no better day than today for her to seek legal counsel. I called her attorney and warned him. It's a firm we've done business with out here in the past."

Still, he didn't ask where the car was, or whether we were going by limousine. Then I saw what he was waiting for: the familiar figure walking toward us, crossing the drive and barely avoiding an airport bus. Struiker said, "I asked Burley to take a taxi out and ride back with us. You mind?"

"Why should I mind?" I was still angry, but I wanted to find out more about Burley, the side to him I didn't know, couldn't pin down. It certainly wasn't his wardrobe. He was wearing the same cheap-looking brown suit he'd worn two days ago and two days before that, but he'd gone back to a shirt and tie since the Shangri-la. I'd never seen him wear anything but that suit. Did he plug away day after day in the same cardboard brown outfit, his camera bag draped over one shoulder on a wide leather strap that gave him the look of being long in harness? And in his lab, did he just hike up the sleeves of the baggy-sleeved jacket and go to work? If you took away the suit and made him wear something else, would that be the end of Burley?

Twenty-Two

"Hi, boss," Burley said, addressing one or both of us. I said, "Hi, Burley," and told Struiker, "The car's that way." They got in the back, and I headed for the hotel. For the first few miles, the conversation was mainly about Trill.

Struiker said, "She's out on bail. Of course you knew that."

"Yeah," Burley said. "Two hundred thou. Not bad, huh?"

"Her lawyer do all right?"

"Oh, sure, he's around. Tall, bald guy, walks beside her like a prince consort when the cameras are clicking, like he's making sure the red carpet they're rolling out doesn't have any wrinkles in it she might trip over. And there she is, her head up like a trooper, but you can see she's scared. She's tough, though. She won't crack, that one, no matter how hard they squeeze her. She's too proud."

That surprised me. Was this the same Trill I knew?

Struiker said, "What would she say if she did?"

"You mean did she do it? I guess so. I'm no mind reader. The only thing is, if she did it, I got a feeling she'd say so."

"You think she knew what she was going to do when she drove back to the hotel? You think she was rational?"

"What the hell do you mean? You think she's crazy or something?"

Struiker said, "I talked to Pamela earlier today. She said when McGuffy went off to Nepal, she was in very bad shape."

"I don't know anything about anything like that."

"Would the McGuffy you know hear voices?"

"I don't know her that well, but she could be the type to hear voices. You know, like a medium, one of those psychics who talk to spirits from the other side. She's not one of these hard, shallow broads you see out here. She's very sensitive. I don't know how to put it to you, but sometimes it's like she can see what the camera doesn't."

"So you'd say she may have heard voices nobody else would hear."

"How the hell do I know? Bob, I don't know what you're getting at."

Struiker said to me, "Mike, let's wait on the hotel. I want to go by the Plaza."

"All right," I said. I'd already passed the usual turnoff, but it wouldn't be far out of the way. Burley said, "What do you want to go back there for?"

"I've got permission to visit the suite. I just want to fix a few things in my mind." He said to Burley, "You don't mind coming along, do you?"

"No. I told Helen not to expect me for dinner."

Struiker laughed. "Okay, I'll buy you dinner, Burley. Anyway, we need to talk. I'm seeing the detectives in the morning. I want to find out what they've got so far."

"You think they may have some kind of evidence to go on?"

"I don't see that. It looks like her word against Pamela's, but a good prosecutor could do a lot to build motive. And when he does that, he'll backtrack over this whole libel matter and bring out everything we were trying to avoid telling Bangor. It could be made to look like a rat's nest of intrigue." He said to Burley, "You might have to take the stand."

"Me?"

"You and Provine. Harv Wallace. What we went into at lunch on Tuesday, what you knew about all the rumors. What Jim knew."

"But that's all hearsay."

"The judge will have to sort it out. They'll want to bring out what McGuffy was doing that triggered Pamela's hysteria. I want to go over that with you in some detail."

"Christ," Burley moaned. "And I was just starting to put it out of my mind."

Struiker said, "One thing that keeps bothering me. Why she decided to come over when she did, when Bangor called me."

I had left the expressway and made a stop, waiting to turn into Santa Monica Boulevard, and behind me I saw Burley leaning over, watching the traffic, too. As I made the turn, Struiker said, "Well?"

"Well, what?" Burley said. "Oh. You mean Pamela?"

"How did she know we were still there? We might just as well have left the day before."

"I don't get it," Burley said impatiently. "How would I know that?"

"The only people who knew we were leaving at two were you and Provine, and of course McGuffy, who was taking us to the airport."

"Well, hell. Sure, Bob, I was blabbing it all over town. Half of Los Angeles might have showed up. God knows the place is big enough."

"Well, who would have told her that?" Struiker said, ignoring Burley's sarcasm, talking more or less to himself. "Provine barely knew her, and McGuffy wasn't on the best of terms. That leaves you."

"Well," Burley said, "I might have mentioned it to Harv—I don't remember. You know, just telling him I didn't want to get tied up with any assignments till you left."

Struiker was silent for a moment. We were almost at the hotel. "How well do you know Pamela?"

"A little bit. She's a nice lady when she's not upset. She works hard. Harv Wallace couldn't do without her. She's a pleasure to photograph."

"You've photographed her?" Struiker said in surprise.

"Well, sure, around the office, sometimes when I drop by. Just candids. She has an interesting face. She's no kid. She's got character lines around the eyes and mouth that weren't there two years ago. To me, her eyes are the most interesting thing about her. I've done a whole study of Harv, too, but he's got less variety to work with. I shoot people I'm with all the time."

Struiker said, "You've never done a study of me."

Burley laughed. "I wouldn't have the nerve!"

I turned into the drive and went around to the parking lot. There was an open slot not far from the pool, and I pulled in, wondering how soon I'd be able to get away.

"Well," Struiker said, "this is the kind of thing I want to go over with you and Provine. If you are called to testify, I want you to know what you're going to say. You, too, Mike."

"Me?" I turned around and looked at him.

"According to the cops, you were the last person to see McGuffy before she went to the hotel."

"Boy," Burley said, "I hope this isn't a long trial."

I said to Struiker, "How about you? Will they call you, too?"

He grinned. "Maybe. That's why it's important to make sure we all tell the same story. I don't want any confusion that would prolong my presence out here."

We all got out of the car, and I followed them inside. I was thinking about what my mother had said. Maybe I'd be around all summer after all.

The cop on duty was Officer Persky. He was an older

man who'd been sitting outside the door to the suite in one of the poker player chairs, and the way his face brightened, he'd probably been wishing that three guys from the outside world would show up with a deck of cards. He let us in, warning us not to touch anything, and then stood just inside the door, red-faced and affable, chatting with Burley while Struiker moved idly about the place. I followed Struiker from room to room. There was nothing to see that I could see. The only thing that seemed out of place was the book I'd been reading when the Laudiceks had showed up two days before. It was on the library floor. Perhaps I'd dropped it there in responding to Bangor's knock. The pieces of glass I'd brought in from the balcony, where she'd knocked the drink from my hand, were no longer in the trash can in the kitchen, and I couldn't find Bangor's bottle of brandy anywhere. The lab technicians had taken them as evidence, I assumed, leaving nothing except the book to remind anybody that the Laudiceks had been here.

When we came back into the living room, Burley and the cop were on the balcony. The drapes had been opened and the sky was dark. Officer Persky saw us and came back into the room. "Your photographer's shooting pictures of the pool. I told him it was all right, since he's not with the press."

Struiker said, "Thanks," and walked past him, leaning over the balcony railing with Burley, looking down.

I said to the policeman, "It's a long drop."

"You better believe it," he said. "You guys from out of town? New York? I grew up in Jersey. Been out here fifteen years. If I'd have known then what I know now, I would have come out a lot sooner. The weather, the mountains, the ocean, you can do anything you want out here."

"I know. I grew up out here."

"You had it all and you left? You nuts or something?" He looked at Struiker, who was crossing to the library. "Her lawyer, huh? You a lawyer?"

"I'm an editor."

"I'm surprised they let you up here. No newspapers allowed."

"I'm not working on the case," I said. "I'm with him."

"Oh."

Struiker reappeared in the library doorway. He was examining the book he'd picked up off the floor. "*Twice-Told Tales*," he said.

" 'This fated evening was an ugly one,' " I said, quoting.

"Huh?" the officer said.

"It's a line from the book. Kind of sticks in the mind."

Struiker looked at me. "Hawthorne was obsessed with guilt," he said, "like Dostoyevski. They both understood what it was to suffer after transgressing society's laws. But Dostoyevski knew how guilt could cut like an ax. Hawthorne was a wimp. He never got beyond the letter A." He closed the book and put it down on a table. "Ready, Burley?" Burley clicked off two more shots and then came back into the room, and Struiker said, "Thank you, Officer. We're finished here."

Officer Persky held the door as we went out. "I always get a charge out of Beverly Hills murders," he said. "Always something doing, the press, the prosecutors, private investigators, lawyers, police brass. You don't find that so much with your ordinary crimes."

"Private investigators?" Struiker said.

"Well, like yourself, sir, for instance. Lawyers, insurance investigators, all kinds."

"You think it was murder?"

"Not for me to say." He pulled the door closed and tested it to make sure it was locked. "But you know, if you have three people in a room and one of them turns up dead, sooner or later somebody's gonna ask that very question."

Struiker grinned at Burley, and Burley nodded. He didn't look well. When the elevator doors closed and we started down, Struiker said, "You see why they decided to go ahead and charge her. An open-and-shut case."

I said, "Maybe Pamela's lying."

He looked sharply at me. "What makes you think that?"

I shrugged. "She had a motive. She was angry at Bangor, too."

Struiker shook his head and leaned against the elevator wall, folding his arms. "She was angry because he was being attacked and wouldn't take us into court. The anger of an anguished wife is quite different from that of a woman who feels she's been wronged, like McGuffy, and is out of control."

"And hears voices?"

"If she was hearing voices back in New York, as Pamela says, it could indicate some serious emotional instability that drugs were only a symptom of. She was abandoned by her family after what happened at Michigan, Pamela says. Very straitlaced, and they felt humiliated, with Bangor's parents just down the street. At that point, in New York, I gather that Pamela was her only friend, the only person she could confide in."

I said, "Did you know she was in the Peace Corps?"

He blinked. "When?"

"After she left New York. She got malaria in Africa."

He snorted. "She told you that? It sounds to me like another example of mixing fantasy with fact, like Raphael. We didn't know what we were into, coming out here." He glanced at Burley, then back at me. "She may still be on drugs, did you know that?" He stood up straight as we neared the lobby level. "She could have ingested something in her car after she left us at the airport, stopped off along the way." As we hit bottom, he said, "That would explain her disorientation upstairs."

That, I thought, and the panic you threw into her. I hadn't seen any signs of drugs around her place, but I supposed it was possible. I just didn't see why he kept taking Pamela's side of things.

We reached the car without Burley having opened his mouth. A couple of times in the elevator I'd wanted to put him on the spot, like asking him how long he'd known Trill or how could he think Raphael was a fantasy if he'd nearly broken his arm. But I owed Burley one for looking after Trill that night, even if he hadn't bothered to call me afterward.

When I dropped them off at the Beverly Wilshire, Struiker said, "Call me in the morning."

"Sure. What time?"

"Before nine."

"No problem."

Tomorrow I recalled, was Bangor's funeral. It was also the beginning of the weekend, and I hoped he didn't have too many errands for me to run.

Twenty-Three

The press army was encamped along the curving road in front of Trill's driveway, maybe a dozen cars and half a dozen TV trucks, and they were held at bay by a couple of police cars arrowed in on the gate. I got through with the help of a kid from the main house who was hanging around, enjoying the fun. He was about seventeen and he had his girlfriend with him. He was tall and gangly and wearing only a pair of long khaki shorts. He said he lived here with his parents and his name was Ricky.

"She went out a couple of hours ago," he said. "She walked out, told the reporters she was my sister. I drove her car up around the bend, out of sight, and met her there. Just like CIA, you know?"

I thanked him and drove up to the guest house, admiring her ingenuity in getting past the press. The desk lamp was burning in her workroom, and I went in to turn it off and noticed that the computer was still on. I started to click it off but then thought maybe I'd better not. Though I'd used word processors, I didn't know much about them. I did know you could lose whatever you'd been working on if it wasn't stored properly. I touched a key just to check it out, and a block of green lettering sprang onto the screen, filling the top half of it and casting a pale glow over the room. I started to turn away when the last line caught my eye:

> a light in your window. I'll be dreaming into the night. R.

I sat down and read the whole type block. The top part was a jumble of notes that seemed to be describing some kind of nightclub setting, and there was a quote, probably from an interview with one of her comedians. It didn't seem like part of his act, exactly, and yet it was hard to tell these days when the jokes are welded to autobiography.

> I used to hear these announcers on radio or TV. You could never be sure what they were really saying, and then it became pretty obvious that they were talking in code. What really surprised me was that I seemed to have some special gift for decoding everything, you know? All these hidden messages! For instance, this guy would be talking about a political leader in the Near East and what most people were hearing was, "For the first time, Syria's president makes his way to the NATO conference today," but what he really was saying was, "For the first time, a serious president makes his way to the NATO conference today." So, hey, I began to hear a whole new world out there. And like hey, this president is serious! Hey, this man is not here to tell jokes, not like these other guys. Maybe he's the first serious president in history! And I was one of the few people in the world who knew! And little things began to occur to me, things I'd never thought of before. For instance, would the proprietor of a bawdy house be called an improprietor? I mean

There was a sudden break in the type block at that point, followed by a couple of lines that made no sense at all and then what looked like something else entirely. A message:

> Hi. I'm back again. There's a full moon tonight. I'll be through by five and there are a couple of steaks for the grill. If you haven't heard from him by then, come up. If I haven't heard from you by seven, I'll know he's back. Put a light in your window. I'll be dreaming into the night. R.

R for Raphael.

Or *R* for Ricky? Was Ricky planning to dump his girlfriend if Trill put a light in her window?

I looked at my watch: 8:15. I read the message over again and then got up and went out onto the deck. It was spooky, I thought. Somehow the computer genius, or all-around genius, had linked up his and Trill's computers. It was scary, kind of like mind control. A higher order of communication, a cocaine experience. I knew computers were linked up all the time, but what made this unnerving was that it seemed to me to override the ordinary forms of communication I'd been used to, as if Trill and I could be talking, the ordinary old sound waves moving across the space between our eardrums, but all the time there was this other super message center, with messages coming off the green machine any time of the day or night from Raphael's aerie in the sky, where he could look down at night and see the light in her window and dream away, pale green computer dreams. I didn't like it. It frightened me, Trill being so susceptible to suggestion and all, facing a murder trial and maybe back on drugs. I stood out there in the smog-filled sunlight as it groped its way out of the western sky, and then I heard her car pulling into the garage beneath the house. I ran up through the kitchen and the living room and met her coming up the stairs. She was wearing short white shorts, a red and white striped shirt, and a head scarf and dark glasses. She smiled up at me when she saw me. She was carrying something in a brown paper bag.

"Hi," she said. "I knew you'd be back. We had a fight."

"With the reporters?"

She laughed, coming inside. "No! They thought I was somebody else, and by the time they figured it out, I was inside the gate. No, I had a big fight with Raphael." She turned around and looked up at me. "I went over to see him. I was getting bored working."

I kissed her lightly. "What did you fight about?"

"You, mostly." She colored a little, then went toward the kitchen. I followed. "I've got a couple of steaks. They're Raphael's. I got so angry, I said I was taking them. I said if that's the way he was going to be, he deserved to go hungry." She emptied the sack on the kitchen counter and laid out the steaks side by side. They were an inch and a half thick, and absolutely prime.

"Those are Raphael's steaks?" I said.

"Yes. I figured you'd be hungry."

"I am. But I don't know if I want to eat some other guy's steaks."

"Don't be silly," she said. "Why don't you make a salad while I go out and start the grill."

It was dark by the time we'd finished eating. There was still the smell of charcoal and grilled meat, and we'd been watching the biggest moon I'd ever seen as it sailed mistily through the haze. We were sitting on the deck floor with our backs against the wall beneath the bedroom window. We couldn't see much of the city from there, but the sound it emitted was a steady roar, of traffic, of a hundred thousand voices—as if the moon were a satellite dish bouncing back all that distant noise.

She'd been telling me about meeting Bangor again in Hollywood, the newly married Bangor who'd seemed scared of her when she'd showed up at a studio party and smiled and said, "Hi." She was frank to say she'd pursued him relentlessly until he gave in.

"You resumed the affair." I was getting tired of hearing about her and other guys.

"I got him into bed again, yeah," she said. "Is that what you want to know? I loved his body and his cocaine. He'd say he was old, and I'd say, no, just weathered to a fine perfection. Bang, bang, I used to say. Hey, Bang, hit me again."

Jesus, I hated hearing this! "But it stopped at some point."

"Oh yes, things did begin to drift, and that's when I concocted that crazy satire for the alternative paper. After that, he came to me and tried to buy me off. Drugs or Dollars, that was the name of the game. I don't know why I didn't take the money and run, except it was him I thought I wanted, I don't know why. I can see now it was as much anger as love. If it isn't overdramatizing, you could say it was a kind of madness. Burley said it was madness."

"Burley?" I sat up and looked at her. I was incredulous. How could he say a thing like that?

"He just worries about me. He's helped me a lot." I settled back. I had to have that talk with Burley. "Anyway," she went on, "whatever it was, I was still hooked on him. It was Pamela who stopped it. She'd been after him ever since the newspaper satire, and Bangor was making up all kinds of stories about helping me overcome the drug habit. It's true I'd had a drug habit. It went with me all the way from Michigan to the steps of the sacred temple of Pashupatinath, but he'd helped me into it, not out of it. Now he was saying he couldn't go on seeing me, it was too dangerous and he wanted to stay married. He said the habit had destroyed my mind, which was what he loved most about me, and he couldn't do anything more for me. That was crazy, because I was fine. I'd kicked it in Nepal, and that was crazy, too, because most freaks go there to get drugs, not kick them. I had some help, of course. Then it began all over again out here, and Bangor was the reason, and it made me furious because he was still supplying me but he kept airing these antidrug shows and saying no to drugs. But everything Struiker was so worried about in that quote he'd already said to me, and I'll bet to Pamela—how he admired young people doing drugs to explore shocks of life in a world where there's no peace or serenity, trying desperately to come to grips with themselves the inner way. I read what he said on TV and I wanted to kill him. I'm glad he's dead." She looked at me. "No, I'm not. But I am."

"Wait a minute. You read it? You didn't hear it on TV?"

"No, Harv Wallace gave me the quote. It was printed out on a cocktail napkin from the Polo Lounge."

I thought, First Harv Wallace offers her a job, then he gets her the assignment, then he feeds her the quote. Why? Deliberately getting her into deep water? Mad because she won't go to bed with him? But didn't he know how upsetting this would be to Pamela? How unscrupulous could the guy be?

I reached out and took her hand. It was cold, as if she'd just come out of a freshwater pool. "I read the message from Raphael," I said. "On your computer."

"Raphael's dreaming," she said. "He's on drugs half the time. He doesn't like his life. He doesn't think he's getting anywhere. Here he is, practically running a big business, and he's afraid he won't make it. It's the Hollywood work ethic—insecurity and panic. He's been very worried about me during all this. I think he's afraid he's becoming too dependent on me. He looks to me for reassurance. He's very manipulative. I wonder sometimes if he really cares for me or if he's just wholly self-absorbed. You know how small children can't see the difference between themselves and exterior events? They think everyone else and everything that happens are part of themselves and caused by themselves. I wonder if Raphael is like that. In adults, it's a sickness." She moved closer. "Did you mean it when you said you loved me?"

"I don't know, Trill. I think so. I feel very close to you. I was afraid last night I might be starting to need you."

"Needing isn't loving."

"I know, that's what scares me. Last night, I just felt I wanted you so much."

"I think I love you. I didn't love Bangor, I know that now. I love Raphael, but like a brother. A brother who just doesn't quite get it, but you love him, anyway."

"Trill," I said, "I hate to think of going back to New York and leaving you."

"Oh, Michael," she said, and reached up and kissed me, then kissed me again when the phone rang, then got up to answer it in the bedroom. I could hear her end of the conversation from out there.

"Oh, no, I'm fine," she said, and then, "Yes, he is." She listened for quite a while. "I understand. But I'm all right, really. . . . Yes, absolutely." Another long pause. "Well, really, that's not necessary. All right, I think that's best. And please don't worry. I'm glad you called. Good night."

She came back and sat down. "That was Raphael. Apologizing."

I'd been watching the moon. It was quite distinct now, and the clouds had become vividly alive. So Raphael did care. Well, I decided, I cared more. "Let's go in," I said. "I want to make love to you."

"Screw, you mean."

"I don't mean screw." Was I starting to love her? Something held me back, partly the old fear of commitment, I suppose, partly wondering exactly who she was. Fear of making promises, yes, but at the same time I felt I needed something deeper than Connecticut weekends with Gisele if I were to really get involved with a woman. I wasn't sure that woman was Trill, though. I hesitated to move into what might be mind-blowing shadows and dark mysteries. I preferred the light. I liked the clean feeling I got from simpler, less convoluted involvements. I remembered my straightforward conversation with Becky the other night, and the Scandanavian girl whose name I couldn't recall. But that was sisterly, with Becky, wasn't it? And if my weekends with Gisele were as essentially carefree and uncomplicated as that, leaving aside the sexual element of course, did that mean sisterly, too? Was sisterly enough for me? Was there any more to that interlude with the Scandanavian that night than a passing infatuation with the seat of her pants? What more did I want? Why was I here?

I lost the thread of what I was thinking then, overcome with a longing for whatever it was I saw in Trill, mysterious or not, strange or not, and I took her in through the kitchen to the bedroom, where the closet door was a continuous skein of bright, colorful beads and the rug on the wall was like an Indian desert full of sacramental sand sculptures telling stories of the gods, and the moonlight from the big-sky window lay on her flanks like snow on the foothills of the Himalayas, or the steps of the sacred temple of whatever it was.

It was mystical and it was great, but in the morning I came back to the Western world with a bang. The sky was bright and my brain was registering three disturbing facts: Struiker. Saturday. And worst of all, it was 10:15. Was it possible that he wanted me to call him on a Saturday? I rolled over and looked at Trill. She was immobilized in her usual position, on her right side, her body slightly curled, sleeping dead-out. We had made love, the first time sacramentally, ceremonially, in a trance, and then very early in the morning, in a wild dream. She had looked up at me with the moonlight and a half-awake, sassy grin on her face and said, "You want to fuck me like a dog?" I had groaned inwardly. I couldn't think what she meant at first, and no, whatever it was, I didn't want to do it like a dog because I didn't want to lose this feeling I had that made me feel like a person, yes a person full of strong desire and bright lights and tenderness and a terrific wish to merge and then I came in a rush and lay on top of her panting like one, and finally we had slept.

I sat up and looked at the clock again: 10:20. I went into her office. The little red light on the computer was still burning brightly. I'd forgotten to tell her she'd left it on. I went over and touched the keyboard and the blank screen flashed green. There was another message below the one I'd read yesterday. More scrambled code and then:

> Why, oh why? I'm thinking steaks and seeing roses. Where are you? Love, R.

I let the message burn and took the phone down onto the deck and plugged it in. I called the Beverly Wilshire and there was no answer in Struiker's room. Then I called the police department and got Detective Braun's phone number and called that. He wasn't there. I explained about Struiker and they gave the call to a sergeant.

"I don't know where your lawyer is, sir," the sergeant said, "but Detective Braun was called to the Plaza on an investigation a little while ago. You may be able to find him over there."

I left Trill a note and drove down to the gate. The same kid, this time wearing swim trunks and dripping wet, came around the main house and waved. I waved back. Somehow I made it down the short, winding drive past the ranks of media soldiers, and then it was all downhill into Beverly Hills.

Twenty-Four

There were a couple of uniform cars in front of the hotel, and an officer told me I'd find Detective Braun around at the rear, by the pool. I parked back there and saw Struiker standing away from the crowd talking to a tall gray-haired man who turned out to be the hotel's vice president in charge of public relations. Detectives Braun and Bannister were over by the pool with two uniformed cops and some evidence technicians and a group of reporters, three of whom now detached themselves and came over to talk to the PR man.

Struiker said, "It's nothing. They found a key last night, that's all." What did he mean? A car key? The rooms all used those electronic key cards. He was studying me. "Where were you? I called your sister's. Her friend said you hadn't been there since Wednesday. She asked me if I was your father."

I didn't know whether he'd called my parents or not, so I said, "To tell you the truth, I got waylaid last night. Met an old girlfriend for dinner and stayed over. I don't know what happened to me this morning. I've been waking up at five or six in the morning every day out here." I knew there was a chance my picture would be in the papers, showing me coming out of Trill's driveway, but I didn't care. "What is it, a key to the suite?"

He was watching a TV truck leave the parking lot. "Some hotel thief took it. Or some kid, found it and tossed it there for no reason at all."

"What kind of key is it?"

He looked back at the pool. I had a feeling he didn't want me around. So why had he told me to call him? Then I realized he was watching Detective Braun coming toward us from poolside.

Braun said, "The key's clean. No prints." He looked at me. "Enjoying your stay?"

I was in the middle of a yawn, and nodded. "I guess you could say that."

He said to Struiker, "I have to write this up, for what it's worth. What say we continue our conversation later? Although you've got just about all I've got."

"Thanks, I'll give you a ring." As Braun walked away, Struiker said to me, "You think Bangor fell nineteen stories and then had time to wipe off the key before he died? Anyway, what would Bangor want with it? Can you picture him using a freight elevator? It's an oxymoron."

I said, "It's a key to the freight elevator?"

"The one outside the suite, at the end of the hall. People throw money in the pool. They collect the loose change from the water every night about nine or ten o'clock. At nine-thirty this morning, somebody thought to tell the cops about finding the key."

"So it had to be left there yesterday."

"Apparently. It doesn't mean anything."

"Is that what Braun thinks?"

"He's curious, like all cops. The freight elevator makes only three stops, the basement, the lobby floor, and the suite area. If someone wanted to get to and from the suite without being seen going through the lobby, that's how he might do it. Through the basement."

"You think there may have been someone else up there, besides Pamela and Trill?"

"I'm telling you what Braun thinks."

"Wouldn't a professional thief put the key back where he got it, make a copy or something?"

"Maybe. It's been missing since Monday, two days before Bangor died. Why would the killer take it on Monday? To keep it from being connected to the murder? So you steal it two days before and discard it two days afterward."

"But why the pool? Why not toss it in some shopping mall garbage bin, just make it disappear? Seems like somebody wanted it found."

Braun and Bannister were leaving now, and so was the rest of the press. Struiker said, "Forget it. People always throw things in pools. When they found the key, they also found seven dollars in change. They give the money to the homeless, did you know that? A new theory on the distribution of wealth. Saves the homeless the trouble of having to come around and fish it out themselves. Come on, let's get the car."

I led the way, wishing he'd let me know when he was kidding. "So then why is everybody out here if the key doesn't mean anything?"

"Slow press day. The murderer's been charged but justice isn't quite ready to take its slow but inexorable course. This makes a perfect next day's lead: 'A mystery key was found yesterday in the murder pool.' Has a nice, crappy ring."

"Maybe the killer wanted the key to be in the papers but couldn't throw it in the pool because Bangor's body was down there and people were all over the place." I pictured the pool, the fountain going, and Bangor's body looking like a piece of ornamental statuary that had been vandalized. I shuddered. "So whoever it was had to come back and do it later. Got out on some balcony and—"

We had reached the car. He said, "Who was the last person you saw up on that balcony?"

I stared at him, a picture in my mind. The pool with the sun low in the sky, no body, just the fountain going, and a shiny key sailing from a height of nineteen stories and plopping into the water. And on the balcony, a man in a cardboard-brown suit, shooting photographs. I said, "You don't think it's meaningless at all!"

He looked back at me without expression. "Who were you really with last night?"

I had to swallow to keep from gagging. "Trill," I said. "But Burley—my God!"

Struiker pointed at the car. I could hardly unlock the door. I walked around to the driver's side and got in, my mind going sixteen different ways.

Struiker said, "Did you go directly to McGuffy's place after you dropped us last night?"

I stared at him. "She wasn't home. She was at a friend's."

"When did she get back?"

"Eight o'clock, something like that."

"Burley left me about ten. You were with her all night?"

"Me and the press. They were still outside the gate this morning."

He said, "Burley couldn't have been up in that suite on Wednesday because McGuffy saw him when she came down, that's what she told Braun. It has to be somebody else. Unless she's lying. Why didn't Burley tell me he'd seen her when I asked him to find her, I wonder."

I said, "He *could* have been upstairs. She was getting into her car. He could have followed her down."

"Pushed Bangor, gone down the freight elevator, and still found her out front? Not unless she had to change a tire." He looked at me accusingly. "How do you know she was getting into her car?" He took a deep breath. "You told McGuffy the Laudiceks were in the suite, didn't you?"

"It just slipped out."

"Giving me phony phone numbers so you could fall into

bed with her. Phony numbers are bad enough, but getting involved with her is incredibly bad judgment. Look what it did to Bangor. And because you were emotionally entangled, you sent her back here, and that could be the death of her."

"She couldn't have killed him."

"Why not? She's a big strong girl and she was feeling trapped."

My temper flared. "Damn right. She was scared to death after that ride out to the airport. Like Mr. Kim. She was paralyzed."

He smiled. "You can't forget Mr. Kim, can you? Except he didn't hate his dentist; he wanted his approval. McGuffy was feeling violent enough to hit Bangor on the nose, so what's a little push off a balcony?"

"She couldn't. She wouldn't."

"Then who? Pamela? Burley? McGuffy's the one with the motive."

"It had to be somebody else."

"Well, Braun thinks that's a possibility, all right, although if this were a horse race I think he'd put his money on McGuffy. He thinks she has a winning stride. How is she in bed?"

I wanted to hit him but I let it ride, feeling the anger seep out of me—most of it anyway. I still wanted to shake him up. I said, "It could have been Raphael."

"Raphael?"

"He's real."

Struiker shifted in his seat, interested. "No shit."

I said, "Burley knew he was real. He threatened to break his arm if he didn't leave Trill alone."

He was smiling now, but not his eyes.

I couldn't shut up. I said, "Burley knew all about Trill. They go way back."

"To what?"

"I don't know. I get the idea they both hated Bangor."

"What else do you know?"

"The quote. It came from Harv Wallace. It was written out on a napkin."

"What else?"

"When you told Burley to find Trill, he'd already found her. They left the hotel together and he was with her for several hours."

He looked out the window. "When were you going to tell me all this?"

"Whenever it mattered. Most of it didn't seem important because Bangor was dead and couldn't sue us. Now I guess it does."

"You guess." He opened his door but took his time getting out. "Drive around in front of the hotel and wait for me. I'll put in a call to Burley, tell him we're coming to see him."

I started the engine. "Wouldn't it be better to call the detectives?"

He looked back in the window. "And tell them what? That Burley was up on the balcony yesterday?"

I drove around to the entrance and waited. When Struiker came out he said, "I told him about finding the key. He said, 'Sounds like somebody else was up in the suite.' I said, 'Maybe it was Raphael.' He said that would surprise him because Raphael didn't exist. I asked him why he went to the hotel on Wednesday. He said he thought he might be able to get Pamela off my back. I said, 'At three o'clock? My plane was leaving. What made you think we'd still be there?' He said he didn't think about it. I thanked him for wanting to protect me from Pamela and for taking good care of McGuffy afterward. He had no reaction to that. All he said was the pictures he took of the pool were on his light box, ready for me to look at. Let's hear what he has to say when he's had a little time to think. He's at the photo lab. Turn right."

"Old shoe," I said, starting the engine and nosing down the drive.

He said, "I've known Burley for a long time. It's disappointing, his not being straight with me. I expected you might fabricate a few games, but not Burley."

We were heading south. "So where is this place?"

"He said to take a right at Pico Boulevard, then go a mile or so to a long, low building saying BGM PICTURES. For Burley Gerard Moore."

"Gerard. That puts him in a whole new light."

"The Gerards were the original family of wealth in Little Rock, his mother's family. Burley grew up rich but left school nouveau poor."

Turning onto Pico, I was nearly cut off by a deep tan in aviator glasses driving a white Porsche. He needed my lane to make a right into the Twentieth Century–Fox lot. I thought of Trill that first afternoon, the guy blasting his horn at her in the middle of traffic. Then I remembered something she'd said one of the first times we'd talked on the phone. "Trill told me once that her father walked into the ocean."

"And her mother was a mermaid and they lived happily ever after," Struiker said. "Mike, I wish you'd get your head out of bed and stop believing everything McGuffy tells you."

Wanting to defend her, I said, "If it's true, it's a terrible thing to have happen."

"Her father walks into the ocean, her reluctant lover threatens to sue her and then jumps off a roof. She was not meant to lead an uneventful life undeserving of pity."

I needed to change the subject. "So tell me what you think. How do you see this thing?"

He said, "Tell me first about Raphael."

"Not much to tell. He lives in the hills above Trill's place. He sends her messages by computer. He's a computer genius, she says, does work for USC and various companies. He also does drugs and mopes a lot. Just like in the article."

"Have you met him?"

"No, but I ate his steak last night." Struiker stared at me

without comment. "If Trill wanted someone put away, Raphael would probably do it, just for the intellectual exercise. He seems to be hung up on her. And so far he hasn't got an alibi."

Struiker sighed. "The trouble with you literary types is you like to fantasize. Raphael may be real, but the Raphael you're talking about as a possible suspect doesn't exist. You have no earthly reason to think he'd have any interest in committing violence and mayhem. McGuffy, on the other hand, obviously has no self-control at all. Yes, Pamela could get violent. Burley, even Provine, they have violence in them someplace, although I suspect it would have a harder time getting out. Harv Wallace, he's too smart, too savvy. He might hire it done. But he vents his rage every day, in his column, and occasionally by getting pretty young women into trouble."

"All right," I said, "but let's say Trill didn't do it. Who would you think?"

"First of all, myself," he said. "I didn't like the way Bangor powdered his hair, but that wasn't my only motive. I wanted to save generations of television viewers from boredom, not to mention the jury if he took us to court."

"No, really. Who?"

"Well, all right, let's start with the man who inexplicably felt he had to visit the scene of the crime before there was a crime, and this assumes something else inexplicable, that he was conspiring with Pamela to kill her husband. Burley was in his lab when he learned from Harv Wallace that Pamela was coming over to see me at the hotel. Pamela had made sure Wallace knew that, so that Burley would have an excuse if he was seen there. Earlier in the week, he had gone down into the hotel basement and stolen the key to the freight elevator. If he met a bellhop on his way upstairs, he'd say he was security. Pamela would open the door and tell him Bangor was in the bedroom full of brandy, and that would be that. She'd go down to the lobby and ask for some aspirin for her poor husband's headache, while Burley did what he came to do. She'd be down there when it happened and could write her own script. She's probably always wanted to play Ophelia. He'd go down in the elevator and get rid of the key. But instead of all this, when he arrived at the hotel with the key in his pocket, he saw McGuffy coming out. What should he do? He's told Pamela he'd be right up, but now he's stuck down there with McGuffy. Later in the week, he finds himself standing on the balcony with a familiar key in his pocket. He drops it into the pool, as a memorial offering to his good friend Bangor."

"So who killed him?"

He shrugged. "Pamela's up there all alone. But what if she isn't? Let's say Burley really did want to rescue me from the wicked witch. Say Harv Wallace hangs up the phone and goes to the hotel with the elevator key in his pocket. Tired of younger women, he's secretly lusted after Pamela for years and now they're in league. He goes up, but before he can take care of Bangor, there's a knock at the door. Pamela goes to answer it, he hides in the closet, nothing new for him, and surprise, it's McGuffy, so why not make her look like the killer? When she leaves, he whisks Bangor off the balcony. Bangor beats him to the parking lot by only sixty seconds and Pamela's already on the phone, calling security."

"What about the key in the pool?"

"Two days later, he's up in the *Inquirer*'s news helicopter, whetting his appetite for eyeballing scantily clad flight attendants of either sex lounging about their swimming pools. The copter makes a pass over the hotel and he lets the key fall."

"Either way, you've got Pamela plotting her husband's murder. That seems to be what the key inevitably shows."

"Unless it was stolen by a thief or a prankster and McGuffy's guilty as charged. Right now, she's the one who's going to trial. Of course, there's always a chance that somebody simply wants Pamela to appear to be guilty, but that someone would have to have known Bangor was going to be killed as early as Monday, when the key was stolen."

So now it was my turn. "Okay, say Pamela plans to kill her husband and wants to make it look like someone else did it. She steals the key, intending to leave it in some conspicuous place afterward. She'll kill Bangor, feign unconsciousness, and wake up, the bereaved widow. But when Trill appears, she has a better idea. Accuse Trilla McGuffy and later toss the key in the pool, where a kid might be expected to toss it."

"Except she wouldn't. To make it work against McGuffy, she'd have to make the key disappear," Struiker said. "So would Burley or Wallace."

I was only half-paying attention to the game. I was looking at the numbers on the buildings. Something was wrong. "The numbers are way too high," I told him, "and getting higher."

Now he was looking, too. "We've gone past it. Turn around."

I waited for an opening, made a U-turn and headed back. "Unless she did have a confederate, and there was a falling-out, and he wanted to cast suspicion on her, like you said, and away from Trill."

"Burley, you mean." Struiker was frowning, watching the numbers. "Let's get back to motive and opportunity," he said.

"Well, if you just want to back off and look at everybody, the only one I know who wanted anyone dead was Jim Provine. But he wanted to kill Harv Wallace."

Struiker grinned. "Well, all right, then Provine was the third presence in the suite, and he planted the key to cast suspicion on Wallace because everybody knows about those voyeuristic helicopter flights." He sobered. "You're talking about the items in his column? About Jim's wife?" I nodded. "Jim's a hothead, all right. But he doesn't belong in this. He barely knows Pamela at all. Wallace knows her well. Burley admires her. He took her picture."

"Burley's a puzzle. Wednesday night, there was some kind of standoff between him and Trill. She seemed almost afraid of him."

Struiker sat back and glared. "You mean to say you were with them?"

"Burley went out to arrange for her lawyer to take her downtown to see the police. When he came back, at first she seemed glad to see him. Then she got very nervous."

"McGuffy's an actress," he said. "She wouldn't make a dependable witness. She lies, or she makes up things she wants to be true. Slow down now."

We were approaching the Fox lot. I said, "Burley must have said turn left on Pico."

"He said turn right. Keep going."

A block or so on the other side of the Avenue of the Stars where Pico Boulevard begins a gentle bend, the numbers were still too high, but at least we were going in the right direction. "Why would he say right when he meant left?" I said.

"Why would he tell me he hadn't found McGuffy when he had?"

"He's getting old?" Burley was at least ten years older than Struiker. "He's getting nervous? The old shoe is no longer steady as a rock?"

"We're getting closer," he said. I shut up and started watching. Five blocks later, there it was, a one-story brick building painted white, with the typical orange tile roof. Most of it seemed to be a storefront office with two large windows beneath a sign reading M&M REAL ESTATE. There were two doors, one to the real estate office and one marked BGM PICTURES. I parked and we walked across the street. Burley's door was locked, but there was a handwritten note taped to the little window. It read: "Waited and had to go out on a call. Back soon. Ask next door. Burley."

Twenty-Five

We went into the real estate office and confronted the only occupant, a bald man behind one of the six desks. He wore a yellow vest and a blue and white striped shirt open at the neck. He looked up warily. "He's gone out," he said. "Here's a key if you want to wait for him." He pushed the key across the desk.

Struiker said, "Were you here all day Wednesday?"

The man looked annoyed. "Sure I was. I'm here every day."

"Was Burley here?"

"I think so. I don't keep track of the boss."

"He owns this place?"

"Sure. He bought me out and changed the name three or four months ago."

"M&M. Moore & Moore." Struiker looked at me. "Sounds like Greed & Greed." He asked the man, "I'm thinking between two and three o'clock Wednesday. Was he here then?"

"Let's see. His car was here. Yes, it was here when I got back from lunch, about two-thirty. It was gone when I went out an hour later."

"I thought you said you were here all day."

"Well, sometimes when we run out of salespeople, I have to show a house. I was here all day Wednesday except for lunch until about three-thirty. What is it? Are you the police? He in some kind of trouble?"

"Not as long as I'm around," Struiker said, and reached out and took the key.

We let ourselves into Burley's lab. There was a small office up in front with a long worktable, a leather couch, and two filing cabinets. Off a hallway leading to the rear were three doors. The two on the left led to darkrooms with signs reading KEEP OUT and PLEASE KNOCK. The door on the right opened onto a large room with a long table, a couple of light boxes for viewing slides, and a storage cabinet that was the height and length of the room and was filled with wide, shallow drawers holding photographs. Each drawer bore a handprinted label. Struiker turned up the lights and pulled out a drawer marked L. Inside were some portraits and several large envelopes containing negatives and prints, all of Pamela Laudicek. He spread the dozen or so mounted enlargements on the table and bent over them. Only two of them were smiling. The others were simply arresting: thoughtful or brooding or challenging in some way. Burley was right—all of them had a haunting quality.

I went down the line until I came to a drawer that was labeled NEPAL. "Burley was in Nepal," I said.

Struiker said, "Burley was everyplace."

"Trill was in Nepal."

A chair scraped the wood floor as Struiker sat down. "Well, take a look."

The drawer slithered with plastic sleeves, twenty color slides each. I pulled the drawer out of the cabinet and put it down on the table near the larger light box, turned on the box, and started to remove a dozen or so color transparencies from its translucent surface. They were all a shimmering blue, and in most of them the blue was guitar-shaped. "Here're your pool shots," I said. The all-blue ones were extreme close-ups. Within the arc of the pool, you could see coins glittering on the bottom, pennies and nickels mostly. All of them were sharply defined in the underwater lighting. I looked around and found a viewing lupe, and noticed a nickel that had grown a snout. A key. It wasn't there in all the transparencies, but then I couldn't be sure I was looking at the same part of the pool.

I went through all the shots until I found a matching pair. The coins in both transparencies were in exactly the same position, but in one of the shots was a key.

"Here's your key," I said, "before and after."

Struiker got up and looked. "Poor old Burley," he said, "always dependable. Saying look, here's proof I threw the key in the pool." He turned and went back to his art shots.

I pulled the transparencies off the box and started going through the slides from the drawer. They were either of people or landscapes. It was several minutes before I came to the shots of the three little girls. None of the photographs was exactly like the one on my wall at home, but about halfway down in the next sleeve I thought I saw a familiar face. The shot had gone awry. The camera had been tipped at an angle, as if accidentally. It showed only one of the little girls. She was looking up with an expression of annoyance, as if the earth itself had shifted beneath her feet. In the foreground was a much larger face in profile, so close to the camera that it was out of focus. With the viewer, I examined the face closely. It was Trill, and she was laughing as she turned her head away. The blur that cut off most of her hair could have been her hand trying to block the shot.

I showed the slide to Struiker.

"It's McGuffy, all right. I'd know that goofy smile anywhere." He looked up at me. "So they were together in Nepal. What, about two years ago?"

"Maybe less."

He stared down at the plastic-covered slides scattered over the bright surface. "Call her," he said.

"What'll I say?"

"Tell her not to let anyone in the gate until we get there." Before I could move, he looked up again. He seemed to be trying to make up his mind whether to hit me or not. "No," he said, "tell her to get out of that house immediately. Tell her to drive to my hotel and wait there for us. Tell her to stay there all day if she has to. And tell her not to stop for anything, most of all Burley."

I made the call and we headed for Trill's, cutting straight through the glass and brass wonderland of noontime Beverly Hills toward the canyon drive that would take us upward.

"He had the key in his pocket on Wednesday when he drove up to the hotel," Struiker was saying. "Seeing McGuffy, he panicked and the key flew out of his mind. He remembered it later, maybe not until he was up on that balcony with his camera two days later, and he dropped the key into the pool. The wonder is he bothered to wipe it clean, since he left us such a clear message in his lab, but by that time he was thinking differently. He'd been part of a conspiracy to kill Bangor and he'd changed his mind. It had to be McGuffy that changed it for him, her being accused of the murder. They go back a long way, and when she came out here and met Bangor, it was Nepal all over again. She went back to her habit and Burley went back to trying to save her.

"Pamela was the other half of the plot. Whatever arrangement she had with Burley, when she accused McGuffy, she broke their agreement. Burley couldn't handle that. When he decided to drop the key in the pool instead of making it vanish, he was declaring that the partnership had ended. You could say he was pointing the finger at Pamela. The fact that he took those pictures and left them for us is an indication of that. Today when I told him the key had been found and we were coming over, he told me to go the wrong way on Pico Boulevard to give himself more time."

"Shouldn't we stop and call the police?"

He grinned at me. "Nothing's happened. This is pure conjecture, baby."

We crossed Wilshire and Santa Monica, leaving the Beverly Hills police station behind. Ahead of us was the Beverly Hills Hotel and Sunset Boulevard, then the long climb up the canyon. "Don't worry," he went on, "Burley's probably on his way to Mexico. He always liked it down there. He spent several years in Veracruz."

"You weren't thinking that way back at the lab."

"I wasn't breathing the clear, invigorating air of Beverly Hills."

"Well, what were you thinking then?"

"That if I'd gone completely around the bend and loved somebody, and it looked like life was over just as it seemed to have started, then I'd like to clear out and take her with me. And if she wouldn't come, I'd take her with me by force, and if that didn't work, I'd just start killing people."

"Life was over? How?"

"If I were Burley? He grew up rich, but turned poor. If he made a deal with Pamela, you can be damn sure it included lots of Bangor's money. He'd be in the catbird seat. Maybe he'd have Pamela, too—I don't know what their agreement was. Then when McGuffy was charged, all his old feelings for her came back. He'd been protecting her for years, but now she became an obsession. The law is full of this kind of irrational behavior. Grandiosity. The beginning of madness. The brain lighted up, egomania running rampant. Bangor had the beginnings of it, but he didn't have a cause that would light him up and make him a god. He was a fake emotionally. Not Burley. By the time he got up on that balcony last night, he was bursting with life and authority. I can see him out there with the key in his hand. Should he drop it or not? If he did, and if he could prove it with his camera, he'd be telling Pamela to go to hell, and you and me and the rest of the world right along with her. At that moment, he must have felt he had all the power in the universe. Popes stand on balconies. Caesars. Madmen with automatic weapons. He hadn't felt such power in years, not since he was a rich kid in Little Rock. He could whisk McGuffy right off the planet, take her out of all this, and himself, too. That's what I mean by around the bend. But afterward, on the elevator, he didn't say a thing, did you notice that? He must have been having second thoughts. He'd spat out Pamela, all right, but what did he do for an encore? He was coming down fast. He was just Burley, after all, not Superman. Burley didn't rescue damsels from their tower and ride off with them into the sunset. Burley was just an old shoe. His life was over."

We were winding upward now, and I was using both sides of the road. Although we'd met several cars, I'd had time to get out of their way. But the road was narrow and steep and more often than not tended to curl back on itself, like a ferret, like a rattler.

"I could be a hundred and eighty degrees wrong," he went on. "All this is based on feeling. He might not be heading for McGuffy's at all. Right now, he could be stalking Pamela back in Beverly Hills."

"Pamela? Why?"

"By accusing McGuffy, even though she may have had no choice, Pamela had done something either very stupid or very deliberate. Either way, if I were Burley, I'd have to wonder whether she deserved to live."

I said, "You carry a gun?"

"Of course not. I don't borrow trouble."

"Well, what'll you do, reason with him? Tell him he's going up against the established order?"

"I'm just hoping McGuffy's out of there and Burley's down at the airport."

"But you don't believe that."

"It all depends on what he felt like when he hung up the phone after I called. Was it all really over? Or did he have one more chance? Obviously, it wasn't over, at least not quite, or he wouldn't have sent me right on Pico. He'd have waited for us, old reliable gone wrong. He didn't do that, and I think what motivated him was his obsession with rescuing McGuffy. He must have felt that he could take just one more step and have her forever."

"So that's it? And you don't have a plan when we get up there?"

"Are you kidding? I'm too busy praying that some Mexican gardener doesn't back his truck out in front of you."

I'd been praying, too, asking God to do me a favor. I wanted her to be out of there. She'd sounded funny on the phone. "Hotel?" she'd said. "Where? Why?" Like a wakeful child in the night asking whether she was really going to heaven when she died. "Burley?" she'd said. "Why should I be afraid of Burley?" And finally, "Well, all right, all right! But get there as soon as you can. I don't want to sit around for hours and hours in some hotel lobby, I don't care how classy it is."

We were almost there. I could see the vehicles scattered up along the side of the road, more press than ever. I hoped I wouldn't see Burley. Maybe the kid would be there, Ricky. He'd say, "Oh, she drove out of here twenty minutes ago," and there'd be no Burley at all. I slowed, swinging around the final curve past reporters and photographers, and then hard to the right and into the drive, ready to brake at the police barricade.

I screeched to a stop just in time to avoid hitting one of the two uniform cars blocking the entry, Mars lights flashing in the sun. A cop came around one car, yelling, "Where the Christ you think you are, on the freeway?" but it was the big metal gates beyond him I was staring at. They stood ajar, as if they'd been blasted inward. One gate was buckled but remained upright. The other sagged at a forty-five-degree angle, wrenched from its support. I got out, looking through mangled wrought iron at the road running through the trees past the main house. Four more cop cars were parked up there near the house, and beside them I saw the kid and an older woman, probably his mother. Without thinking, I waved, and the kid waved back. Then I heard

Struiker's door open and the squawking of a police radio, and I turned and saw the officer right in my face, like the keeper of the gates of hell. "You got business up here, buddy?" he asked, casual but insistent. He was about my age and had an Oklahoma drawl.

"You'd better ask him," I said, nodding toward Struiker. But Struiker had started toward a car parked off to one side, a long black Continental. A limo rental with a chauffeur, I thought. But then the door opened on the opposite side and I stared. The chauffeur was heavily veiled but unmistakably Pamela Laudicek, and the passenger getting out and walking around the limo toward Struiker was Nels Barbidoux.

The media was closing in on the two police cars at the entrance to the drive, cameras clicking and whirring, and the young cop was still trying to get my attention. "You media or what?"

I held up my hand, holding him back like traffic, and moved off around the car. "Let me talk to these people just a second, okay?" I said. I went over and said, "Hi, Nels," at the same time nodding at Pamela. She nodded back. Beneath the veil, her face was almost invisible.

Nels glanced at me, interrupted but used to that. "Hello, Mike." He sounded tired. He gave me a quick smile that crinkled away the little pouches under his eyes, then turned back to Struiker and said, "We were on our way to the funeral, up the hill a couple of miles. We heard the sirens, and you know an old newshawk can't resist that."

"Old fire dogs never die, they just howl away," Struiker said, and Nels laughed.

"I offered to go in and try to talk Burley down to reality, but they wouldn't let me. Too risky for the girl, they said. I flew in last night. Anton tell you I was coming?"

"What time?" Struiker said.

"Late, too late to call you, and I couldn't reach you this morning."

"You're early for the funeral. It doesn't start for several hours."

Nels looked at the pavement. "Pamela wants to go up and use the chapel." He looked up. "She's quite spiritual, did you know that? I guess that's why I'm still hanging around her."

Struiker said, "I didn't know you had a spiritual side."

"Mountains," Nels said, smiling at him. "You zone in on some sinister, scary peak, it's dark, there's ice and the rock's no good, you go kind of transcendental. You've got to have something to hold on to. Even God." He nodded wearily. "I'm glad you're here, Bob. Maybe they'll let you talk to Burley. I'll go with you if you think it would help."

Struiker shook his head. "No, you've got your hands full. How's Mrs. Laudicek taking all this?"

Nels said, "Very strong, surprisingly strong. You can see. She's the one doing the driving." He hesitated. "I'd better go." He said to me, "Nice work, Mike, on the libel case. Sorry it didn't end there." He backed away, and we watched him go around the car and get in beside Pamela. The Continental backed slowly out, a black honeycomb swarming with media bees, and then took off up the hill.

Struiker turned around and said to the young cop, "I'm meeting a client here." He handed the officer his card. "I'm a little late."

The cop glanced at the card and handed it back. "Little late is right, sir. We have a hostage situation down there. For your own safety, I can't let you go any farther. That's the lieutenant's order."

"I think my client's the hostage taker," Struiker said.

The cop said, "Just a minute," and got on the radio. "Lieutenant, I've got the offender's lawyer up here. You want him to come to you?"

"Affirmative," came the reply.

The cop said to Struiker, "We took an officer to the hospital a little while ago, but you'll be out of the line of fire if you just keep back of those trees and go in the back way. Park where those police vehicles are but leave them room to get out."

He pulled his patrol car over, and I drove carefully past it and then past the wreckage of the gate. "Damn it, why didn't she leave when she had a chance?"

Struiker shook his head. "Maybe there wasn't time. On the other hand, she always has her own reasons, you know that. Like Pamela."

We were approaching the main house, and I was looking for a parking place. "I didn't know what to say to Nels."

"He'll be all right. It's just a funeral."

I pulled in under the trees, and as we got out, the kid came around the house and ran up to us, already talking excitedly. "Trill called down and told me not to let him in the gate, but he went right on through. Really incredible! The alarm went off and the cops at the gate took off after him, and when they did that, the reporters did, too, and that's when the shooting started. I was in my room. I couldn't believe it. This one cop was hit in the arm, then more cops came, but there's been no more shooting. They're just sitting and waiting. The lieutenant keeps talking to him on the phone, but nothing's going on."

Struiker said, "You know him, do you?"

"Oh, sure," Ricky said. "Burley's been here lots of times, sometimes twice a week. He's a really friendly old guy. He took my picture once."

"How many cars up there?"

"Oh, four or five. Some other cops are up in the woods behind the house."

"How did the policeman get shot?"

"It was right at the first, right after the first car drove up there. The other cops were turning back the reporters, yelling and swearing and everything, getting them back in the street, and Burley broke a window out and everybody started shooting."

"Just one car?"

"Yeah, at first."

"Where were you by then?"

"I was still upstairs, watching out the window."

"Who fired first, could you tell?"

"All I know is, he broke out a window and the shooting started. I don't know who started it."

An officer came around the house and said, "The lieutenant's waiting," so we walked around past the pool and an umbrella table that held remnants of the family breakfast. The sun was high overhead, bouncing off the water. It was getting hot.

Struiker said, "It's raining back home. Fifty-five degrees. Where would you rather be?" I didn't bother replying. How could I tell him I didn't want to be here, but right now it was the only place in the world to be? There was no doubt in my mind what his answer would be, though. He'd called it exactly right so far. He looked made for this day and this place.

Twenty-Six

The lieutenant was in the dining room. He was seated at a highly polished table beneath an ornate chandelier aglow with the sunlight flooding a large, white-curtained window. He looked like some military governor sent by an occupying army to maintain order. The table held two phones and radio equipment crackling away, some papers and coffee cups, overflowing ashtrays and uniform hats, and several heavy-duty nightsticks. From here, he could look through the window and see the coach house past the fringe of the trees and the four police cars angled crazily before it and the officers crouched behind the cars. The coach house, a couple of hundred feet away across the sun-drenched field, made a low dark rectangle against the woods. The noonday sun glittered off the hoods of the cars. The lieutenant appeared to be about Struiker's age, with the same gray at the temples, but a head taller.

"So you're the lawyer," he said, getting up and shaking hands, glancing at Struiker's card. "I'm Lieutenant Marx." The young cop we'd come in with sat down at one end of the table, pulled a phone toward him, and started making calls. "I hope you can persuade your man to go before the judge and clear this up before it's too late and somebody else gets hurt. We've been talking back and forth for twenty minutes but it's like trying to talk to the Vietcong. I don't seem to be getting through to him. What am I doing wrong? Who is this guy, anyway?" He reached down and picked up a piece of paper. "He says his name is Burley Moore. The youngster who lives here says he's a photographer and a charming fellow. Who is he really? What am I dealing with?"

"A solid citizen, Lieutenant." Struiker was doing the low, slow drone. "Before this week, he never broke the law in his life."

"So what brought you up here, Mr. Struiker? He call you or what? What set him off?"

"It has to do with his friend Miss McGuffy, more or less a domestic dispute. What's the situation up there now?"

The lieutenant glanced toward the house up the slope. "I've got fourteen officers up there with a sergeant, five of them in the woods above the house and a man underneath the deck. I've got two more officers upstairs here, rifles with telescopic sights, and all of them have orders not to move or fire unless I tell them to do so personally. I'm on the phone with him every few minutes, and he's a lot calmer than he was. The hostage is okay, but I have an officer being patched up at the hospital, condition fair. Took one in the shoulder. The captain should be here any minute, and we have a police helicopter standing by."

"Situation well in hand."

"Well, he's not heavily armed, thank God. But he's got a heavy-duty pistol and says he's prepared to hold out for a month if he has to. A month? I told him he's got two hours. He wants a helicopter ride over the border and says he plans to take his hostage with him." He hesitated.

"What is it?" Struiker said.

"I'm not sure." He glanced at me, then said, "How well do you know these two?"

"Well enough. I've known Burley Moore for fifteen

years. Mr. Lindenthal here knows the girl better than I do. Why?"

The lieutenant moved his finger around the rim of a uniform cap on the table. "It's just that we may have a second hostage up there. I got him to put Miss McGuffy on the phone for about twenty seconds. She's distraught, to say the least. From what I could understand, there's this friend of hers, apparently been shot. He's dying, she says. She's hysterical and it's hard to make sense out of it, but I conclude that in the initial exchange, before I got here, this friend ran out of the house and was wounded, and now he's either someplace inside there or down on the side of the hill. Bleeding, she says. She keeps insisting he's bleeding to death." He swore. "I've forgotten his name." He looked over at the young policeman on the phone. "What was it?"

The cop said, "Gabriel?"

"Raphael," I said.

The lieutenant looked at me. "That's it. Well, you know more than I do and more than Mr. Burley Moore does. He claims to know nothing of this." He said to Struiker, "I don't know what to think. I had a couple of men crawl down along the hill, and they didn't find a thing. But if we've got a wounded hostage up there, we ought to try to go in and get him out."

Struiker said, "Let me talk to my client."

The lieutenant nodded at the younger cop, who hung up the phone he was talking into and began dialing. The lieutenant said to Struiker, "Tell him to come out quietly and we won't hurt him. Somehow they never believe me when I tell them that." The other cop talked into the phone, said, "Hold on," and held up the receiver.

Struiker took it and said, "Burley, how are you?" He listened for a moment. "Burley, it all comes down to one thing. Do you want representation or not? Because if you do, I'm here to look after your interests, and if you don't, I'm going home. My daughter is finally flying back to England in the morning and I'd just as soon be there to see her off." He was silent for more than a minute. The young cop got up and went to the window and peered out. The lieutenant moved over to the doorway behind us for a smoke.

"Well, forget her," Struiker said into the phone. "She's no good. She's self-destructive and unreliable; she's proved that to you in a dozen ways." He listened. "I know, but it's better than going to jail for the rest of your life, and it's sure as hell better than spending it in Mexico."

A pause. A glance at me. "Raphael?" he said, and nodded. "Well, I don't know, either, but if he's up there someplace bleeding to death, we should get him to a doctor. What's McGuffy doing now? Where is she?" He listened. "Tell her I want to talk to her. Burley, you know better than that. Let her talk. Everybody deserves to speak their piece before they die." A pause. "Well, I'll discuss that with the lieutenant. But Burley, remember, when the big boys get here, they may not be so willing to sit around and debate the issues with you. You're going to have to shit or get off the pot. . . . All right, put her on. Wait a minute. Burley, I'm coming up there to see you as soon as Helen gets here. Yes, Helen, she's on her way." He glanced at the lieutenant. "Well, it could be the last time you'll see each other unless you change your mind. Getting out on bail is harder to do if you're dead. Right. Okay."

He sat down in the lieutenant's chair, leaned back, crossed his legs, and waited. "How are you, doll? I know, he's bleeding. Listen, we're going to get somebody up there to get him out. Trilla, dear, listen. How's Burley doing? No, this is important. On a scale of one to ten, how firmly is his mind made up?" He was silent for a moment. "All right, listen, I'm coming up. Yes, right away. You're not drugged or tied up or hurt, are you? Good. What? Oh, hello, Burley." He uncrossed his legs and put both elbows on the table. The young cop came back and sat down, and the lieutenant came over and put his cigarette out.

Struiker said, "I was just telling McGuffy, I'm coming up. I'm not going to wait for Helen. Yes, it'll be better that way. . . . Burley, sit down and try not to think about it. I'll be right there. And listen, Burley, you've got one more chance before the goons from Washington show up and start going crazy. . . . All the way, all the way if you want me to and are willing to cooperate. All right. All right. I'll be coming up the drive to the house. You'll see me, I'll wave. You'll recognize me by my irresistible smile. . . . You have to trust me, baby, I'm all you've got. Ciao."

He handed the receiver back to the young cop and turned to the lieutenant. "He's making very little sense, but he's in much better shape than McGuffy is. I think I can get him out of there, but I need a clear field. Everybody pulls back, and then I go. Can you do that?"

"Pull back?" the lieutenant said. "How far?" Like a Civil War battleground, I thought, with distances measured in yards and inches.

"Just clear the field, pull back out of sight. He doesn't know about the people up behind the house, and that's fine as long as they stay invisible. But no action of any kind, is that agreed?" The lieutenant nodded. Struiker got up. "You want to go, Mike?"

I looked at him, startled. "Yeah, sure," I said, thinking of Trill. "But won't my being along make him nervous?"

"Once we get up there, he'll accept the idea. Take your coat off and roll up your sleeves. That will remove some of the threat." He turned to the lieutenant as I took off my jacket and hung it over a chair. "Tell the cars to be gone by the time we're halfway there. That should cut his anxiety in half. I want everybody out of sight. If I yell or break a window or something, they can come running. Otherwise, I never want to see them again."

The young cop got up, hitched up his pants, and said briskly to the lieutenant, "They ought to take a weapon along, sir."

Struiker turned, giving him a level look with no encouragement in it. "No, thanks," he said, "that's for heavy-action types like you who think with their hormones.

Come on, Mike, let's take a walk." We went out of the room toward the front door, me rolling up my sleeves.

"Aren't you going to take off your coat?" I said.

"No," he said, reaching for the door. "He already trusts me."

It was hot in the sun, and the cars didn't look as if they were going to leave. The crouching cops kept turning their heads, watching us walk slowly up the drive, and all I could think of was that cops must have very strong thighs, do a lot of knee bends. Trill didn't seem real to me. Burley did. To tell you the truth, I expected to get shot any minute. I pictured myself lying there with all hell breaking loose around me. I wasn't a bit worried about Struiker, though.

I could hear the first faint crackle of the radios. Burley probably had been hearing that for the last half hour, through the broken window in Trill's living room. I thought I saw him, just a quick look before ducking out of sight. The window was one of the three above the pair of garage doors at the end of the drive, the one nearest the stairs, one sash broken out. On the right of the house, a long, shallow window full of plants ran the width of the kitchen. All the living room windows had bullet holes in them. I guess nobody wanted to shoot at the plants. The four squad cars glinted in the overhead sun, their motors idling, the sharp punctuation of the radios louder now as we strolled up the sloping drive.

"How did he sound on the phone?" I asked.

"You mean did he sound like he'd start shooting when we walked in the door? No, he's calm enough. Actually, he sounded glad to talk. I think it's begun to occur to him that Trilla McGuffy was a poor choice as a hostage. I think she's making him nervous."

I didn't intend to talk about it, it just burst out of me. "What the hell is he to her? Is it like Bangor?"

"They evidently mean quite a lot to each other."

"Lovers? Like Bangor?"

"It's possible. They tell me the moon over Kathmandu

can be seductive, and she was in need of comfort, after Bangor. After New York. Both of them were hard on her, and Burley can be kindness itself. It must have been an emotionally fulfilling time, meeting each other in the shadow of Mount Everest."

"Funny," I said. "She didn't want him to take her picture in Nepal."

"She might have been afraid he'd steal her soul away. Maybe she was that fragile."

The police were moving out now, wheeling sedately into line as at a parade, and the first car was coming down the drive toward us. We moved over onto the hummocky grass. I said, "You want me to try to talk to her or what?"

"I figure Burley doesn't want Raphael to die, whether he shot him or not. It may not make any difference in the end, but he'd probably rather be blamed for taking a hostage and shooting a cop in the shoulder than for plotting a murder and letting a young man die. Better one more shooting than one more murder."

"So you want me to try to get Raphael out?"

"Yes."

"Burley's got to hate it, seeing me here."

"Not necessarily. You look better to him than those cops do."

The cops driving by didn't say anything, didn't look at us. What do combat troops on their way to R and R say to the reinforcements coming up the road? Jeer, don't they? Taunt them about what's in store? They weren't doing that. Maybe they were thinking what fools we were, or that we were robbing them of a surefire way of getting their rocks off in combat. I said, "Why didn't you tell the lieutenant about Burley? I mean about Bangor?"

"I didn't want to confuse him. He might not have let me come up here. Besides, if I'm going to be defending Burley, it's not my job to make him look guilty, is it?"

"Are you going to defend him?"

"On this? I might."

"On the murder."

After a pause, he said, "Cut the conversation now. I don't want him to think there's anything wrong. Just look happy. Let's see what happens."

For an instant, I saw Burley's head and shoulders in the broken window again. No expression. Apparently, he wasn't worried about being picked off. He trusted us, or at least Struiker. Even so, he didn't stay there long.

Then we were crossing the grass where the police cars had been. It was full of cigarette butts and empty Diet Pepsi cans. The sun bore down, and I was glad to be without my coat. Struiker didn't seem to mind his. He was hardly perspiring. He swung along easily, a happy camper on a hike.

It was hard not to talk. Hard not to say something, anything to take my mind off where we were going. I tried to spot uniforms under the trees alongside the house, the way a kid on a trip looks for all the state plates or makes of cars, but it was hard to concentrate. I kept imagining things, crazy things.

I was half-afraid Raphael was going to rise up from the noontime shade of the woods and come staggering out to meet us, all bloody. Or Trill would come out the door and run down the stairs, and there'd be all that golden shower of hair and no face, just a blank, as if there'd never been a real Trill at all. Or Burley. He'd look down at us and grin and say, "Just kidding," and take our picture, take shots of all the cops guzzling Pepsi. And then he'd vanish, and I'd be out on the water, in a sailboat, and this would be a dream.

It had to be the sun, I thought.

We were getting close, and I thought, Oh, God, let there be a Raphael, bloody or not, not just some ghost image on a screen. Let there be a Trill, please, and a Burley, let them be real, and let Nels have his Pamela if that's what he wanted, and put Bangor back together again, and let me be a happy camper, too.

And then Struiker touched my arm. He had stopped

about twenty yards from the coach house and was staring up at it, looking almost into the sun.

Fifteen feet above us, in Trill's broken living room window, Burley's stoical visage reappeared.

Struiker said softly, "There are two high-powered rifles trained on him right now. I hope the lieutenant meant what he said about giving us leeway." He called out, "Burley, I'm coming up."

"He stays out there," Burley yelled back. "Just you."

"Aw, Burley, come on," Struiker said, shielding his eyes with his hand. "It's hot out here. Besides, he has to help me get Raphael out of there. Or Raphael's body. Where is he? How bad is it?"

"Is that why we've got this truce, to collect the wounded?" Burley yelled. "I thought you were coming up here to help me."

"I'll help you if you'll let me," Struiker said. "Mike will carry Raphael out of there, and we'll bring up one of the cars to collect the body. Then we'll talk, okay?"

"I don't give a shit," Burley said. "Only there isn't any body."

Suddenly, Trill was there behind him, and she was screaming, "There is! He's dead. He's bleeding!" Burley whirled around and they both vanished for a moment. When he returned, he was breathing hard.

"I don't know where he is," he said. "Anyway, that's the least of my problems. Bob, come on up. We'll talk first."

Struiker said, "He may die, Burley."

"I could give a fuck. I didn't shoot him."

"We could prove that if we could find the body and examine the slug."

"Oh, shit," Burley said, "do I need complications?" He seemed to be having trouble getting his breath.

Struiker moved closer to the window and the stairs. "We're coming up now, my friend. We'll talk while Mike looks around the place. I promise you, no hanky-panky."

"There better not," Burley said.

Struiker glanced at me, and we started for the stairs as Burley watched, thinking God knows what. All the way up to the door, every step I took, I made sure I didn't falter or flinch. But I have to tell you I was also making sure that I kept pace with Struiker. At that moment, he was more than an inspiration. He was also between me and the window.

Twenty-Seven

That's where they were now, over by the broken window, Struiker and Burley, both in suits, Burley's brown, of course, and no tie. They sat on two folding camp stools, one red, one blue. The canvas and wood stools were low to the floor and made him less of a target, Burley said, scratching his jaw with the muzzle of a pistol as big as the Ritz. It looked larger than a cop's .38, maybe a .45. He handled it like a camera, the way anyone else would use a telephone, like an ordinary tool to get the job done. The first thing Struiker said when he saw the stools was, "I see they have portable ones now." But Burley wasn't laughing.

When we had entered, Trill was sitting in a corner next to the Early American couch, her back against the wall between the living room and the kitchen. She hadn't moved, had barely acknowledged us. Burley had directed me to sit down against the same wall, at the other end of the couch, beside the kitchen doorway. The kitchen had no door, so he had turned the kitchen table on its side and shoved its top against the opening as a barricade. This seemed to me a futile exercise, especially if the cops came in both ways, and shooting. But then the whole escapade seemed doomed, and made me sad.

There were three openings near that corner of the living room: the barricaded kitchen doorway, which led to the deck, where a cop was supposedly hiding, and next to it the door to the bedroom with its big bed and bigger picture window, and next to that the door to Trill's workroom. The workroom blinds had been closed. From where I was sitting, I could look in and see the faint outline of the computer, and the empty chair before it, and the piles of notes Trill had been working from. I wondered whether *Esquire* was ever going to get that story.

I couldn't see much of Trill. Our backs were to the same wall and we were separated by her maple-wood couch with its ruffled, flowery pillows. Ruffles didn't look like Trill to me, but today she was wearing them, too. She had on some kind of playsuit like little girls wear, a dumb pink thing that went ruffling across her chest and came down to midthigh. I couldn't imagine why she'd put on such a thing. It wasn't your usual hostage wear. Probably she'd meant to put in a long, hot day at her computer. But it was pretty obvious that she no longer cared what she was wearing or even what was happening. Her head was down and her face was blotched red from crying, and she still hadn't reacted to me, almost as if she didn't know who I was. Well, I didn't really know her all that well, either. In an awful way, it was as if we'd barely met, as if I didn't know the real Trill yet and might never. That hurt.

She was slumped against the wall, tears in her eyes and drying on her cheeks, the blond abundance of her hair shriveled as if singed by fire. When I came in, I'd been surprised to see that her hands weren't tied. In the hour or so they'd been up here together, she could have brained him with something while his back was turned, like the rappeling hook beneath her bed. She could have broken out of the place and run. Did he think she was too hopelessly confused by events to cross him? Was there some kind of understanding between them? Was it trust? Because he seemed to need her, had, all the way back to Nepal? Or did he have some hold over her besides the gun? Was it Raphael? Was Raphael the real hostage, the one that was keeping Trill in line? Using a hostage to control a hostage? Did he have the wounded Raphael tied up somewhere, maybe below in the garage? Earlier that had seemed uppermost in Trill's mind, that terrified vision of a sainted Raphael shot and bleeding. Nobody else had seen him. If she was disturbed the way Struiker thought, in that first clash with the police she might have conjured up some shocking, screaming scene in which Raphael had run outside and been hit in the cross fire. I stole a look at her. Her head was still down and the tears were still coming, being squeezed out of her eyes. She didn't look much like the Trill I knew.

"So what do we do now?" I heard Burley say. He sat facing the window, where he could watch the outside stairway and the open field below and still keep an eye on Trill and me, and on the kitchen doorway. For ten minutes, I'd been listening to them talk in short sentences with long pauses in between. And all the time, I'd been glancing at that multipronged rappeling hook beneath the bed. I couldn't keep my eyes off it. It was fastened to one hell of a lot of neatly coiled nylon cord that made it suitable for swinging down a vertical rockface. What was it doing here? A fire escape? And then I remembered Trill and her Sherpas. She'd lugged Nepal and its mountains around with her for thousands of miles. As long as that damned hook was there, it must have meant Nepal wasn't over for her. She could always cling to the memory of it when things got rough. Did she remember Nepal now? What were all the tears for? Just pure fright? Raphael? If she didn't remember me all that well, she might be thinking of anything.

They had started out talking old times, Struiker recalling the days before *Beyond*, when he and Anton Black had come out to California on business and spent long evenings with Burley and his wife at the clubs or the Hollywood Bowl or just drinking into the night at Burley and Helen's house. He wasn't that big on reminiscence, so I figured it was by design, like that opening comment about the camping stools. Softening Burley up, maybe Burley going along with it to soften him up, too, working on each other. I had to admit that Burley was a lot brighter and more devious than I'd ever suspected. Old shoe indeed. Old crocodile shoe was more like it.

Now they were starting to get down to the issue at hand. Neither one of them had mentioned Bangor or the key. "She's in no condition to go to Mexico," Struiker was saying. "She needs professional help. She'll just be a burden to you."

"She'll go if I say she goes. Anyway, I need her now, to get there."

"It's a crappy life down there, Burley. Besides, they'll extradite you."

"Not if they can't find me, they won't."

"Why would you risk her life like this?"

Burley shifted uneasily on the stool. "That's up to me to decide."

Struiker got up, putting his hands in his pockets. "Sit down," Burley said. He hadn't taken his eyes from the window.

Struiker didn't move. "I just want to stretch my legs. That fucking stool was never meant to hold a human being."

"Sit on a chair then." There was a chair beside the long coffee table that had been pushed up against the wall beneath the other two living room windows. That's where the telephone was that Struiker kept eyeing.

"I don't want to sit," Struiker said. "I want to walk out of here with you. Let me make the call."

Burley looked around at me, then up at Struiker. "The only call I want you to make is to get that helicopter up here. They've got half an hour."

Struiker sighed and sat down on the stool. "Then let's get Raphael out of here." He turned to me. "Mike, he's got to be someplace near the house or inside, either up here or down in the garage."

"He's not up here," Burley said.

Trill looked up, her eyes red and smudged with tears. "He's dead and bleeding," she said, as if she no longer cared.

"Then start with the garage," Struiker said to me.

Burley stood up and backed away from the window, the gun loose in his hand. "All right. But when you're ready to come back up, go outside and stand where I can see you and wait till I give the okay."

Struiker said, "If you find him, take him outside and I'll have the lieutenant send a car up. One car, Burley, okay? One cop. No weapons. Okay?" He was stating the terms of a contract, keeping them simple and explicit, keeping Burley's anxiety to a minimum. "Ride back as far as the main house, Mike, and give me a call. I want to know Raphael's condition."

I got to my feet, wondering what Burley would do if I grabbed that hook lying beneath the bed and threw it at him. Shoot me, probably. I crossed the room to the front door and went down the stairs, trying to unwind. I couldn't see anything down at the main house, no police cars, no nothing. The dining room window where the lieutenant was glittered in the sun. It was weird, knowing they were just sitting down there with all that latent force, invisible and waiting.

I raised the nearest garage door and saw Burley's car. I remembered it from that first night at the airport, the big, solid tan Buick Electra. I walked around and looked at the smashed grill, then the bent and ripped fenders and the deep scratches raking the sides. He'd driven it through the heavy metal gates as if it had been a tank. I wondered whether he'd made the decision about possibly throwing his life away at that moment. Or earlier, when Struiker had called about the key and he'd gone out and gotten in his car. When had he decided everything was over? Because I still wasn't convinced he was committed to going the hostage route. He just didn't look to me like a man with that much hope. But then I guess he never had.

I looked underneath the Electra and then inside it. I didn't have a key to the trunk, but neither did Raphael. I did the same with the Mustang convertible. Actually, if I'd had to guess where Raphael would be, it would have been the convertible. Just walk over and fall in. But I shuddered at the thought of his bleeding all over Trill's upholstery. Maybe Raphael had shuddered, too, and that's why he wasn't there.

I stood there and softly called his name. "Raphael? Raphael?" I felt like an idiot, but I still stood there listening. Had he heard me? Was he lying mortally wounded in some corner of the place, trying to make himself heard? Or was he hiding there, keeping quiet, afraid I'd come to finish the job? Where would a computer genius go to die?

I settled down to work then and went over the whole garage, lifting dusty old lengths of plywood and rolling aside a stack of barely used tires and looking inside large cardboard barrels that contained peat moss or yard fertilizer, until there was no place left for him to be concealed. Then I went over and sat down on a plank stairway. It rose about four feet out from the wall next to the deck and ended at the ceiling. It occurred to me that it was directly beneath the bedroom. I went up and found the trapdoor that had to be there. I gave it a push and it moved. I raised it a couple of inches but could see nothing but darkness. Then I reached up and touched the darkness. It was the heavy blue Persian rug on the bedroom floor.

I closed the trapdoor and sat down again. I was sweating from the heat up there near the ceiling, but also from the thought of what I had to do next. Go up there and crawl along the bedroom floor, get that hook out from under the bed and do something with it. My God, what? I could get us all killed.

Then I saw him standing in the gloom at the bottom of

the stairs. I stood up and yelled, "Raphael!" and hit my head on a rafter, and he was up the stairs before I could sit back down, gripping my arm and jamming his hand over my mouth. I heard Trill scream, and a lot of running overhead, and Burley yelling. Then there was a sound on the floorboards above me like an anchor being hauled up, and a great smashing and tinkling of glass. The big window, I thought. What was going on? I heard Trill cry out and someone fall heavily on the bedsprings, and heard her wail in the stillness that followed.

I looked at the guy holding his hand over my mouth, his face next to mine, and even in the semidarkness of the garage I could tell he was about Raphael's age and that he didn't look weird the way I'd been afraid Raphael would look. I had the damnedest feeling I'd seen him before. Is it possible, I asked myself, that I've known Raphael all along? Then I saw the epaulets on the blue shoulders and realized that he was in uniform.

"Jesus Christ," I said, but it came out muffled. He took his hand away from my mouth and eased himself downward one step, looking up at the trapdoor where Trill was still sobbing. He looked as if he'd found what he'd been looking for all his life. All at once, I knew who he was. The young cop who'd been on the phone in the dining room.

I whispered, "I thought you were Raphael."

His eyes came down and looked at me. "Hell," he said softly, beginning to grin, "I ain't even Gabriel."

Twenty-Eight

Trill had quieted down some, and Struiker and Burley were talking in low tones in the bedroom. Every once in a while, I could hear her muffled sob as the cop explained in whispers how the lieutenant had sent him up through the trees after they'd seen me enter the garage. "He wanted to know what the fuck was going on," he said. "We didn't want to use the phone, maybe screw things up, but you know, you can sit on your ass only so long." I nodded. I was thinking the lieutenant had made a big mistake. For some reason, I didn't like this guy. I was thinking this man was trigger-happy.

He was shaking a finger at me and saying, "Now we got him. Let me up there, and I'll go on up and get him."

I shook my head. "There's a rug over the trapdoor. They're right in the room. Before you could get out from under the rug, he'd have plenty of time to deal with you."

"All right then, here's what we'll do. You go up first and leave the trapdoor open. Then stand clear and I'll handle it."

I shook my head again. "It's too dangerous. Too many people up there might get hurt."

He laughed softly, shaking his head. "Well, shit, I guess there'll always be cops and civilians. Now listen, I want to know the whole layout. He's only got this one weapon, right?"

I said, "I may be just a civilian but I pay your salary. I don't think the lieutenant would go for this. He promised. No violence."

"You let me worry about that," he said. "I'm gonna go for it. Get out of my way."

I shook my head slowly. "No," I said. I could hear somebody moving around overhead. I said, "Never."

The cop studied me for a moment and then he took out his pistol, holding it down along his thigh, pointed at the floor. "I'm ordering you, buster," he said quietly. "You're interfering with the law."

There were lots of jarring little movements and creakings overhead, and I put my finger to my lips. All at once, the trapdoor shifted and a crack of light sprang into view. The cop dropped down, ducking under the stairs as sunlight burst through the ceiling and Struiker said, "Mike? Mike, are you down there?"

I glanced up. The light blinded me. I said, "I'm here." I didn't move. I didn't want to leave the way free for the cop to come bursting up the stairs.

Struiker said sharply, "Well, what's going on? Is Raphael down there?"

I decided the hell with the cop. I went up and let down the trapdoor and stood on it, sealing the cop down there for good.

"You find him?" Struiker said. He was standing in front of the big window with the sun coming in, his suit jacket off, and it took me a moment to realize that there was no glass in the window, only tiny sunlit fragments scattered over the floor. Burley, in his rumpled brown suit, was sitting against the wall opposite the door, over where the Oriental rug made a mountainous heap, not Everest but a lower Himalayan range.

"No," I said. "I thought I saw something move and let out a yell, that's all. My God, what happened?" I turned and looked at Trill. She was on the bed, curled up in the pink playsuit, with her eyes shut and her thumb in her mouth, like a huge baby doll. She opened one eye and looked at me, then closed it. There was a large welt on her left temple, just above the eye. Had it started her screaming or stopped her?

Struiker said, "She thought you'd found Raphael, and when Burley prevented her from opening the trapdoor, she threw the rappeling hook at him. She missed. He hit her with the pistol. You'll notice he doesn't have the pistol now."

Burley had his head down and his arms draped over his knees. He looked as if he might have been crying, though his eyes were dry. His hands were empty and lifeless. They seemed unsuitable for holding a weapon anymore, much less working one properly.

"I called the lieutenant," Struiker said. "He'll be sending up a car in about ten minutes. Just one car, just one cop. No press, no handcuffs, that's part of the deal." He was droning, but only because he was tired. He leaned back against the wall and closed his eyes. It was very bright in the room. "Then we'll go downtown and see what we can do about all this. It will be a lot easier this way, Burley." He opened his eyes and looked over at me. "When we get down there, we'll go over everything."

The murder? I wondered. Pamela? The key? All of it? Then this might be the last of Burley. Did he know that's what was happening? Had he said anything yet?

Burley began to cry. He put his head back and cried, his whole body shaking. Struiker didn't move. "Christ," Burley said finally, wiping his eyes, "I'm not worth shit." He took out a handkerchief and blew his nose. "I didn't even know I hit her. I feel like I was the one who got hit. Oh, Christ, look at her now, like a kid with her thumb in her mouth." He was thick-tongued and sounded beyond caring what happened to him now.

"What about Raphael?" I said.

Struiker looked at me as if he couldn't believe I'd said it, and Burley, suddenly aroused, said, "Shit. You guys, I keep telling you and you don't listen. You think there's a Raphael? It was a joke. It started out as a joke! I said to Trill, 'Who's this guy in the story?' and she said, 'It's a joke. I just made him up.' And I said, 'Well, as long as you made him up, why not let him say this stuff about how great cocaine is? Let's take Bangor out of the story altogether. It doesn't need him, anyway.' And she said, 'Oh, no, Bangor stays and the quote stays.' But later, when I reminded her about Raphael, she said, 'Oh no, he's my friend. He lives in my neighborhood.' She wanted him to be real. She was even trying to convince me. But I knew what she was up to, and I wasn't buying it."

I heard the bed squeak, and I looked around. Trill was walking toward the door, moving stiffly, as if what Burley was saying offended her. She went into the living room and disappeared. I looked at Struiker. He shrugged.

"You guys think you know everything," Burley went on, staring across the room after her. "Well, you weren't there in Nepal, when she was so far down on her luck, it didn't look as if she'd ever make it back, and there were times I didn't know if I could, either. Some of those nights when she'd be on a high like you've never seen, and I had to hold her down to keep her from running up the street. And then when the lows hit her, it was awful. It took six months before she even started to come out of it."

He looked up at Struiker, but the sunlight hurt his eyes and he looked away. "You weren't here when her dad came out, either, like he was hunting for his long-lost little girl. And when he didn't like what he saw, the life she was leading, Antichrist, he says, he left town that night without a word. Except he hit her, right in the face, trying to get her back to God." He swallowed, his mouth dry, his tongue still giving him trouble. "And so she said he'd walked into the ocean. That was her story then, after that, but I guess she had to replace him with something. That was Raphael. Only she knew she couldn't get away with that with me." He looked up at us, squinting. "You guys, though, you went for it, didn't you? She put it past you."

Yes, I thought, I went for it. She had made him so real for me: the messages on the green machine, the phone call, Christ! Even the steaks. Who had called her last night? Probably Burley, upset and wondering how she was. Had she really thought she was talking to Raphael?

I heard a single high beep from the next room. Her computer, she'd turned it on.

Burley was rubbing his forehead now, his head down. "You were right, Bob, about the key. I should have gotten rid of it. I just wanted to teach him a lesson he wouldn't forget, that's all, even if he died learning it. Pamela had it all planned out, and there was more money than I'd ever made in all my life, and all I had to do was tip him over the railing and she'd say he fell and nobody would even know I'd been there. It all seemed so easy." So he and Struiker had talked about it. "You're right," he went on. "When she said Trill did it, I got shook. I'm a rescuer, Bob, did you know that? I'd helped her come back in Nepal and again out here, and I thought I could pull her out of this, too. So I threw the key and made the pictures, to make it look like somebody else was in on it, put it back on Pamela. I was going to tell all about it if I had to."

I could hear Trill typing now. The keys made a soft clatter, clatter, clatter, like a tiny Chinese doll dancing on wooden clogs.

I got up and walked to the doorway and turned to look into her workroom. The blinds were still closed and it was glowing the familiar green. She was sitting in front of the computer and she had stopped typing. Her hands were on her lap and she was just sitting there comfortably. There was a block of green type on the screen, then below that a line or two that I knew was a mishmash of letters and symbols, then a short message that would be signed "R."

I walked over and stood behind her to read it. It said, "Trilla McGuffy of La Grange, Illinois, and Nepal, can't you see how mistaken you are? I'm bleeding, I'm dead. Don't you think you've taken this whole thing about as far as it will go? Come and meet me. Love, R."

I said, "Trill?" I waited, but she didn't answer, didn't move. I turned and walked out. As I reached the bedroom doorway, Burley raised his head and stared at me, bug-eyed. Then he cried, "The gun. Get the gun!" and started getting to his feet, stumbling over the rug. I whirled around just as the gun went off, and I stopped. I had this terrible feeling, as if it had gone off at me.

Burley cried, "No!" and ran into me, shoving me into the workroom doorway, and we both stared. She was slumped sidewise in the chair, her head tilted toward me. Then Struiker pulled me aside and moved past us into the room.

I turned away, and the next thing I saw was Burley, going toward the telephone on the coffee table in front of the living room windows, saying softly, "I need an ambulance," repeating it over and over as if he was memorizing it. I watched him pick up the phone, then heard a noise behind me, a footfall grinding little bits of glass. I didn't know what it was. I turned around. In the bedroom, in front of the open trapdoor, was the cop. He was crouching in firing position, holding his pistol out in front of him aimed straight at me. He waved the gun, directing me to get out of the doorway, out of his line of fire. I shook my head no. My mouth was open but I couldn't get my voice to work. It was so quiet, I could hear Burley dialing.

When I didn't move, the cop crossed the bedroom and kicked my legs out from under me. I fell, my left shoulder slamming into the kitchen table. I felt a wrenching pain in the shoulder. I looked up and saw Burley holding the receiver at his side. He was staring at the cop and the pistol in the cop's hand. The cop said, "Police!" but Burley didn't move. He gave a little sob, a kind of hiccup, then slowly brought up the receiver and pointed it at the cop like a gun.

I made a lunge for the cop's legs and heard Burley say, "Bang! Bang!" but the next bang was lost in the explosions: one, two, three, four, very fast. Then the cop and I were down on the floor and he was cursing and hitting me with the pistol, and then he stopped when somebody yelled, "Freeze!" I looked up. There was another cop in the kitchen doorway, the one who'd been hiding beneath the deck. Other cops were pounding up the front stairs, the ones from the woods behind the house. Then I saw Struiker standing in the doorway of the workroom. He was staring down at me as if appalled by some jury's stupid verdict. He was holding Trill in his arms. And I had the clear impression that he was the one who was dead, and bleeding.

Twenty-Nine

I didn't go down with Struiker to talk to the detectives. Why should I? Anyway, he told me I could talk to them later, when the goose egg behind my left ear was gone.

He'd come back to the main house to tell me Burley had died of his wounds in the hospital, talking right up to the end, while I'd sat on the glass-slatted porch in the afternoon sun, waiting to hear. The police and the media were all gone, of course, and I knew I'd be leaving soon. To pass the time, I'd been looking at the paper and drinking lemonade, pampering myself. Not that I was feeling bad physically. Oh, I had a patch of gauze over the goose egg and my left arm was in a sling, but nothing was broken. Ricky's mother had made the lemonade, and then she and her son had gone out to the pool to wait for Ricky's father, who was due back in town later in the day. I was glad they'd left me alone. My head ached, and every once in a while I'd start shaking for no reason. Otherwise I wasn't feeling bad. I wasn't feeling anything, if you want to know, and that bothered me because I couldn't seem to do anything about it.

I'd found what I was looking for in the paper, Bangor's funeral. It had already started up at Forest Lawn. Just a couple of miles away, Nels had said. I'd decided to go. Not the service. I didn't want to hear the words, just take a look. Just be there.

So after Struiker left to go downtown, I said good-bye to Ricky and his mother and drove up and walked around to the chapel. I'd left my sling back at the house. When I saw the line of cars leave the chapel, I followed it to the burial site. I stood back under the trees until it was all over, watching them getting into their cars, Nels and Pamela, Jim Provine and his wife, and all the rest, and the press vehicles and the two police cars. Then I walked over to the fresh mound of earth with its imposing headstone and said hello to Harv Wallace. He was alone, writing something down. He looked up in surprise and then, not sure who I was for a moment, blurted out, "You don't say?" Then came a grin of recognition.

"Well, hello, I didn't know you were here." He leaned toward me and gave me a short laugh. "You are here, aren't you? Let's establish that first, whether you're really here. I get this wonderful feeling at funerals. Look around you, some folks are here and some folks aren't, and who's to be sure who's here and who's not? Or who's going to be here fifteen years from now?" He put away his writing pad and his pen. He seemed uncharacteristically nervous, and not pleased to see me at all.

I said, "I see Nels Barbidoux is back in town."

"Yes," he said. He took out a cigarette and touched a lighter to it. "It's an item, but I can't use it yet, for sentimental reasons. They're old friends, of course, but it'll come as a surprise to most people. Strange, isn't it? I wonder if they can really resume, you know what I mean? After this? But you never know."

I didn't want to talk about Nels and Pamela. I wanted to talk about Trill. But I had to start with Pamela. "I hear it was Pamela who got you to recommend her for that assignment."

He gave me a sharp look. "Trilla McGuffy? Where did

you hear that?" When I didn't reply, he said, "Yes, I did it as a favor to Pamela. Old friends again. Everybody said she and McGuffy were enemies, but they'd known each other for a long time." He chuckled and glanced off into the trees.

"So you knew about—"

"The differences between them?" He looked back at me, the eyes sly. "Sure, I did. But the assignment wasn't about Bangor. Good God, if I'd had any idea!" He lifted his eyebrows. I was starting to ask him something else when he said, "Hell of a day to have a funeral. Hell of a day. They would have called it off if they could. I was over there, you know. Yes, got stopped at that banged-up gate. Waited a while. Couldn't get in and decided to come up here. They called me from the paper on my car phone just before the service began and told me he'd given himself up. And then driving over here to the burial, the last thing to do for poor old Bangor, I pick up the phone again and they tell me about Trilla McGuffy and poor old Burley. I hope he pulls through."

I nodded.

"Well, I didn't mention it to anybody else—one death is aplenty at a funeral." He sighed. "Well, you knew her. You knew both of them, didn't you? It's a shame. I worked with Burley for years. Good, good friend. Old friend." He threw his cigarette down and ground it into the grass and the dribble of fresh earth that had spilled over from Bangor's grave. "It's funny. It started me thinking. About the article, and everything that's happened to all the people involved. It's like we're all on a caravan, on our way to some place of final importance, and we're trying like hell not to fall apart on the way. I'll tell you something. For a long time, I haven't been certain I'm living in the world. I get out of the shower and the top half of the mirror is misted over, and I look and I can't see my head. It's just drifting off, like it's leaving me. How much longer, I ask myself, is the rest of me going to be here?" He glanced at me, to see whether I'd been overcome by this unburdening.

I stood there thinking about his head misting off, and then he said, "How's this? Michael Lindenthal, successful young editor from the great *Beyond*, showed up at the funeral of Dr. Bangor Laudicek, erstwhile archenemy of his celebrated monthly, and asked me how I had managed to write a daily column for all these years. My answer was, 'Birth, and avoiding death as long as you possibly can. All very necessary to a long and flourishing career.' "

He stepped closer and put his hand on my shoulder, and his eyes lighted up. "You know, six months a year for the last three years, I've had a passionate affair with a great young beauty. Does wonders for your morale. But if you're anything at all like me, the other six months will be full of pain and resentment, and eventually it'll kill you." He slapped me on the back a few times, then took a deep breath of the air that was full of the scents of fresh sod and fresh flowers. "Well, best to be going. Can I give you a lift?"

I said, "You offered her a job once, didn't you?"

"Who? McGuffy? Why, I might, I might."

"You knew you couldn't hire her. Not with Pamela there, and knowing how Trill felt about Bangor. Of course, at the time she was a great young beauty."

He chuckled. "Well, you know. Sometimes you just like to see what happens."

"Is that why you gave her the quote? Just to see what would happen?"

He looked at me as if he didn't understand. "You're a strange young fellow."

"You're a strange old man. You like to get in there and mix it up, don't you? Put people together and see what happens when you light a match. Just out of curiosity. Just to see if they'll burn."

He turned away, glancing up at the sky. I could see he was sore, but he was keeping his famous temper in check. "You've got the wrong idea, sonny. I don't make things happen. I just keep my eyes open, and when they happen, I write them down."

I said, "I don't think you know what it is you do anymore. You know what I think? I think she didn't want to be one of your great young beauties. And when she turned you down, you couldn't stand it. I think you knew exactly what might happen when you did Pamela that favor, and then when you did her another one by passing along that cocktail napkin. It's been found, did you know that? it's probably in Pamela's handwriting. Now you're going to leave here and go home and start writing it all down."

His head was turned away but I could hear his breathing, loud and raspy. His scalp beneath those wisps of white hair was glowing. He started to say something and choked it off, and then he said it again, like an afterthought: "Well, best to be going." And he turned and walked away, not looking back.

I watched him heading for his car, and I was feeling better because I was starting to feel something. On the one hand, I was seeing Trill sitting before her green machine in that absurd playsuit, with that message on the screen from someone who existed only for her and the gun in her lap I couldn't see, and I was beginning to miss her, really miss her. But I also felt oddly at peace. After all her turmoil over Bangor and her struggles with Burley and her standoff fight with herself and the rest of the world, now it was as if she'd finally gotten in a last word.

I watched him get into his car and drive off and I thought, You missed it, didn't you, you fat, dumb, conniving, screwed-up Hollywood reporter, you missed it. Maybe you're getting it on the car phone now, the way they called you earlier about Burley giving up his hostage, then about the dramatic shoot-out between a police .38 Special and a telephone. And right now maybe they're telling you how he died and how the uniform car pulled up while you were staring up at the funeral sky, saying to me whatever you were saying, and the two officers quietly halted the departing cars and made the arrest, right behind your back. Because of Burley, as he lay dying. Because of what he'd told Struiker, the things Struiker had come back from the hospital to tell me before he went downtown to talk to Detectives Bannister and Braun.

Of course I'd already known most of it. He'd put her down on the pillowed maple sofa, ruffles to ruffles, dust to dust, and turned toward the cops breaking down the front door and running with rifles into the room. The young cop ran down the stairs to meet the lone squad car already coming up the drive, and then Burley had made a sound and raised a hand. Struiker bent down and told him they'd have him in a hospital in no time, and Burley looked up, unbelieving and somewhat amused, and told him to look under *N* in the photo file at the lab, and Struiker said, "*N* for Nepal? I already did that," and Burley said, "No. *N* for nothing. That's all I've got now. No Mexico. No McGuffy. No Nepal. No nothing."

I'd sat up then, leaning back against the overturned kitchen table, while the medics took care of Burley and then me. He was still talking, his voice growing fainter as they carried him down the stairs, and while I rode to the main house with the lieutenant, Struiker went ahead in the wailing ambulance.

When he'd finally come back from the hospital, just the two of us sitting on the porch, Struiker said, "Bangor suspected Pamela had a lover; that's when she decided to kill him, for the money she wouldn't get if he took it into his head to leave her. He might have at that, if he'd found out about Nels. Of course, she imagined she had them all wrapped around her finger. She'd gotten Wallace to assist McGuffy into troubled legal waters, and she'd almost persuaded Bangor to take us into court. Now she went to work on Burley, who was so full of pain he couldn't think straight. He'd been going around the bend for years, you can see that now, can't you? He'd always hated Bangor for what he'd done to McGuffy. Now he could teach him a lesson. And, of course, he'd finally have the kind of money he'd once expected to inherit from his father.

"The plan was simple enough. Burley would come up on the freight elevator while Pamela was pouring more brandy into her husband. She'd put in an appearance in the lobby while he did the deed, and then Burley would disappear and so would the key. Instead, McGuffy arrived, and Pamela decided on a new course of action. As soon as McGuffy was out the door, she nudged a stupified Bangor off the balcony and called security. Meanwhile, Burley was sitting downstairs in his car, paralyzed because McGuffy's empty convertible was parked at the front entrance. When she came out of the hotel, she told him she'd slapped Bangor around, and all his protective instincts were aroused. To get her out of there, Burley took her for a drink, just what she needed after the scene upstairs, and then he got her to the Shangri-la. You showed up almost on time."

He waited, as if he was expecting something from me. I wasn't sure what. Was he just telling me how right he'd been? I was a little surprised about Nels, but not much. I said, "Pamela gave Harv Wallace the quote?"

He said yes and explained about that, and then he went on. "It wasn't until Pamela accused McGuffy, though, that Burley really went to pieces. He didn't know which way to go. Like all the others, he was wrapped around Pamela's finger all right, but now he held McGuffy's fate in his hand, just like God. And that's what he felt like, standing up on the balcony last night taking the key out of his pocket. By then, it wasn't just a key, it was McGuffy's life. He'd already saved it once or twice, by getting her off drugs, and he decided he couldn't abandon her now. So he let the key fall and recorded the event. Then this morning after my phone call, he went over the edge. He thought it would be the great escape. He didn't know she'd resist the idea, didn't know she'd gone over the edge, too. But first he left the transparencies of the key on the light box and told me where to find them. Burley was always a perfectionist when it came to photography."

By this time, Struiker was up and walking slowly around the porch, as if he was addressing a jury that was taking a dip in the pool. I guess he drones sometimes when he talks to a jury, too. Even chats, makes little asides, filling in the details. "Nels was in Nepal, you remember his telling us that? The year he made his first try at Everest, his second piece for the *Geographic*. Afterward, in the foothills, quite a local celebrity, he met McGuffy and her rappeling hook. She told him about Pamela, this friend of hers back in New York who wasn't doing too well as an actress and needed a magazine writing assignment. Nels went home and looked her up, and that's when their affair began. Burley was in Nepal, too, of course, shooting the preparations for the climb. He stayed on and got to know McGuffy intimately. He was immediately drawn to her because she needed rescuing. As you know, he didn't meet Pamela until she came out here, went to work for Harv Wallace, and then got married. I wonder if part of the reason he went along with her plan was that she had a problem and needed rescuing, too."

Interesting but trivial, I thought. I got up and removed the sling from my arm. All I had wanted to do at that moment was go up to the cemetery, to Bangor's funeral, and somehow be there with Trill, sort of represent her. Then maybe I'd begin to feel something.

"Leave the sling on for a while," Struiker said. "Your shoulder will heal faster."

"Thanks. I don't really give a damn right now."

He stared at me. "What's the matter, Mike? It's over. The police are on their way up there right now, to arrest her after the ceremonies." He looked at his watch. "They've already begun."

"I know that."

He smiled, but he looked as if he wanted to slap my face. I couldn't take my eyes off him. What did he want from me? Some kind of kudos for solving a mystery? Burley had done that for him, hadn't he? He seemed to be searching his mind for something I didn't know, something that would blow me away. Finally he said, "What you don't seem to see is what's been going through Pamela's mind the last couple of days. She's been deciding whether she had to kill again. It looked like she might have to kill Burley, before he talked."

I didn't want to hear any more of this. I went over and looked out at the pool. Ricky and his mother were just sitting out there, talking. I decided that after the funeral I'd head for Laguna Beach. Tomorrow would be a good day for a long, long sail.

Struiker's voice came from behind me. It had a new edge, as if he'd finally found something to get excited about. "Pamela's amazing. See how she engineered all this. Even picking the suite as the killing ground. Coming up there at the last possible moment, asking me if they could stay when we left for the airport because her husband needed rest. Florence Nightingale, managing everything. Even this morning. The bulletin about Burley taking a hostage and shooting the cop was on TV by the time we were looking at the pictures in the lab. She must have gotten Nels into the car and headed right up there. Maybe she was hoping she'd be permitted to talk to Burley. If she had, there'd have been a tussle over the gun and Burley would have been dead by the time we arrived." He was silent for a moment. "Well, do you see it all now? Pamela may be a murderer but she's also an amazing woman. All that beauty, all that energy. Power. Power over Bangor and Wallace and Burley, and even Nels. What she couldn't have done if she'd kept her head on straight."

Another moment of quiet. I didn't look around. Then I heard him at the door, saying he'd see me later at his hotel. I nodded, but I was pretty sure I wasn't going to be there and pretty sure he knew it. I waited until I heard his taxi leave, then went out to the pool to say good-bye. I didn't tell the kid about Burley dying, though. He'd find out soon enough.

No Nepal, Burley had said, no Mexico, no Trill, no nothing.

Driving up to the funeral, I got to thinking about what it had all come down to, for all of us. No Bangor, no Burley, no Trill. Nothing for Nels, either. All of us had lost something, been done in in some way. Dead or bereaved or arrested or bereft somehow. Even Struiker, if he could see it. I thought maybe he could see it now.